MW00325170

Praise for Andre Norton and Jean Rabe

"This collaboration between the late SF and fantasy grand master Norton and prolific fantasy author Rabe (the Finest trilogy) touches upon aspects of Norton's popular *Dragon Magic* while telling a unique story about a young girl's unusual coming of age. A good choice."

—*Library Journal*

"This long-delayed sequel honors the classic elements of Norton's 1972 young adult fantasy *Dragon Magic* while taking on a decidedly modern air. ... Rabe *(The Finest Creation)* has built on Norton's estimable groundwork to produce an action-packed, satisfying young adult story that will be very accessible to modern teens as well as now-grown fans of the original Magic books."

—*Publishers Weekly*

Also from Tor Books by Andre Norton

A *Taste of Magic*
(with Jean Rabe)
Quag Keep
Return to Quag Keep
(with Jean Rabe)
The Crystal Gryphon
Dare to Go A-Hunting
Flight in Yiktor
Forerunner
Forerunner: The Second Venture
Here Abide Monsters
Moon Called
Moon Mirror
The Prince Commands
Ralestone Luck
Stand and Deliver
Wheel of Stars
Wizards' Worlds
Wraiths of Time

Beast Master's Planet
(omnibus comprising
The Beast Master and
Lord of Thunder)

The Solar Queen
(omnibus comprising
Sargasso of Space and
Plague Ship)

The Gates to Witch World
(omnibus comprising
Witch World,
Web of the Witch World, and
Year of the Unicorn)

Lost Lands of Witch World
(omnibus comprising
Three Against the Witch World,
Warlock of the Witch World, and
Sorceress of the Witch World)

Grandmasters' Choice
(Editor)
The Jekyll Legacy
(with Robert Bloch)
Gryphon's Eyrie
(with A. C. Crispin)
Songsmith
(with A. C. Crispin)
Caroline
(with Enid Cushing)
Firehand
(with P. M. Griffin)
Redline the Stars
(with P. M. Griffin)
Sneeze on Sunday
(with Grace Allen Hogarth)
The Duke's Ballad
(with Lyn McConchie)
House of Shadows
(with Phyllis Miller).
Empire of the Eagle
(with Susan Shwartz)
Imperial Lady
(with Susan Shwartz)

BEAST MASTER
(with Lyn McConchie)
Beast Master's Ark
Beast Master's Circus

CAROLUS REX
(with Rosemary Edghill)
The Shadow of Albion
Leopard in Exile

THE HALFBLOOD CHRONICLES
(with Mercedes Lackey)
The Elvenbane
Elvenblood
Elvenborn

MAGIC IN ITHKAR
(Editor, with Robert Adams)
Magic in Ithkar 1
Magic in Ithkar 2
Magic in Ithkar 3
Magic in Ithkar 4

THE OAK, YEW, ASH,
AND ROWAN CYCLE
(with Sasha Miller)
To the King a Daughter
Knight or Knave
A Crown Disowned

THE WITCH WORLD (Editor)
Four from the Witch World
Tales from the Witch World I
Tales from the Witch World 2
Tales from the Witch World 3

WITCH WORLD: THE TURNING
I *Storms of Victory*
(with P. M. Griffin)
II *Flight of Vengeance*
(with P. M. Griffin &
Mary H. Schaub)
III *On the Wings of Magic*
(with Patricia Mathews
& Sasha Miller)

THE SOLAR QUEEN
(with Sherwood Smith)
Derelict for Trade
A Mind for Trade

THE TIME TRADERS
(with Sherwood Smith)
Echoes in Time
Atlantis Endgame

By Jean Rabe

The Finest Challenge
The Finest Choice
The Finest Creation

DRAGON MAGE

ANDRE NORTON AND JEAN RABE

The characters and events portrayed in this book are fictitious. Any similarity to real persons, living or dead, is coincidental and not intended by the author.

Dragon Mage
Copyright © 2008 Andre Norton and Jean Rabe
This edition published 2018
All rights reserved.

No part of this book may be reproduced or stored in a retrieval system, or transmitted in any form or by any means, electronic, mechanical, photocopying, recording or otherwise, without express written permission of the publisher.
Published as a service of the Ethan Ellenberg Literary Agency

Cover design by Matt Forsyth

ISBN-13: 978-1-68068-093-5

ACKNOWLEDGMENTS

I am grateful to Bill Fawcett, who encouraged me to write this book and who packaged this project, and to Sue Stewart, for taking such wonderful care of Andre while the two of us schemed on this tale.

Thanks to Brian Thomsen, my wonderful editor, who managed—as always—to make my tale a better one.

And to Tom Doherty, my publisher, for saying yes to *Dragon Mage*.

Special thanks to John Heifers, who graciously and generously lent his eyes to the first draft of this manuscript and taught me a thing or three about old baseball players, potatoes, and Mesopotamian stew.

FOREWORD

Late in 2003, Andre Norton did some housecleaning, and as a surprise, sent me a beautiful framed piece of needlework depicting the four dragons from her book *Dragon Magic*. The artist, whom Andre said she sadly could not recall, had rendered the piece to look just like the lid of the puzzle box in her book, and gave it to her as a gift.

Andre couldn't keep the piece any longer, as she was closing her High Hallack Library and planning to move into an apartment. She said she simply had too much stuff for too little space. And though she cherished it, she said this piece needed a new home. She knew I loved dragons.

I'm looking at that needlework piece now as I write this, a bit of treasure that holds a special place in my heart and in my home.

Andre and I chatted quite a bit about *Dragon Magic* and the needlework dragons, and she said she'd like to see a sequel to that book. We started plotting, and then both of us got busy with other projects, including editing an anthology together about Renaissance fairs.

In the fall of 2004, we started talking about the *Dragon Magic* sequel again. She was happily settled in her new apartment, and was looking forward to working on that book with me. We discussed plot elements and dragons and the heroine of the tale—since *Dragon Magic* focused on boys, four of them— we figured it was time to give a young lady a turn in the spotlight.

The characters and antagonists agreed upon, she sent me off to do a little research on the ancient Middle East. However, before we could truly knuckle down on the project, Andre became ill, and she died the following spring. I had considered the project buried with her, but Bill Fawcett convinced me to finish what Andre and I had started.

I had always enjoyed working with Andre, as she was an amazing teacher—and a wonderful friend. This is the third book I collaborated on with her, and it is special to me because *Dragon Magic* was one of my favorite books—I have three paperback copies in various conditions and with different covers sitting on a shelf in my office.

She had a knack for portraying young characters, and though the book was written more than thirty years ago, it seems to have "aged" little.

Because I so enjoyed that book, Andre suggested we incorporate a few elements of it into this sequel. I won't tell you what they are—you will have to unearth those on your own.

Jean Rabe

DRAGON MAGE

Dear Sig,

I sure miss you. Being pen pals isn't as good as being side-by-side adventurers. And what adventures we shared!

I wish Wisconsin wasn't so far away.

School's okay, history class is the best. I think I'll get an "A" in it for a change. Dad said he'd take me to Stone Mountain if I get an "A." That will be fun, but not near so exciting as when you and I took a trip. And I bet there isn't a dragon at Stone Mountain ... well, not a real one anyway. Bet the real ones are all gone.

Do you think you'll ever tell anybody where we went and what we saw? I don't think I will. Nobody would believe me.

Send me a picture of all that snow!

Keep in touch.

Until our paths cross again,
Kim

1

Slade's Corners

"**I**'m in hades," shilo said, staring out her bedroom window, gaze locked on Big Mick's Pub across the street. Mick, a scrawny, elderly man with a bulbous nose, struggled to put out a large sign advertising tonight's fish boil.

A wheezing fan teased Shilo's short red hair, but it did little to cool her. Her bedroom was on the second floor of an antique store. The store was not air-conditioned, nor were any of the rooms on the floor above it—not a single window unit hummed in the entire building. (Initially, she hadn't expected that to be a problem, as she'd envisioned Wisconsin a cold place ... but in the heart of July it felt every degree as oppressive as her native Marietta, Georgia.)

No air-conditioning, no ceiling fan, and no swimming pool for ... well ... probably a light-year distant. She figured that by noon the heat would be enough to melt the rubber soles off her favorite pair of tennis shoes.

Still, it wasn't the heat that made her say she was in Hades.

It was her big room with its creaking wooden floor and high tin ceiling painted eggshell white.

It was the antique store.

It was Slade's Corners.

Maybe it was Wisconsin itself.

Her dad had died one month ago, of a heart attack the death certificate-in-triplicate read—two days after his forty-ninth birthday and two days before her fifteenth. She hadn't seen her mother in eight years, not since the Tuesday afternoon that the divorce papers were served.

Her mother lived in Portland now, in the company of a bass clarinetist she'd taken up with three Christmases past. She hadn't bothered to come to

1

the funeral, or to call with a word or two of sympathy. Shilo's older brother lived in Atlanta and had a job in the Braves' marketing department, which he'd landed after graduating from college last year. He said he'd love to have Shilo move in with him and his new wife, but there just wasn't room in the condo, especially with a baby on the way.

After the funeral and all the paperwork from the hospital, funeral home, and attorney was finished, Shilo's grandparents drove her and her three suitcases and four smallish boxes of belongings from Marietta to Slade's Corners. She would have rather lived in a closet at her brother's place than to have this big room atop a sprawling antique store in muggy, boring, don't-blink-or-you'll-surely-miss-it, No-wheres-ville, Wisconsin.

The antique store was the largest building in Slade's Corners. Three stories tall, it stretched a hundred feet across and half again that deep on a patchy grass-dotted lot, and would have been considered good-sized in most any city.

The town, if it could be called such, was four blocks long and a few blocks off a state highway that stretched from the shores of Lake Michigan to Beloit. In addition to the antique store, it consisted of a dozen or so aging houses; a small and relatively new tire store that rarely had customers; a white clapboard church with peeling paint; and an Irish tavern aptly named Big Mick's Pub.

The antique store was covered with shingles, like someone had bought far too many for the roof and didn't have anything else to do with them. The shingles were speckled gray and worn on the edges, much like the couple who owned the store—Shilo's grandparents.

Shilo had been living with them for three endless, unbearable weeks.

For excitement, she'd discovered she could hop on a rusty bike she'd found in the garage. She'd ride it a mile to the east to visit the dog kennel on the hill where a pleasant woman raised little white dogs that yapped incessantly. Or she could ride a few miles farther, past an orchard being plowed under to make way for new homes, and on to the bustling community of New Munster. (On a good day New Munster looked twice the size of Slade's Corners. It had a tiny post office with a soda machine out front; a gas station with a soda machine out front that only sold Pepsi, when someone bothered to stock it; a small grocery store with irregular hours; a beautiful Catholic church with an adjacent cemetery; and way too many taverns.)

Riding her bike to the west wasn't an option. Slade's Corners dead-ended in a cornfield.

At night Shilo either listened to music on her iPod or read. Her grandparents didn't have cable—cable didn't exist in Slade's Corners—and they didn't want to spend their money on a satellite dish. They had recently bought a rabbit-ear antenna—for five dollars Grandfather was proud to say—which they'd set atop their too-small color TV (recently being ten years ago). Grandfather had wrapped aluminum foil around one ear, supposedly to improve the reception.

"I'm in Hades," she repeated.

Shilo hated this place more than she'd hated anything, and she hated her mom for not caring and her dad for dying and relegating her to this second-floor room where it was so hot it was difficult to breathe.

Tears spilled down her freckled face and she buried her head in her hands.

She hadn't cried at her dad's funeral; she was too numb. Now it seemed like she cried every day, so hard that her shoulders shook and the bed jiggled from the force of her sobs.

"Three years," she whispered when she finally came up for air. "Only three."

In three years her "sentence" here would be served and she would be released. She would be eighteen and could go where she wanted and do what she wanted.

She had money in a trust—it was all clearly spelled out in the will. She'd get it on her eighteenth birthday, and then she'd pack her three suitcases and be on her way.

She'd pick a university somewhere out East, maybe North Carolina, and get a degree in history. Her father had been a history buff, passing his erudite obsession to her. She loved to peruse all of his books, which were at her brother's now, dog-earring the pages of the ones on ancient Egypt and George Washington and the American Revolution, disparate topics that fiercely held her interest.

"Shy…"

Shilo groaned.

"Shy…we're opening!"

She slipped into the bathroom and splashed water on her face, deftly avoiding the mirror. She hoped her eyes weren't red and wouldn't give her away, but she didn't want to look at her reflection to see for certain.

"Coming, Meemaw."

She put on four silver earrings, two for each ear, and followed that with a simple gold bracelet, a pewter cross on a thin chain, and three rings on her right hand—all given to her by her grandmother, and all antiques. Her favorite was a silver one set with a smooth piece of turquoise. Her dad had called her a magpie on more than one occasion because she wore so much jewelry.

She put tour rings on her left hand, one a piece of clear red plastic that wrapped around her index finger like a snake. She'd won it at a carnival in the spring, while on her first date. Two were 14-karat gold bands from her grandmother on her mom's side, one with two small sapphires. The last was a high school ring she wore on her thumb, the back of it wrapped with yarn to make the opening small enough so it wouldn't fall off.

The ring belonged to the boy who took her on that first date, and who gave her his ring on their eighth...a few days before her dad died. Dad had been furious she was "going steady" at her age, but he let her wear the ring nonetheless. The boy had come to her father's funeral, and she forgot to give the ring back to him that day. Well, she hadn't forgotten, but now she wished she would have returned it—she'd probably never see him again.

"God, don't let me cry anymore."

"Shy..."

"Be right there, Meemaw."

Her grandparents had asked her to work in the antique store until school started; she'd be a sophomore this year. She agreed, since there was nothing else to do in Slade's Corners and she felt like she owed them something because they took her in.

Besides, the work wasn't difficult. She dusted the antiques—some of which she found pretty, waited on the infrequent customer who accidentally found the exit off the highway, and watched her grandmother take inventory and check the books. Her grandfather was always inspecting this stamp collection or that baseball card collection, dozing at his big roll-top desk as he did so.

Surprisingly, the days, like this one, passed quickly.

"Coming to the fish boil with us? We want to get there early, Shy, before the crowd."

Shilo pretended to study the figurines on an eye-level shelf. The past two Friday nights she'd managed to avoid the dinner ritual. The thought of boiled fish made her practically gag.

"Shy..."

"Uhm, I'd rather not, Meemaw. I'm not very hungry. I think I'll just fix myself half a sandwich and read."

Her grandmother smiled sadly and flipped the sign hanging in the front window to CLOSED. "Maybe next Friday, then."

Shilo nodded. "Next Friday, Meemaw." She'd come up with another excuse then.

A half hour later her grandparents walked across the street for dinner.

A moment after that, Shilo slathered peanut butter and strawberry jelly on two pieces of bread, folded them over, and devoured them. She followed those with a handful of cheese puffs, four chocolate chip cookies, and a big glass of milk. Then she borrowed a leather-covered western off the "sale" rack and climbed the stairs to her room.

She sat on the bed and looked out the window and up at the dusky sky. It had started raining shortly after the store closed. Rivulets of water, colored blue and pink by Big Mick's neon sign, shot through the screen and ran down to pool on the ledge; she worried that the wood might warp, but she had to keep the window open at least a little in this heat.

The pub had a good crowd, cars parked in front of it, and probably around back, and filling the nearby church lot. Shilo suspected there were more people in the tavern than in all of Slade's Corners and perhaps New Munster put together. Big Mick's drew nearby farmers who'd come in from their fields, and people on their way home to bigger towns along the state highway and who appreciated the pub's low prices. Friday night was always busy, though for the life of her Shilo couldn't figure out why anyone would want to eat boiled fish.

Fried? Sure. She'd been to lots of Friday night fish fries with her dad. Golden brown breaded pieces of cod or perch and tall glasses of sweet tea. Those were good memories.

Grilled or smoked halibut and swordfish. Yeah, she'd had fish fixed those ways before.

Boiled?

She felt bile rising in her throat and she spun around, putting her back to the window and closing her eyes. She listened to the rain hitting the screen and the shingles, and heard the persistent honking of a distant car horn. Faint music drifted across the street from the pub, a blues piece that might have been Wynton Marsalis. Yeah, it was Wynton, wailing away on "Thick in the South." Her Meemaw had probably played it on the jukebox.

The rain suddenly came down harder, drowning out Wynton's trumpet. It rat-a-tat-tatted out its own rhythm, which Shilo found oddly pleasant and soothing. For a moment she thought she heard something else … an unfamiliar voice.

Someone calling to her?

The light flickered in her room; that was nothing unusual. When it rained hard in Slade's Corners, the power often went out.

There! Shilo heard it again. Someone *was* calling, but not to her. She heard the words "Sig … Sigmund." That had been her father's name. She crept to her bedroom door and peered out into the hall. The light was flickering there, too. She found a flashlight in the end closet, turned it on to make sure it worked. Then she turned it off and waited for the voice.

It came again moments later, so soft she wondered if she imagined it.

No, not her imagination.

"Sig … it is time."

It wasn't Meemaw's or Grandfather's voice. The tone was low and almost sultry, sounding whiskey-tinged like it could have belonged to a woman jazz singer. Shilo was intrigued and wanted to hear more. The voice might belong to someone from Slade's Corners, someone who'd come in downstairs—her grandparents didn't always lock the doors—someone who was looking for her father. But Slade's Corners was so absolutely teeny that anyone in it would know that her father was resting in peace in Marietta. Too, they would know that the antique store was closed.

"Sigurd Clawhand …"

Sigurd?

"Who's Sigurd?" she whispered.

So the mysterious voice was not calling to her father after all, but to someone she'd never heard of. And it wasn't coming from downstairs in the antique shop like she'd first thought. It was coming from above her.

The lights went out and a shiver passed down her spine.

2

THE PUZZLE OF SIGURD

"Sigurd clawhand, heed my call. It is time."

Shilo crept down the hall, flashlight on and aimed at the door that led to the third floor, which served as the building's attic. Meemaw had taken her up there two weeks past, telling her that this building had once served as a stagecoach stop, and that the people who came to Slade's Corners slept on the third floor by propping themselves up in three-quarter-length beds. Depending on the time of year, they either sweated or froze until the next coaches showed up to take them to their various destinations. There were no fans then, and the windows were small. Shilo figured she would've died if she had to sleep up there in the summer. Then she wondered if anybody had died here; maybe their ghosts haunted this place. Maybe it was a ghost calling for Sigurd.

The attic had intrigued Shilo though, with all of its boxes, barrels, and unusual objects arranged in no discernible pattern. She'd thought she might like to poke around in it sometime. She just hadn't intended for that time to be now. She shivered at the thought of going up there in the dark, searching for whoever was talking. It was like something out of a Stephen King movie.

"Don't go up there alone," she whispered, as if she were giving advice to a character in a horror film. "The monster's upstairs and it'll get you." Like said movie character, she ignored the warning.

Shilo reached for the door handle just as thunder boomed and the lights flickered on. She let out a great sigh of relief and turned off the flashlight. She hoped the power would stay on, but she intended to take the flashlight up with her—just in case.

The door opened, the hinges complaining with an ominous squeal, and each step creaked as she went up. Shilo didn't think there was an inch of floor in the entire building that didn't creak or groan in protest when she stepped on it. Halfway up the stairs she stretched and barely reached the string that dangled down from a bare lightbulb. She tugged it carefully; the string had several knots in it—evidence it had been pulled too hard in the past and had snapped as a result.

The light came on and spiders skittered to the shadowy edges of their webs. She could smell the oldness of this place, in the wood of the building itself and in all the things stored here. The smell was neither pleasant nor unpleasant, but it settled firmly in her nose, and she swore she could taste the staleness.

"Sigurd ... Sigurd Clawhand."

Shilo froze. This *is so very much not a good idea,* she thought. "Don't go up there alone," she repeated. But she took another creaking step, and then another, the string from the lightbulb brushing her forehead and making her jump. She nearly lost her footing and took a tumble. Grabbing the rail with her free hand, she noticed that she was trembling all over and that her breath came unevenly. Her chest felt tight and her tongue felt thick, and she swallowed to try to work up some moisture.

She should wait for Meemaw and Grandfather to come back from their precious fish boil and get them to come up here with her. They could all search together for the whiskey-voiced woman who called for someone named Sigurd. The name sounded ... Norse, she decided, like Ragnor and Leif and Jarli. She should wait.

Shilo sucked in a deep breath and continued up the stairs, cringing at each creak of the wood and telling herself she wasn't a frightened girl. She was fifteen years old, an age that was considered an adult in some cultures. *An adult wouldn't be afraid to go into the attic on a stormy night,* she thought. Shilo shook her head. An adult would be smart enough not to come up here alone.

The stranger in the attic might be dangerous.

"Who's there?" Shilo asked.

A heartbeat later she repeated the question louder and with the small measure of authority she'd summoned.

"I ... said ... who's ... there?"

No answer.

She walked to the center of the attic, threading her way between boxes of old kitchen tools and wooden fishing lures—all properly labeled and waiting for price stickers. She edged past a spinning wheel, from which cobwebs hung rather than spun wool, and made her way past a shelf filled with hand-thrown clay bowls with funny marks and drawings on the insides.

"I said... who's there?" This time there was a tinge of anger to her voice. She tapped her foot in irritation. Since she'd bothered to come all the way up here in a power-flickering storm, the least the stranger could do was show herself.

Shilo peered into the corners... as much of the corners as she could see. So much stuff was piled up it was a wonder the floor didn't give way and send everything falling into Meemaw and Grandfather's living space. Included were old glass lamps, wooden wagons, tin weather vanes, easels, glass and cloth Christmas decorations, and ceramic lawn ornaments—which she strongly doubted were antiques. In the mix were rocking chairs and rocking horses, unicycles and tricycles, turn-of-the-century dresses in clear plastic bags, Hula Hoops hanging from nails and covered with webs and the husks of dead insects, and much more.

Her gaze lingered on a grandfather's clock that was missing the pendulum, then moved to a bench—devoid of dust—where pieces of pocket watches were spread. A large enameled basin sat atop a delicate-looking stand that was made of some dark wood. And there were boxes and bins stacked everywhere.

The old sea chest was positioned directly beneath the last fluorescent light tube. Meemaw had pointed it out to her the day they'd come up here, telling her that things from her father's childhood were tucked inside, things that maybe should have been given away or sold years ago. Things that Meemaw had clung to and that maybe Shilo might want.

Shilo stepped toward the chest, no longer noticing the floor creak beneath her feet. A stool sat in front of it, on a faded rug braided from rags.

She hadn't heard the voice since she came up here. Maybe she'd never really heard it. Maybe it was part of a song playing on the jukebox across the street, drifting in through a crack somewhere.

She sat on the stool and put the flashlight between her feet, wanting to keep track of it just in case the lights went out again. The chest had some dust on it, though not so much as other things in the attic. Fingerprints were clear around the latch and on the top, and Shilo remembered that Meemaw had placed a little red truck in Dad's casket; she'd said it was a favorite toy. Meemaw had probably gotten into the chest before driving down for the funeral.

Tears welled in Shilo's eyes, and she shook her head. *No more crying*, she told herself. She'd cried an ocean in the past three weeks. Meemaw was going to open the chest for her before, but Shilo had declined. "Later," she'd told her grandmother. Meemaw seemed to understand.

Forgetting all about the voice and the storm and the advice she'd given herself not to be up here alone, she leaned forward and lifted the catch. The chest must have been something to really look at once, all mahogany and brass, old and shiny and magnificent in the cabin of a ship's captain. Cleaned up, it would fetch a good amount of money, Shilo was certain.

She released a breath she'd been holding and lifted the lid. The fusty scent of old things wafted up and made her cough.

"Toys." Lots of them, all dating back some thirty-five or forty years. "Why would Meemaw keep all of this stuff?" *Sentiment was fine,* Shilo thought, *but too much of it simply took up too much space.* Her father was dead and buried, and these toys should find a new home. She'd talk to Meemaw about putting some of these things up for sale in the store. Old toys were highly collectible now; she knew that from perusing eBay when she was in Marietta, where the Internet and e-mail existed.

'These gotta be antiques. I'd forgotten they actually made these things." Shilo referred to an assortment of eight-track tapes lined up in a lidless shoe-box. The Beach Boys' *Endless Summer,* Boz Skaggs' *Silk Degrees,* three Rolling Stones, Neil Diamond—arghh, her mother had played him all the time— Moody Blues, two Monkees, the Cowsills, and one cracked Lovin' Spoonful. There were 45s in another box, which she took out and sat on the floor beside her. "Oldie moldy music," she said. But her fingers lingered on the Rolling Stones. "Them and Neil Diamond've been around forever."

Shilo doubted the eight-tracks would sell, as no one could possibly own something that played those big, bulky tapes anymore.

"What's this?" She picked up a stack of baseball cards that were held together by a rotted rubber band. "Grandfather should go through these." She set them on the floor next to the 45s.

An Etch-A-Sketch came out next, and she fiddled with the knobs to discover that it still sort of worked. There was a worn baseball glove, a baseball hat, and a yellowed letter to her father written by someone named Kim, who asked him to send a picture of snow. There were several board games, too: Dogfight, Jeopardy, Stratego, and Monopoly, this latter game likely to fetch several dollars because the box was in great shape and it looked like all the pieces were there. She spotted a pinewood derby car that her father had likely made, and this she put next to the flashlight, deciding to keep it in her room.

Old roller skates, a G.I. Joe, a single croquet ball and the head of a croquet mallet. "Why ever would you keep these? Useless without the whole set." There was a stack of Archie comic books, all with deep creases down the middle like they'd been folded and stuffed in a back pocket, and all too worn on the edges to be worth anything. There were a couple of Supermans farther down, in slightly better shape. At the very bottom was a puzzle box, the cover showing four dragons—red, blue, silver, and yellow-gold.

She stared at the puzzle for several moments before reaching in and taking it out. Then she set it on her knees and regarded it curiously.

There weren't any words on the box, like a title or copyright line. Even that many years ago they copyrighted stuff, she knew. There were no words to say who had manufactured it or when or where it had come from. And there was no broken seal around the edges. All the puzzles she'd seen in stores had seals to keep people from opening the boxes in the store and losing some of the pieces.

So the puzzle was a puzzle.

And more than that, it made Shilo a little mad. When she was younger, shopping in the mall with her dad, she pointed to the puzzles in the toy stores and drugstores, wanting ones with puppies and ships and fields full of flowers. But her father wouldn't let her have even one, tugged her away from the toy aisles and tried to interest her in new Barbie dolls.

She had lots of Barbie dolls when she was younger. All of them donated to Goodwill when she hit junior high.

"No puzzles," he'd told her. "No puzzles ever."

He said they were too expensive, though she knew they weren't. He said they took up too much space—particularly if you had a bunch of them. All she really wanted was one or two. He said that the pieces would get lost and that the whole thing would be worthless, money thrown away. Well, she had to concede that part was true.

She opened the box and immediately decided there weren't enough pieces to complete the picture on the cover. Yes, lost pieces made a puzzle pretty worthless.

"Dad was right." Shilo started to replace the lid, then stopped herself. Holding the lid in one hand, she brushed the fingers of her free hand over the pieces. Her skin tingled where it met the wood. "A wooden puzzle." Too bad it wasn't all there; she bet wood puzzles were antiques for certain.

There was a layer of paper on top of the wood, and the puzzle had been printed on that. It made the pieces thicker than the cardboard puzzles her

11

friends had. The paper was curled on the edges of some of the pieces, making them look like dried fish scales … or dragon scales. She stirred them with her index finger. They felt odd, some of them cool to the touch in this summer-hot, stuffy attic.

A chill passed through her as she turned more and more of the pieces over, seeing the vibrant red that belonged to the red dragon, the lake-blue pieces, the silver ones. The yellow-gold pieces shimmered under the fluorescent lights, like metal had been powdered and mixed with the ink.

The lid slipped from her grip, and now she moved the pieces with both hands, while she looked for something flat she could spread them out on. Might as well see just how much of the puzzle was missing.

"Sigurd Clawhand … I have need of you."

Shilo had been so engrossed in the puzzle she'd forgotten that the real reason she'd come up here was to find the speaker. Startled, she leapt to her feet, the bottom of the box overturning and spilling the pieces on the rag rug.

"Shy?"

Shilo spun and saw her grandmother.

"Shy, are you all right?"

Shilo opened her mouth to warn Meemaw that a stranger was in the attic—or a ghost. But her throat had gone instantly dry, and no sound came out.

"Sigurd," she heard, finally realizing the voice was in her head. "Sigurd, you must hurry."

3

DRAGON DREAMS

"Oh! I didn't mean to startle you."

Shilo's grandmother stood at the top of the stairs, shaking her head as if scolding herself, her gray-blue hair haloed by the fluorescent lights. "I didn't see you in your room, but I saw the door to the attic cracked open."

She laughed lightly, the sound like that made by the tin wind chimes that hung from the store's front porch. "Let me help you pick up that old puzzle."

"You don't have to, Meemaw. I'm the one who dropped it. I just hope I didn't lose any of the pieces."

Her grandmother laughed again. "Child, pieces of that puzzle were lost a long time ago." She bent and started picking up the ones that belonged to the red dragon. "Got some old puzzles on the sale rack downstairs, not antiques, but from the sixties and seventies. If you want to work a puzzle, take your pick from those. They look to have all their pieces."

Shilo opened her mouth to ask her grandmother why she'd kept this particular puzzle if it was missing pieces. But then she'd need to ask why her grandmother had kept all these other things in the sea chest, including the head of a croquet mallet.

"You know, Shy, your father concocted such interesting stories about this puzzle. He said when he put part of it together it sent him to some ancient land in the far, far north … farther north than the Upper Peninsula, I'd gathered."

Shilo grabbed the silver pieces and tossed them in the box. "From a puzzle? He made up stories?"

"I remember quite a bit. Lots of years ago, Shy. But the stories! My, they were vivid. Said snow spread everywhere, and that there was a huge forge and a master smith where he went. He said there was a chair that looked like a throne, and that men fought a silver dragon." She pointed to the silvery pieces. "Said the dragon looked just like the one in the puzzle. It was the first time he had ever told such wild stories to me. I think he just had dreams that got a little too real and scary."

The far north ... Shilo shivered, feeling instantly cold in the insufferably hot attic. A wind came out of nowhere, whistling around her ears and setting her teeth to chattering. Her grandmother seemed not to notice, and continued:

"Ah, I swear if your father had a nose like Pinocchio it would have stretched all the way across the street and to the front door of the pub."

Shilo picked up one of the silvery pieces. It felt like ice, and she dropped it into the box. Her fingertips were pink where they'd touched it. The cold wind stilled, and after a moment more her fingers warmed. The attic returned to its sweltering state.

"Said he watched them slay a dragon, the master smith and someone else."

"Meemaw, did he mention someone named Sig or Sigurd?" Shilo scooped up the rest of the pieces and put them in the box. Her grandmother added the few she had in her hands, and Shilo put the lid on. Still, Shilo didn't set the puzzle back in the sea chest. She kept it balanced on her knees. "Sigurd, that's the name, Meemaw."

Shilo watched her grandmother's expression draw forward, like her face was pinched.

"Well, that's the name he said the master smith called him. He must have told the whole story to you, too."

"Maybe," Shilo answered after a moment. "Maybe when I was younger."

"Sigurd Clawhand."

Had her grandmother just repeated that name? Or was it the stranger talking again?

Shilo stared at the puzzle box lid. The blue dragon looked stiff and strange; its head was curled a bit. It had a cone-shaped horn midway down its nose. The silver dragon was coiled and rearing. It had a red tongue and eyes so green they looked like wet emeralds. "And he, my father, said this puzzle ..."

"Fool thing, that puzzle." Shilo's grandmother made a clucking sound. "Back when we lived in Georgia, there was an old man next door, quite the world traveler he was. He up and died, and your father said he found the puzzle in the house. He shouldn't have been poking around things that weren't

his. But he was a good boy for the most part, and I forgave him that little transgression."

"Fafnir," Shilo said.

"Pardon?"

Shilo somehow knew that was the name of the silver dragon, the one her father claimed to have watched slain.

"Maybe Dad did tell me something about all of this, Meemaw." But Shilo didn't remember that. She'd remembered him reading to her—books by Dr. Seuss and Clive Cussler, and history books, of course, and the Bible. She never remembered him talking about dragons and puzzles. "And about Sirrush-Lau." That was the name of the blue dragon. How did she know that? And how, too, did she know that Sirrush-Lau was called by priests, intending to set it against Daniel... the Bible's Daniel? But Daniel killed the dragon. How did she know that? Her fingers trembled and the box jiggled in her hands.

Her grandmother had been talking, and Shilo was so caught up in the unfamiliar memories that she missed part of it.

"...Ras, why he claimed that his name was Sker...Sherkar...ah, yes, Sherkarer of Meroe, and that the puzzle whisked him away to...well, that was all back almost forty years ago, Shy. I'm surprised I remember what I do. Kim, I think he was Korean, and he said he went to the Far East. Actually, all the boys went to Anthony Wayne School, and I don't think they went any farther than the playground. Certainly not to the Far East or to the Far North. And there was Artie, he was my favorite of your father's childhood friends, even though he wasn't the best of influences. A real scallywag! He told some whoppers, too, close to rivaling your father's. He said the puzzle took him to Old England and that there were tribesmen, Picts, Romans, and some famous folks—Artos Pendragon, Modred, Vortigen. Quite colorful."

"Pendragon, the man who was a dragon," Shilo whispered. "The red dragon on the box."

"Arthurian, Artie's tale was. History was never my strong suit. Your father loved history, though. Surprised he never taught it. He would have been good at it. Now antiques are another matter; those are pieces of history that I can manage." Her grandmother's eyes were watery. She pushed a strand of gray hair behind her ear and picked up the Etch-A-Sketch and other things Shilo had taken out of the chest. She carefully replaced them, then plucked the puzzle box off Shilo's lap.

"Quite the tale-spinners those boys were. Artie's stories about the High King and the Saxons, and three beautiful goddesses guarding a hidden grave. Maybe the goddesses are watching over your father's grave now." She put the puzzle back in the sea chest and closed the lid. "All of those things that belonged to your father, they're yours now, Shy."

She brushed at a spot on her dress, a tiny piece of potato salad from the fish boil. "Don't stay up too late. I want to open a little early tomorrow. Got a carload of women from Racine coming by to look at our Beatrix Potter figurines." She patted Shilo on the head, then made her way to the stairs. The floorboards didn't creak under her feet. Shilo wondered if her grandmother knew just where to step or if the old building liked her so well it didn't protest her passing.

"Meemaw…"

Shilo's grandmother stopped and looked over her shoulder.

"Why did you keep the puzzle? Since some of the pieces are missing?" There, she finally asked the question.

A smile played at the corner of the old woman's lips. "Why did I keep any of it, Shy? Your father thought there was something special about that puzzle. Said after he and his friends put it together in that old man's house, and then went back to get it, they couldn't find it. Funny, but it turned up some years later. Bill, your uncle Bill, he was six or seven, and he found it in your father's closet. Your father was in high school at the time, and he was so surprised… and a little nervous… to see it. He said Bill was too young to play with it. But Bill wouldn't give it up, and he never could get it together right. He lost quite a few of the pieces. Your father was very upset. I don't think your father ever quite forgave Bill." She sighed and ran a hand through her hair. "I should have thrown it out, Shy. It's no good without all the pieces. Your father said it was a magic puzzle, but there's no magic in this world. I shouldn't've kept it. Shouldn't've kept a lot of things. Maybe next week you and I will go through that old chest and start pitching."

Shilo's grandmother started down the stairs. "I want to open early tomorrow."

"I'll only be up a little while longer," Shilo said. She glanced at her watch. Nine! Where had the time gone? She stood and yawned, deciding to pass on the old western tonight and go straight to bed.

"Sigurd Clawhand."

Shilo whirled, looking into the corners of the attic. She'd forgotten to tell her grandmother about the voice.

"Where are you? In my head?" Shilo demanded. "Who are you?"

The floorboards creaked when she shifted her weight back and forth on the balls of her feet.

There was no answer.

"Sigurd's not here!" *And he never was,* she added to herself. He was a make-believe persona of her dead father.

She took a step toward the stairs, then stopped, thinking she saw something over by the Hula Hoops. Nothing, she decided after a moment, just a cobweb moving.

"Sigurd's not here," she repeated. Then she turned back to the sea chest and opened it again, retrieved the puzzle, and shut the lid. She hurried from the attic, flicking off the lights and scampering down the stairs, forgetting the flashlight and deciding not to go back up and get it when she finally remembered it. Maybe she'd get it tomorrow, when it was light out. Maybe she'd get it the day after.

Why had she grabbed the puzzle?

She set it on her bed and slipped into the bathroom, taking a cool shower and washing her hair and dressing for bed. Her nightgown was too short; at one time it came down to her ankles, but now it hit just below her knees. It was old, and all the pink flowers were faded and the fabric was worn thin. But it was her favorite, and it was the lightest thing she had.

It was still so intolerably hot.

She ran her fingers over the top of the puzzle box, then slid it under her bed. Shilo turned on the fan and raised the window higher. It had stopped raining, but it was still wet outside, the lights from the pub reflecting on the wet blacktop road out front. The grass and leaves smelled sweet.

She turned off the light and lay on top of the covers, the fan ruffling the hem of her nightgown and her damp hair. Shilo was tired, but she had a hard time drifting off to sleep. She kept thinking about the puzzle, wondering why she'd put it under the bed, why her grandmother had kept it, why her father had taken it from the old man's house, and why her fingers had felt so cold when she touched one of the pieces. The memory of the chill wind that had whipped around her helped cut the heat.

She closed her eyes and half expected the mysterious voice to call for Sigurd Clawhand again. But all she heard was a moldy country-western tune, playing so faintly on the pub's jukebox that she couldn't catch all the words. It took a half-dozen more songs before sleep finally claimed her.

Then the dreams came, and though they played out in her mind, they belonged to someone else.

Shilo saw an oriental boy in raggedy clothes bleached from the sun. At one time the clothes had looked fine; she could tell that by their cut and by the traces of embroidery around the neck and ankles.

"The Slumbering Dragon, Shui Mien-Lung, golden dragon, imperial dragon, the Son of Heaven of the House of Han," the boy recited.

Shilo looked close and saw more embroidery on the back of the boy's jacket. It was a dragon similar to the yellow-gold one on the puzzle box. Was the boy Kim? The friend of her father's that Meemaw had mentioned?

"There are three kinds of courage," the boy said. Shilo couldn't tell whom he was talking to. "Courage in the blood." A face appeared in the air above him, becoming red with anger. "Courage in the veins." The face turned blue and lost some of its ire. "And courage in the spirit. The face did not change color this time, but its eyes sparkled intensely, and the boy's voice became stronger. "I have the three kinds of courage, the virtues of a hero. You'll have to find them, too."

Shilo couldn't make out the details of the buildings behind him. They were hazy on the edges, as if the boy stood in front of a huge watercolor painting where the artist had feathered the lines. There was sweat on the boy's forehead and circles of sweat under his arms, so Shilo knew he was someplace hot.

He knelt and combed the sand around his feet with his fingers. She thought the design random, but after a moment she recognized five claws on a curled foot. The leg extending from it was straight like a road.

"Empty is the clear path to Heaven, crowded the dark road to Hades. When the mantis hunts the locust he forgets the shrike hunts him. Take care what hunts you, Shilo." She shivered at the boy's words and nearly woke up. But sleep held her tight.

"My dragon was the First Minister and General in Chief to Emperor Liu Pei." The boy gestured and a sword appeared in his hands, a beautiful curved blade with a sleeping dragon etched on it. "The Slumbering Dragon, mine was called. Yours can never sleep, Shilo, at least not unless you help. And yet if you value your life and want to hold on to your father's memories—if you don't want to risk everything you know, you must never heed her call."

"Never what?" Shilo whispered in her sleep.

"Sigurd Clawhand..." the mysterious voice said.

4

MISSING PIECES

The next morning, shilo heard the voice again. It WAS gusty outside and she'd opened the window all the way. The sounds of rustling leaves and clacking branches from the oak in the front yard, and from the hammering—Big Mick was on his roof replacing some shingles—made it difficult to hear the call for Sigurd. Too, she tried to ignore it and started humming to add to the noise.

She dressed quickly and took the old western downstairs, putting it back on the sale rack in the store before breakfast and deciding there was really nothing there she wanted to read. So she decided a long bicycle ride to the little library next to the Laundromat would be in order this morning—if she could convince her grandmother she wasn't needed in the antique store for a while. In truth, she wanted to look through the abysmal history section and see if she could find anything on Norse mythology and dragons, and failing that, Pendragon and Britain.

Shilo's grandmother gave her the entire morning off, and though Shilo loved books, she perused the shelves in the library in less time than it took her to ride the dozen miles to get there. "Could've fit most of this in a bookmobile," she muttered as she filled out the application for a library card and put her selections on the counter. The return trip was longer, the sun higher and hotter and the books in her backpack slowing her a little. She'd checked out one book on Leif and Thorvald Eriksson, a book on Arthur Pendragon ... the only books they had on either subject, plus two somewhat recent best-sellers she'd forgotten the titles of by the time she made it back to the antique store.

She'd picked up the best-sellers so she could set them out on her desk. Let her grandmother spot them and not the others. Let Meemaw think she was reading fiction rather than looking into Norse and English dragon mythology—though she couldn't say why she didn't want her grandmother to know that.

Besides, she told herself she might actually read the best-sellers.

After making her grandparents chicken salad sandwiches and a pear salad her father had liked, she spent the afternoon working in the antique store. There wasn't a single customer for her to wait on, though her grandfather said a man came in shortly after they'd opened and bought the largest collection of Bowman baseball cards on display, including a mint Babe Ruth. They'd all be going out for steak dinner on a paddleboat cruise this coming Friday night to celebrate.

Shilo looked forward to that, pleased she wouldn't have to come up with another excuse for missing the fish boil.

She helped her grandmother close the store and fix a stew for dinner. Grandfather coaxed her into a few games of backgammon before she excused herself for a date with her books from the library. She closed her bedroom door, and for the first time clicked the latch.

"Maybe I'll start with Leif Eriksson," she said to herself. Except she didn't crack open a single book. Instead, she tugged the puzzle out from underneath her bed, sat on the floor, and studied it.

It wasn't a woman who'd been calling for Sigurd Claw-hand, though the voice was female. And it wasn't a ghost. It had been the puzzle talking—Shilo knew that now. Perhaps she'd known it from the instant she'd taken the box out of the sea chest in the attic. The puzzle or something in it was responsible for the voice. She carefully lifted off the lid and then unceremoniously dumped the pieces on the floor. Nothing called to her at the moment, and nothing felt odd about the pieces as she turned them over and separated them by color.

She hadn't intended to look at the puzzle today... or maybe for several days. She just wanted it nearby in case her grandmother really did go back into the attic and started pitching.

"So why shouldn't I let Meemaw throw this out? It's obviously not all here." *But the box might be worth something because of its age,* she thought, *even though there wasn't any printing on it.* She looked closer at the lid, just to be certain. Maybe she'd missed some fine print in the attic last night under the fluorescent lights. No, nothing. Nothing anywhere on the lid or on the bottom. Nothing on the back of the pieces that she could see. Meemaw had said the old man who'd originally owned it was a world traveler. So perhaps the puzzle came from some foreign country that in those long-ago years didn't print copyright or artist statements.

Or maybe the print was on the puzzle itself, down in one of the corners. And while all the pieces weren't there, maybe enough of them were so that she could find the words. But why was that important to her? Why did she care where this worthless old puzzle came from?

Because her father had thought there was magic in it? Was that why?

Or maybe she cared simply because it had belonged to her father ... well, belonged to him after he'd swiped it from the old man's house.

"I shouldn't care at all," she said, reaching out to scoop up the pieces and put them back in the box. But she didn't scoop them up. She stopped herself and leaned back on her hands and sighed, stuck out her lower lip and blew out a breath that traveled up her face and teased the curls against her forehead.

"I don't care about this stupid puzzle."

... But those words were a lie. She glanced at the library books and told herself she should be reading one of them. Or maybe she should go to the living room and see if the aluminum foil-covered rabbit ears were miraculously bringing in one of the channels out of Milwaukee or Chicago.

"Waste of time, a puzzle is."

She leaned forward, hands fluttering over the pieces, her fingers lingering on the silvery ones, as they'd felt icy to the touch last night. Now they just felt like paper and wood, and nothing looked metallic about them under the light shed by her desk lamp.

Closing her eyes, she listened, waiting to hear the voice calling for Sigurd. She heard the faint clacking of branches, the breeze outside slight now, the wheezing whir of her oscillating fan, the chime of one of the grandfather's clocks from the antique store below, and soft, soft music drifting across the street from Big Mick's. The latter was a bubble-gummy song about catching a train to Clarksville, and the rhythm was quirky enough to distract her. When it was over she listened even harder, hoping to find the whiskey-tinged voice in the gap between records.

But there was nothing, and Shilo was both relieved and disappointed. While the voice frightened her a little, and while a part of her didn't want to hear it ever again, the voice also made her curious...a puzzle she wanted to solve.

Her dad had seen the silver dragon, or so his tale to Meemaw claimed. So those were the pieces she started with and within several moments she'd put together its head and hind haunches. There were a few pieces that looked like they belonged on the dragon's underbelly, but nothing that quite went together, with pieces missing in between. And she couldn't find a single piece of its tail. There was a green background behind the silver dragon, and most of those pieces were there. None of the border had the writing she was looking for, so she took the green pieces apart and put them back in the box. Next, she tried to put together the red dragon, finding it much more difficult to work with than the silver. There were more pieces to it, however, and she eventually put it all together, except for a chunk of its neck and its left front claw.

The color was amazing, bright and shiny despite its age. She'd thought the ink on the paper would have faded some. Maybe it had...maybe at one time it was even more vivid. Next came the yellow-gold dragon, which appeared to be missing about half its pieces.

"I see why Dad got mad at Uncle Bill," she said. "Would've been pretty all put together."

She heard the muted chime of the grandfather clock again, and she counted the "bongs." Eleven! She glanced at the small clock on her desk to confirm the time. She should dress for bed and throw her shorts and tank top in the hamper. A shower was out of the question now, as the water running might wake up Meemaw and Grandfather. This wasn't that big of a puzzle that it should take so much time! Where had the hours gone?

"Enough," she said. "Gotta get to bed."

She pried the red dragon apart and put it in the box, then she took apart the silver. But she didn't put those pieces away. She stared at them, like she was staring at something under a microscope. Then she glanced to the yellow-gold pieces and took apart the few she'd managed to hook together.

A moment more and she mixed the silver and yellow-gold pieces, finding that they fit together.

She didn't expect to make a picture out of it, but there was something compelling about the puzzle, and she just couldn't put it away yet. Maybe she was intrigued simply because it had belonged to her father. But there were other things up in that old chest she could have brought down, like the pinewood derby car or the G.I. Joe.

"Now this is odd." By rearranging some of the pieces and turning a few she'd put together, a leg had taken shape. She kept going, moving things this way and that, and only faintly registering the "bong" of the grandfather's clock downstairs. It was midnight.

Past midnight when she'd managed to create four legs and the start of a belly, the silvery and yellow-gold pieces blending together under the light of her desk lamp and looking a shiny beige.

She was pleased with her success, but a little upset that she was spending so much time on this worthless thing. Her father might only have been in the single digits of age, nine likely, when he'd found this puzzle. At the very outside he would have been eleven or twelve, she figured, doing the math in her head. He'd put together the puzzle in Georgia, and he moved to No-wheres-ville, Wisconsin, when he was in junior high. So, no more than twelve, and here she was three years older and it was taking her forever to play with these pieces.

Shilo didn't hear the clock strike one. And she didn't notice the music stop from the pub, which typically forced the stragglers out before one-thirty, as Big Mick was getting up there in age and had his limits.

She had the stomach and back finished, and a scaled tail that looked a little bit like a snake but was straight like a stick and ended in something that might have been a tassel. The neck was next, followed—after the clock "bonged" two—by the head. The pieces fit so snug, like they were truly meant to be together, but the dragon she'd created in the end didn't look at all like any of the four dragons pictured on the lid. In fact, it didn't look entirely like a dragon.

Its head was definitely serpentine, with wicked-looking curved horns that came forward over its eyes. The front feet were feline, like a lion's, and the back feet were clawed, like a bird's. Looking at the tail more closely now, she thought it might have been a scorpion's tail straightened out. So it was a mish-mash of creatures, just like she'd mishmashed the pieces together.

But somehow the dragon looked right, and it looked proud and powerful.

In fact, it looked just like the one adorning the massive gate across the courtyard.

Shilo trembled in fear and awe.

Her chest went instantly tight and she tried to gulp in air.

She wasn't in her bedroom any longer.

She was in a courtyard—looking at that dragon image on that gate!

It was no longer night, though it was heading that way. The setting sun turned the sand-colored buildings that ringed the courtyard golden. The air felt warm ... hot! Easily as hot as Slade's Corners had been. But it was a different heat, dry and intense like she imagined the flames of a furnace would feel against her skin.

Her senses were overwhelmed.

She fought for breath and tried to take it all in. The buildings were at the same time primitive and opulent—for the most part simple in design, yet bedecked with tiles and paintings, the walls between the designs smoothed. Blood-red flowers cascaded from window boxes, palm trees stretched above roofs, and the shadows cast by their trunks created amazing patterns on the dry, flat ground.

There wasn't a single television antenna or telephone pole, not a single indication of anything modern.

Sounds came at her from all directions—music spilled from somewhere above and behind her, but it wasn't from a radio. The instruments she didn't recognize, and the words she couldn't understand. Goats and sheep bleated. She couldn't see them, but she knew the animals weren't too far away because she thought she could smell them. People chattered everywhere, in rich accents that sounded almost tuneful. They walked from one building to the next, through the gate, a couple pausing directly in front of her to gape. The woman thrust a finger toward Shilo and said something that sounded unpleasant. "Kuri! Kuri!" she repeated as she tugged with her free hand on the arm of her male companion.

The woman was dressed in a gown that went from her shoulders to her ankles, an off-white shade that reminded Shilo of the ceiling in her bedroom above the antique store. It had pale green braid around the hem that brushed the tops of her slippered feet. The man was dressed better for the heat; he had on something like a skirt that was tied at the waist. Like the others she saw in the courtyard, the two were dark-skinned, but they weren't black. Their hair was brown and oiled, and they both wore hoop earrings made of a light-colored wood.

The woman continued to point at Shilo, but the man firmly led her away. Others in the courtyard were looking Shilo's way, too, some with simple curiosity, some with fear.

No wonder! Shilo realized. All of the men and women, even the children in the courtyard and down the streets that emanated from it, were dressed similarly to the couple who'd stopped in front of her. All the women had long, dark hair, though some of them had their hair tucked into nets that looked similar to pictures of medieval hats she'd noticed in history books. They looked exotic and elegant, and here she was in tennis shoes, shorts, and a tank top, curly red hair cut close, and her skin pale in comparison to theirs.

"I look like an alien."

A group of men tromped her way. They might not mean her any harm, she thought, but she wasn't going to stick around to find out. She stood and whirled, seeing a narrow street behind her, well shadowed because of the height of the buildings. She raced down it.

People shouted behind her, maybe the men who'd been coming toward her. She still couldn't understand a single word.

Where was she?

And perhaps more importantly... when was she?

5

THE CITY ON THE RIVER

Shilo ran south. Darting past people who pointed at her and called out in the foreign tongue, she slipped by what she guessed were homes, as there was laundry strung outside curtained front doors. Then there were stretches of nothing but walls, made of the same sand and bricks as the buildings in the courtyard, but not nearly as fancy and lacking any of the ornate decorations.

As dissimilar as this place was to Wisconsin or Georgia, she saw some of the same traits of unfortunate neighborhoods in big cities...run-down places and beaten-down people.

She didn't hear the shouting any longer, and when she stepped into a doorway, all she heard was the pounding of her heart.

"Relax," she whispered. "Slow down. Take deep breaths. Just relax." But that was one of those things easier said than done.

She felt the heat held in the coarse fabric behind her—a blanket hung in place of a door. Her fingers drifted to its edges, nervously running across the knobby sections. After a moment she put her ear to the blanket, trying to hear what was going on inside the building.

She heard voices down the alley. She sucked in a deep breath and slipped behind the blanket, turning and expecting to see people in the room beyond.

"Empty." She stood in what was likely a kitchen, or a combination kitchen and living room, with a low table and a small fire pit with a pot hanging over it. A shelf next to the pit held crude plates and other pots, and there were jars with dried things in them. Everything was shaded, as there was only one window, and it was high up on the wall behind her. "Empty and small."

She saw one other room, through an open doorway, a bedroom. Shilo shuddered to see the bed was a straw mat with a blanket on it. There was a smaller straw mat next to it, and she guessed this was for a child. Clothes were folded on a shelf by the small bed, and Shilo was quick to enter the bedroom and select a robe. The garment either belonged to a tall child or a woman, and she pronounced it a reasonable fit.

It had long sleeves and a hood, which she put over her head to hide her short hair. The fabric was scratchy, but thankfully it was threadbare in places, so it wouldn't feel terribly suffocating outside. Shilo feared being caught when someone from this family came home.

What was the penalty for thievery here?

She didn't intend to find out.

Stepping back into the kitchen, she reached for the blanket in the doorway, then stopped herself.

"I can't just take this robe. These people are poor." By any standards they were poor. She could tell that by the lack of furnishings, the meager amount of worn clothes, the smallness of this place.

She reached to her right wrist and unclasped her bracelet. It was thin, but it was gold, a belated birthday present mailed from her mother last year... two months late. She placed it on the table, then nudged it toward the center, where the wood was darker and the gold would stand out.

"I hope gold's worth something here."

She listened at the blanket, not hearing anything nearby. Another deep breath, she poked her head out, and when she didn't see anyone, she headed out along the alley, toward the setting sun.

The robe had pockets, and she thrust her hands in them. No use people seeing her pale hands and all the rings. In this neighborhood, she might be mugged for her jewelry.

She walked quickly, though she didn't know where she was going. She just needed to go ... somewhere ... find a good place to hide until she could figure out when and where she was and what she might do to get home.

A hill rose to the north. It looked inviting and green, and would have been worth investigating were she not trying to locate a hiding spot. There was a tower, too, and she wished the circumstances were different so she could give it a look.

"Stupid puzzle," she muttered.

Indeed it had been magic, just like her father had said. And maybe the magic in it hadn't let her put it down. Maybe it had forced her to go to the attic and find it and spend God-knew-how-many-hours fiddling with the pieces.

...And her reward for making something of those pieces?

A place that was worse than Slade's Corners. Tears spilled down her cheeks and she choked back a sob.

Water.

She was thirsty.

It was so hot here, and she was sweating profusely. She was becoming dehydrated. Her nerves weren't helping matters.

She might be an alien to these people, a witch or a sorceress. And she worried that if the locals caught her, she'd never see Meemaw and Grandfather again. She'd never look out her bedroom window and watch Big Mick repair his pub and put up signs for his god-awful fish boil.

A place like this had to have a fountain somewhere or a public well, someplace where the common folk could get something to drink. She should've looked for something to drink in that little house she'd entered.

Certainly there had to have been a jar of water somewhere on one of those shelves... but she'd been frightened enough taking the robe.

A few moments more and she walked out on a wider street, one made of cobblestones and worked bricks.

The shadows stretched farther now, darkening buildings that had some ornamentation on them and colorful strings of beads hanging in windows and doorways. To the north, she spotted vendors. Primitive, they reminded her of peddlers she'd seen at a Renaissance fair.

The vendors might have water or something else to drink. But no doubt it would cost her, and she didn't want to give up another piece of jewelry yet... she might need her rings to purchase a way out of this city.

The scent of bread baking hung heavy in this block. Shilo could detect fish cooking, too, and something spicy and inviting. The people passing her, she realized, were paying her no heed. They smelled of sweat and musky perfumes. The men and women were dressed better and looked cleaner the farther west she went, and there was more color and brightness in the robes, and more braiding around the hems. The women here had their right arms and shoulders bare, and their hair was long, several with it wrapped artfully around their heads. Some wore heavy makeup that accentuated their eyes. Shilo caught herself staring at one tall, beautiful woman, and nearly tripped over a stone in the street.

She looked away from the people and paid more attention to where she was walking. Her stomach churned with worry. Would someone realize she'd stolen this robe? Could she find her way home? No, she had to find her way home! She didn't want to live here ... couldn't live here.

And what about tonight? If she didn't find her way out of here soon, she'd have to find a place to sleep. It would be dark soon. Shilo was as tired as she was thirsty.

The puzzle had taken far too much time. She should've left it in the sea chest, never stuck it under her bed. Never pulled it out and played with the pieces. She would be tossing and turning on that old mattress right now if she'd left the puzzle alone.

She'd be safe.

Shilo suddenly felt like she'd been hit with the flu, so hot and dizzy, and all of it due to thirst and worry, and all of it her fault for toying with something so sinister as that puzzle.

Meemaw had been wrong; it wasn't a tall tale her father had told about going to the far north.

It was the truth.

And now the puzzle had taken her somewhere, too. How had her father gotten back home? Since he had, she could find a way, too.

But where to look?

A man bumped into her and quickly apologized, the word mysterious, but his intent clear. She nodded and increased her pace, weaving a little and fighting to keep from retching. She paused only to lean up against a wall when a large family pressed through. For an instant she worried she might be wearing the robe that belonged to one of the women.

"I didn't steal this robe," she whispered, trying to make herself feel a little better. "I paid for this." She touched her wrist where the bracelet had been, then thrust her hands back in the pockets and continued on her way, concentrating hard to walk straight.

She cut down another narrow alley to the west, this one dotted with bricks and stones from a wall that had collapsed. By the time she emerged from it onto a larger street, the sun had set, and the river she saw stretching north and south through the city glimmered like molten bronze.

"Water." She rushed toward it.

There were a few people on the bank, fishermen she guessed, as they were working on their boats. She dropped to her knees and thrust her hands in the water, cupping them and bringing up mouthful after mouthful. She was too thirsty to give it much thought, and she was surprised that it tasted as clean as water out of Meemaw's faucet.

She continued to drink.

She eyed the boats.

All of them were along this shore or the opposite, none out on this stretch of the river. The water made gentle lapping sounds against the bank and the boats. It was soothing and helped relax her. For the first time since arriving here, her heart wasn't hammering in her chest.

"My father found a way home," she whispered. "I can find my way, too."

She stayed at the river's edge until the fishermen on her side had gathered their nets and other belongings and left. Twilight was claiming the sky, and the sounds of the city changed around her. Things were quieter, and she no longer heard the constant shushing of feet against the dirt streets. She heard more music, flutes and stringed instruments, and gentle laughter.

The river was the strongest smell coming to her now, and with it fish and the scent of the wet wood of the boats. Fainter were the odors of dinners being cooked. Shilo was hungry, but decided she needed sleep more than food, and to get some sleep she was going to have to first find a place to hide.

She gazed across the wide river. That part of the city looked ... smaller was the word she settled on after a moment. Lights were coming on in windows, candles and oil lamps, she knew, as electricity didn't exist in this place. The homes on the other side were spaced a little farther apart and were not as large or tall. She didn't see a bridge.

"Why would you build a city on both sides of a river and not build a bridge?" She scrutinized the other side more closely. Maybe the people on the other side were criminals, but the homes looked too nice and well kept up for that. Maybe they were ill and had to be isolated from everyone else. Or maybe they were rich and wanted to be kept apart from the rest of the rabble.

She'd thought it might be better to hide over in one of those neighborhoods: not so many streets and not so many lights as in the part of the city behind her. But she wasn't going to borrow a boat, and she wasn't going to swim across, not knowing how deep the river was and what might be lurking in it.

She stood and stretched and yawned deeply. The water was a little choppy, and so the reflected light danced. She knew from watching the news at home that cities weren't the safest places at night, especially for a young woman alone.

Staying close to the river, she went south.

Ahead were more lights—these lanterns hanging from posts outside one of the large, ornate buildings she'd seen earlier.

"That's a temple." She'd read enough history books to deduce that. It had a "house of worship" look about it, taller than any of the buildings around it, and the front dominated by four pillars holding up a stone roof. It looked almost Roman, but not quite, and the doors set back from the pillars were tall, fifteen feet high or more, made of some polished wood and decorated with carvings she was too far away to discern. The pillars and the front of the temple were a riot of color, and the lanterns gave off just enough light that she could make out images of standing men with lions curling around them ... a lot of lions, half reclining and half walking stately.

She expected guards to be stationed out front, protecting the place from looters. But she couldn't see anyone, and so guessed that the doors were simply locked and that the caretakers didn't have to worry about thieves. A semicircle of steps led up to the pillars, and Shilo walked past them and along the western edge of the temple. There were more pictures of men and lions here, and lots of stylized suns, but she had only the stars to see these by and so couldn't make out much of the details.

The windows were set high, too high for her to reach, and the walls too smooth for her to climb. So this wasn't a place to hide in, she decided. Then she instantly changed her mind when she reached the corner and saw the back of the temple. There were two ornate doors there, no more than eight feet tall and shadowed by the wall of another building.

"Not a good idea," she told herself. But she went to the first door anyway and set her ear to it. Hearing nothing, she tugged on the handle.

The door was heavy, but not locked. She wrapped both hands around the latch and pulled, immediately rewarded with a groan of hinges.

A heartbeat later, Shilo was inside, the door closing behind her and the darkness of the place swallowing her.

6

SHADOWS OF SHAMASH

The dark didn't frighten shilo.

The air was blackest-black around her.

For the first time since appearing in this strange city she felt safe. No one could see her, and she didn't have to worry that someone would notice that she didn't belong.

The air felt heavy in here, as there was no breeze to stir it. She could smell the residue of burned incense, neither pleasant nor unpleasant. It had a hint of orange and reminded her that she was hungry.

Shilo put her back to the door and stood there for several long moments, feeling the polished wood with her fingertips. She could hear herself breathing, but that was it. No other sound intruded.

So very, very tired, she thought.

It would be so easy to sleep here in the dark... curl up right here on the hard floor. She stretched her right arm out to the side and felt the edge of the door frame. She edged along the door, and then the wall, finding it textured like stucco. She followed it, slowly, stopping when her tennis shoes squeaked.

She took them off and put them in the pockets of the robe. The floor was cool and smooth against the soles of her feet. She imagined that she might be walking on polished marble. She glided slowly, coming to another wall and following it until she reached an open doorway. Her eyes adjusted, and she picked through the shadows to see manlike shapes she figured were statues. Touching them confirmed that. She found benches, too, and tapestries. She tugged one of the lighter tapestries down from the wall, stretched out on a bench, and covered herself.

She wasn't cold, but she liked the security of a blanket.

She woke stiff and hot, sweating under the tapestry and the robe, her short hair plastered against her head. The sun streamed in through the hole in the roof, so bright and hot she figured it was late in the morning, or maybe noon...which meant it might be time to open the antique shop back in Wisconsin. She'd slept so long! Meemaw would find the bedroom door locked and would have Grandfather force it open. They'd discover Shilo gone and the puzzle on the floor.

The darned puzzle.

She was surprised she hadn't woken up next to it, having appeared back in her bedroom. Her father had come back from his puzzle journey, and she'd hoped she might accomplish her journey by sleeping...and waking up from this horrid dream.

The bench was hard, emphasizing the realness of this place. She folded back the tapestry and sat, working a kink out of her neck as she took in the room. The statues she felt last night were amazing. Each depicted the same man, carved from a beige stone and painted in places, but all in different poses. The closest and largest statue, at least nine feet tall, showed him in wedge sandals and festooned with bracelets, armbands, and neck chains.

He had a skirt, like the other men she'd seen in the city, and a robe. On top of that, there was some sort of drape that wrapped from his left shoulder across his chest and down to his waist, then up his back to fasten at his neck. His hat looked a bit like the ones the Shriners wore in parades, complete with a tassel. And he had a beard decorated with bones and beads and as straight across as a board at the bottom. The eyes were blank, perhaps the artist intending the man to look like he was sleeping. The eyes of all the statues were that way.

She noticed the same figure on the tapestry she'd pulled down. It was effusively embroidered, with lots of reds and greens.

"So beautiful." She forgot about her predicament for a moment as she studied the intricate tapestry and worked to hang it back up. The other tapestries were equally as fine, one of them catching her attention and drawing her near.

The tapestry was a map, and had it been smaller, Shilo would have tugged it down and put it in her pocket. But it was five feet across and more than three feet tall. The background was yellow, the fabric coarse and knobby in places, and the yellow of it also served to indicate streets.

"This city. Has to be this city. This is familiar," she said, meaning not just the part of the map she'd traveled over to reach the river, but all of it. Her fingers traced the thick braid that represented the walls surrounding the city. It was roughly rectangular, but looked more like the shape of a book opened and laid flat, the north and south borders of the city slightly skewed. On the north edge just inside the main gate, a walled structure was clearly the largest building on the map.

Gates, there were nine of them—three to the north, three to the south, one to the west, and two to the east. One of them would be her way out of this place. This center one to the south, she decided, as it was closest to the river, and therefore closest to her.

She touched it.

The tapestry map had firmly caught her interest, and she was certain there was something she recognized about it. There were not many major streets, three running north—south the full length of the city, plus a fourth that started in the center of a great green swatch of fabric that was roughly in the middle. A park, perhaps. If it was, she thought she should have spotted it yesterday. But she had been panicked, she told herself. There were no doubt lots of interesting things she hadn't noticed.

There were ten blue squares, thickly embroidered to raise them above the surface of the tapestry, and each about the size of her fist. Six were on the eastern side of the river, and four on the west, these slightly smaller. Words were embroidered near them, but she couldn't read them. She couldn't read any of the labels that likely named streets and the river and the gates. She tried to guess where she'd appeared in the city, based on the river and how many streets she'd raced down. She guessed she'd materialized in the north, not terribly far from the great walled building that was likewise labeled and unreadable.

The river!

A gray ribbon sewn across it indicated a bridge. If only she'd traveled north along the river rather than south, she would have seen it. Should have realized there'd be a bridge, she scolded herself. The people weren't likely to swim from one side of the city to the other, and none of the boats she'd seen looked like they could serve as ferries.

She wished her father was here, for the company and for his knowledge of history. Shilo was certain she'd seen this city in one of his history books. But it wasn't from any of the volumes on Egypt, and certainly not from any on the American Revolution—some of those books she knew by heart.

Her breath caught when she spotted something faint on the north part of the map. Rendered in golden threads not much darker than the yellow background was the image of the dragonlike creature she'd fashioned from the puzzle...the same figure she'd spotted on the gate when she arrived in the courtyard. It had to be the northeastern gate, and she stretched a finger up, not quite able to reach it.

"Ishtar. ' The voice that spoke that single word sounded like a cat purring. Shilo whirled so fast she nearly fell over.

The speaker was a young man, maybe a few years older than her, but no more than age twenty. He was dressed like most of the other men she'd seen, in a skirt that wrapped around his waist, But this came only to his knees, and so she could better see his sandals. They laced around his ankles and halfway up his calves. His skin was the color of crushed walnuts, and his bare chest was hairless, oiled she thought, to make it glisten so. His hair was pulled back, and so she couldn't tell how long it was. He had a clean-shaven face and unblinking gray eyes that held her gaze.

"Ishtar," he repeated. He said other words, all of them foreign and pleasant-sounding. He took a step toward her, then hesitated when he saw her shiver.

Shilo looked past him to the only doorway that led from this chamber, the one she'd found her way through in the darkness last night. She could dash through it, maybe catch him off guard. Would he grab her? Chase her? Call for the guards because she'd trespassed in a temple or museum or palace? The statues and tapestries in this room were valuable. Did he think her a thief?

He spoke to her again in his purring voice, holding his hands out to his sides. He wore no jewelry, unlike the men she'd spotted on the street.

"Oh!" She brought her hand to her mouth, realizing she'd brushed back the hood of the robe when she'd slept, and so her curly red hair, pale skin and freckled face, and jewelry-cluttered fingers were in the open.

He took a step back, still not blinking. He'd angled himself so that he stood between her and the doorway.

"Look," she began. "I know you can't understand me. I can't understand you either. But I'm not stealing anything, and I'm not hurting anything or anyone. I just want to get out of here without trouble. Okay?"

He cocked his head, his eyebrows raising and his eyes glittering with a mix of confusion and amusement.

"Nidintulugal," he said, pointing to his chest. "Nidintulugal." He waited, expecting her to say something.

Shilo stood there, shifting back and forth on the balls of her feet, which were sweaty in her nervousness. All of her was sweaty.

"Nidintulugal," he tried again, then pointed to her.

Her eyes widened.

"Oh, you're telling me your name. That's quite a mouthful." She pointed to herself with her right hand, and with her left pulled the hood back up over her head. "Shilo," she said.

He smiled. "Shilo." Again there were more words that she couldn't understand.

"Shilo," she said, "as in the old Neil Diamond song. Not that you've ever heard of Neal Diamond. My mother was nuts about him. Played him all the time. She should've paid attention to the dust jackets, though. Shilo's supposed to have a second 'h' on the end. But then my mother never paid much attention to anything. At least she didn't name me Cherry Cherry or Cracklin' Rose."

God, what brought that out? she fumed. *Why am I babbling to this man who can't understand me and who probably is going to cart me off to some city guard and have me thrown in a dungeon for the rest of my life?*

"Shilo," he repeated. "Nidintulugal." He pointed to himself. Then he pointed to the map, to the northern edge where the gate with the dragon was. "Ishtar."

"Ishtar. Now that's familiar. If I could only remember." *Ishtar, Ishtar, Ishtar,* she said to herself. "And it's not familiar because of that lousy Dustin Hoffman movie."

"Ishtar." He glided toward the tapestry map, leaving the way clear between her and the doorway. She could see the back of his head now; the end of his ponytail reached to just below his shoulder blades.

Shilo didn't run. Rather, she watched him. He moved gracefully like a cat, and still she hadn't seen him blink. Taller than she was, he was able to touch the northern gate.

"Ishtar." His finger moved to the highest gate on the east wall. "Marduk." Then to the lower east gate. "Zababa." The gates on the south wall. "Enlil. Urash." That was the one closest to the river. "Shamash." He paused and stabbed at one of the blue squares, again rattling off words that made no sense. "Shamash." The finger moved from the gate to the blue square. "Shamash,

Shilo." He swept his arm to indicate this room, perhaps to indicate the entire building she was in. "Shamash." He pointed to one statue after another. "Shamash. Shamash. Shama..."

"I get it," she said. "The gate is named Shamash. The statue represents some fellow named Shamash. Yeah, Shamash."

Satisfied she understood, he pointed next to the gate on the west. "Adad." And near the northwest corner. "Lugalgirra."

"I'm not going to remember those. But I'll remember Shamash. And I'll definitely remember Ishtar. '

"Ishtar."

An idea formed and something tugged at Shilo's memory. She would go back to that first gate. She'd appeared in the courtyard facing that particular gate with the image of the dragon on it. The magic of the puzzle had drawn her there. So maybe that was the way home. Maybe if she exited the city through that gate, she'd wind up back in Slade's Corners.

"That's where I'm going, Nidin..."

"Nidintulugal."

"Nidintulugal."

He beamed that she'd gotten his name correct.

"I'm going to the Ishtar Gate, Nidintulugal." She sucked in a breath. *"The* Ishtar Gate. I'm in Babylon. And I'm probably close to twenty-five hundred years in the past."

The revelation hit her as hard as if she'd been punched, and her knees buckled.

7

NIDINTULUGAL'S TOUR

S hilo woke up on the bench, the same one she'd slept on last night. Made of hardened wood, it felt thoroughly uncomfortable now, particularly since Nidintulugal had put her on her side, and the tennis shoe in that pocket was pressing against her hip.

She sat up almost too quickly, holding her head with her hands. Her hood was off, either because it had slipped back or the young man had removed it.

"Babylon. I'm in Babylon."

"Babylon," he said, nodding, his expression intense. He gestured to the tapestry map and drew a circle in the air, indicating all of it. "Babylon, Shilo."

"Nid..."

Footsteps in another chamber silenced her. She looked nervously to the doorway, and Nidintulugal noted her worry. He drew a finger to his lips and held his hand toward her, indicating she should stay. Then he went to the doorway, looked out, and a moment later walked through it.

Shilo closed her eyes and rocked back and forth as she rubbed her palms against the robe. She knew he would tell whoever was here about her, maybe the person in charge. She would be caught and never again see Wisconsin. *I should leave*, she mouthed. *Run far and fast and go to the Ishtar Gate. I should...*

The young man returned, again holding his finger to his lips. So he hadn't told anyone. Why? she wondered. Why had he treated her with kindness, she an odd-looking stranger? Why hadn't he ...

A priest! Shilo was angry it had taken her so long to realize this.

Shamash was a deity, and this was his temple, and the young man, dressed simply and without jewelry, had to be a priest or an acolyte. And priests were kind and helpful, took pity on the unfortunate ... and she certainly was unfortunate at the moment.

"The Ishtar Gate," she whispered. "I need to go there."

"Ishtar."

She nodded vigorously and added "please," though she knew he couldn't understand the word. Shilo counted on her pleading, desperate expression to help.

He pointed to her head, and she pulled the hood up, stood, and wriggled so that the robe's sleeves fell down over her hands.

He offered her a weak smile and went back to the doorway, looking out and beckoning with his cupped hand. Shilo pulled in a deep breath and followed him.

The city looked different under the bright sun. Or perhaps, Shilo thought, she was able to look at it differently because she felt less nervous in the priest's company. He led her north, on a street that ran between the river and the temple. She saw that the building was truly impressive in the daytime, covered with tile mosaics that showed Shamash amid lions and under various depictions of the sun. The color was amazing and sparkling in the light. To her left, the river looked different, too, the water a cerulean blue that matched some of the tiles in the building.

Nidintulugal spoke softly to her as they went, nodding at this building and that boat, gesturing to a group of men standing beyond the temple steps.

"I understand none of this," she returned. "I speak English, and not as well as some of my teachers would have liked."

He was undeterred by her gibberish. "Marduk." He pointed to another building, which had the look of a temple. It was larger than the Temple of Shamash, and the columns out front were shaped like the legs of some beast, ending in talons that gripped steps leading up to massive bronze doors.

"Marduk," she repeated. "King of the gods." She remembered that much from one of her father's history books. "And Shamash, I remember now. He was the sun god. You have a lot of gods. I find the one sufficient." She touched her chest, feeling the cross beneath the robe. "And maybe if I would've prayed a little more often I wouldn't have ended up here."

"Euphrates." He pointed to the river now.

"The Euphrates River! I should have remembered that, too. It's still on the map. But it runs through Iraq now." She shuddered. This beautiful city would be nothing in her time, replaced by a country the United States warred against and dropped bombs on.

Shilo knew about the Euphrates River—not a lot, but enough to qualify for what she called "history lite." She'd taken a course on Middle Eastern Conflicts her freshman year in high school. She had to get permission for it, as it was typically a class for juniors and seniors. She remembered that the Euphrates was in the news a lot because of violence reports.

The river also was mentioned in the Bible, which her dad used to read to her when she was younger. In Revelation the river was mentioned twice, called "the great river Euphrates." It wasn't the river's length or depth that made it great. It was the great apocalyptic events associated with it.

And there was the Ishtar Gate.

She slammed her fist against her waist. She should have recognized the gate yesterday! What a fool she'd been. She'd seen pictures of it in her textbook. Sure, she'd been frightened, being whisked away from her bedroom and deposited centuries in the past half the world away. But she shouldn't have let that fear completely shut her brain down. She should have realized where she was.

"Babylon." She said the word with disbelief.

Iraq sprawled over it now, a city named Karbala squatting squarely on what used to be the western side of Babylon.

"If only you knew what was going to happen to this ground, Nidin. Horrible things, so much death."

He looked at her quizzically, and she waved her hand dismissively. He continued pointing to buildings and features, naming them as if he were a tour guide. That's essentially what he was, Shilo thought, wishing she could thank him for his kindness and wishing even more that she could understand the words.

She thought about reaching in her pockets and pulling out her tennis shoes and putting them on. She silently cursed the little rocks that bit into her soles. But she figured she looked odd enough to the priest, and the tennis shoes with their shiny nylon sides and thick rubber bottoms might scare him off.

Their course was leisurely, and Shilo tried to relax. She couldn't wholly, but it was much better than her hurried trek yesterday. She actually paid more attention to the buildings and the people this time, trying to commit things to memory so that when she made it back home she could tell her tall tale in detail to a disbelieving Meemaw. She listened more attentively today, both to her guide and to everything around her. Behind them, as they were walking east now, she heard fishermen calling to one another along the bank of the river. She heard someone singing, and more flute music, similar to what she'd heard before. There were street vendors calling, and these were the most interesting because of her growling stomach.

Nidintulugal took her by the arm and led her to the closest one, pointing to several pieces of tan-skinned oblong fruit and reaching into the pocket of his skirt and bringing out polished shells. He held them out and the vendor selected three.

"So you barter. You don't use money."

He handed her two pieces of the fruit and kept two for himself. He put one in his pocket and held the other in front of him, digging the nail of his thumb into the end and pulling back the skin. He wasn't demonstrating for her benefit, and didn't realize she was unfamiliar with the fruit. But she copied him, devouring the first piece, then the second. It was sweet and pulpy, and the juice ran down her chin. It eased her hunger, but she wanted more. Nidintulugal ate his second piece, and when he was finished he dropped the skins at the edge of a building, where other dried skins curled amid nut shells.

"Thank you," Shilo said. "For the fruit and the tour, for your company. Really, thank you. For not turning me in somewhere."

Next he took her by the hill she'd spotted last night, the green one that had looked inviting. In full sunlight it looked breathtaking.

"The Hanging Gardens," she said. It was one of the wonders of the ancient world, considered a myth by some, and debated by archaeologists.

The Gardens didn't "hang," not like plants suspended in baskets from patios. Rather they overhung a series of terraces, and were of an amazing variety she doubted would naturally be found together. The terraces were stacked, one above the next, and rested atop cube-shaped pillars and vaults that looked like they were made of baked brick, decoratively enameled in places. Some of the vaults were deep enough to accommodate large trees.

She spotted stairs, and Nidintulugal raised an eyebrow and gestured, asking if she wanted to climb them.

Yes, she thought. She truly did. But she couldn't. She shook her head and continued to stare at the Gardens. Squinting, she spied between trees a primitive machine that pulled water from the Euphrates to quench the Gardens. The machine lifted the water high into the air—the Gardens stretched, she estimated, about two hundred feet at the topmost point—then released it to flow down and through the hill's terraces.

"It's not a myth," she said. "And it's more beautiful than the believers could have guessed." Shilo reluctantly drew her attention away from the Gardens and continued Nidintulugal's tour.

"Ishtar," he said many minutes later. They'd reached the courtyard she had first appeared in, though this time she looked on it from a different angle. Dozens of people milled about, talking and praying; she guessed some even conducted business. There were guards, seven of them that she could see, muscular men who wore pieces of metal plates sewn onto leather vests. Their skirts were dark red and came to their knees, and they wore helmets that looked like beaten metal bowls. It didn't appear that they guarded anything in particular, probably just patrolled the area like cops patrolled a big city park. She suspected there'd been at least a few guards here yesterday; she just hadn't been paying close enough attention to notice then.

"The Ishtar Gate." Shilo couldn't hide her awe of it. Beautiful and impressive, the most amazing thing she'd ever seen. The pictures in her Middle Eastern Conflicts textbook weren't close to this; those looked like watercolor paintings that had faded in the sun. The colors here looked electric. "Magical."

Every inch of the gate was covered with glazed bricks and enameled tiles. The background was bluest-blue and cut by yellow and brown beasts, more than half of them lions similar to the ones she'd seen on the temple she'd spent the night in.

"Nebuchadnezzar," Nidintulugal said. There were many more words that didn't register, but Shilo recognized the name of the king.

He'd built this gate and others, ordered it ornamented and dedicated to Ishtar, the Babylonian goddess of war and love. The Processional Street that still stood in modern times led to it, and along its course on walls and buildings were dozens upon dozens of animals fashioned of glazed brick. On the gate itself were several images of the dragon from the puzzle, the largest at the top of the arch. There were bulls, too, and more lions.

Shilo imagined that all the animals had some significance, perhaps symbols for the various deities, and that processions along this road glorified the king and the gods. A part of her fervently wished she could see one of those processions. But the larger part wanted to go home. Before she walked through that gate, however, she decided she would look as closely as possible at everything in this courtyard, memorizing as much as she could. She felt a little more secure in the company of the young priest, and dressed as one of the citizens, she was hiding in plain sight.

Just one last look, she told herself. *Then through the gate and back to Slade's Corners.*

"Thank you," she told Nidintulugal one more time.

He seemed to understand the sentiment, nodding and smiling, and following her gaze to stare at the main dragon.

"Thank you for this look at Nebuchadnezzar's creation."

"Ah, Nebuchadnezzar." The voice startled Shilo. It came from a thickset man approaching them. He had a braided gray beard decorated with glazed beads, and a shaved head that glistened with sweat. His skin was tanned, though not so dark as most of the others in the courtyard. His skirt was made of a brocade material that looked expensive and thin, nothing like the coarse robe she wore or the simple skirt of her companion.

He smelled of musk and cinnamon, and she immediately thought him some sort of royalty.

Nidintulugal bowed slightly, and the two carried on a brief conversation, in which both of the men gestured to her.

"For one so young to know of Nebuchadnezzar, the King of Babylon, is impressive," the older man said. "Particularly since you come from a distant place."

Shilo gasped. He spoke English! Nidintulugal was taken aback by the man's change in language.

"But while you might know something about this city and its ruler, child, you know nothing of the words. You stare at the gate, but cannot read its inscription."

Shilo couldn't speak. She could understand him, but something wasn't right about him.

He continued: "The inscription is of the Ishtar Gate's dedication. It reads: 'Nebuchadnezzar, King of Babylon, the faithful prince appointed by the will of Marduk, the highest princely princes, beloved of Nabu, of prudent counsel, who has learned to embrace wisdom, who fathomed their divine being and reveres their majesty, the untiring governor, who always takes to heart the care of the cult of Esagila and Ezida and is constantly concerned with the well-being of Babylon and Borsippa, the wise, the humble, the caretaker Esagila and Ezida, the firstborn of Nabopolassar, the King of Babylon.' There's more, but I think that much of a translation suffices for the moment. Don't you agree?"

He folded his hands in front of his waist and stared down into Shilo's wide eyes.

"You may call me Arshaka, girl." He bent slightly forward, bringing his face inches from hers. His breath smelled of pepper and other spices. "And what may I call you and your handsome companion?"

Questions flooded Shilo's mind...so she had a name for him, Arshaka, but that didn't tell her *who* he was. How could he know English? Was she not in ancient Babylon after all? Not the real Babylon? Could she be dreaming all of this? She looked to her guide, who was carefully and curiously regarding the man. From Nidintulugal's expression, she didn't think the priest cared for the rich man. But he was being polite. So she should likewise be polite.

"My name's Shilo, and he's Nidintulugal."

The man straightened, steepling his fingers beneath his double chin. "Shilo—a pretty name, for a pretty girl. And Nidintulugal. His simple clothes mark him as a sun priest. But yours...Where did you come from, Shilo? Certainly not from around here?"

She opened her mouth to tell him, but stopped herself. If this really was Babylon, he'd know nothing of Wisconsin or Georgia or a United States that wouldn't exist for more than two thousand years. Still, he knew English! His eyes were bright blue, and she'd not noticed any other people with that color. Maybe he'd magically traveled here.

"A long way from here," she said finally. "I've come a long, long way, and now all I want to do is go home. '

"You've a Southern drawl about you," he observed. "A soft, sweet accent that would put you from South Carolina or Georgia."

Her expression had betrayed her.

"Georgia it is then."

"Marietta," she admitted.

Shilo sighed and her shoulders slumped. This man *had* to be from the United States, or had visited there. If she was dreaming, his presence was easy to explain. But if she wasn't dreaming...Dozens of questions whirled in her head. "How do you know about Georgia, Mr. Arshaka?"

"I know about a lot of things, Shilo. In fact, I know a great deal about a great many things."

Shilo took a step back, Nidintulugal staying even with her shoulder.

"And I know all about Georgia, Shilo. Come with me and we will talk about the South together. Share some memories of a more civilized place." He held out a hand, as encrusted with rings as hers was. But these were heavy gold bands set with grape-sized stones, the mark of a truly wealthy and important man. She saw a ruby and an emerald, and the ring on his pinkie was circled with sapphires that sparkled like fireflies in the bright sun. She thought any one of them could have paid for every building in Slade's Corners.

"Come, come, Shilo. Let us get out of this heat."

He reached for her, his eyes instantly turning dark and his expression cold. "Come with me, little Shilo and ..."

"No!" She spun and barreled toward the Ishtar Gate.

8

WORSE THAN LOST

Shilo heard the sound of pounding feet behind her, shouting, and the blast of something like a trumpet. None of the ruckus could be good, she thought. It would be even worse if she got caught.

Maybe the wealthy man had meant her no harm, only wanted to help. Maybe she was an idiot to have turned away from him and judged him harshly—insulted him.

…But something didn't sit right with her, and when the instinct kicked in to run, she did just that.

She briefly ran across brick, a walkway directly in front of the gate, but then the ground became pebble-dotted. Her feet hurt. She gritted her teeth and forced herself to keep going, all the while cursing herself for not putting on the tennis shoes that thumped against her hips. Her hood flew back, revealing her curly red hair and pale, freckled skin. Spectators and bystanders paused and gasped, either surprised at her appearance or surprised that someone was running from the guards.

Shilo didn't have to look over her shoulder. Guards were after her. She could hear the horn blast again and a rhythmic chink, chink, chink, which she knew had to be the metal plates of the guards' uniforms shifting as they ran. She ran faster, tears streaming down her face from the pain that lanced into her legs. She was tearing the soles of her feet apart, but she told herself she couldn't stop.

"Faster!" she cried, the word making her legs pump a little harder.

Within heartbeats she was through the gate, narrowly avoiding a net that was dropped by a guard stationed on the wall above. She hadn't noticed the guards posted up there, but then she hadn't looked, she'd been so caught up in the beauty of the gate and the nearby walls. A spear came down in front of her, and she swung to her left to avoid it.

She passed through another walled section, this much smaller but even more opulent. It was like running through a tunnel now, the walls rising up on either side, higher here than in the courtyard, and there were more guards. Another threw a net, which brushed her back.

Two more spears came down.

Why had she run from that man?

The shouting grew louder behind her, and she worried that the whole city was after her. She took in great gulps of air and cried out when she ran too close to the wall. The sleeve of her robe caught and ripped and her arm scraped against the tile. Despite the competing pain, she managed to go even faster.

The tunnel she raced down bisected the city's fortress, and from high windows came the sound of more trumpets and shouts.

"The whole city is after me," she managed through gritted teeth. She held her arm tucked to her right side, which had begun to ache from her efforts. In the back of her mind she was thankful for all those recent bicycle rides she'd taken to see the yappy dogs and to the too-small library. She'd built up some stamina, but it wouldn't be enough against an entire force of guards.

There were several "thunks" behind her, which she guessed were more spears being hurled.

I'm going to die here, she thought. *And Meemaw and Grandfather will never know what happened to me. They'll think I ran away.* She'd never make it back to Georgia to see her brother and his wife, never be able to return the class ring on her thumb.

Finally she cleared the tunnel and the city, the road beneath her widening and turning to nothing but dirt. Grass rose on both sides of the road, green and making shushing sounds in a breeze that did nothing to cool her. To her right farm fields stretched, and she strained to see homes or barns that she could run to.

Why hadn't she returned to Slade's Corners when she'd passed through the dragon gate?

Why hadn't she magically reappeared in her bedroom in front of the damnable puzzle?

Her father had come back from his journey to the far, far north. Why hadn't she returned, too?

She scanned the horizon as she ran, trying to find some feature that might afford her a place to hide. But there were only fields of grass and wheatlike crops, and this road that angled to the east and looked to go on forever. Shilo could barely feel her feet now, the soles numb from the pain. She continued to gulp in air and register the shouts behind her. Just one glance back, she told herself, just a look at how close the guards and the citizens were. She shook her head and bit down on her lip, hoping that pain might somehow give her more speed. If she looked over her shoulder, she might stumble, and then it wouldn't matter how close they were; they'd catch her before she could pick herself up and run again.

One of the shouts was getting louder, and she recognized the voice. It was Nidintulugal, and she did nearly give in and take a look back, but he might be trying to catch her, too. She hadn't covered much more ground before Nidintulugal passed her, his long legs giving him speed and distance. He motioned to her, frantically, encouraging her to keep up with him. He stretched back a hand, and she grabbed it, and somehow she was able to draw even with him.

He shouted to her, and with his free hand gestured to the west, where the Euphrates paralleled the road. Then he tugged her in that direction. Shilo picked up her knees as she ran, and made thrashing sounds cut by her sharp, soft cries. The ground uneven and littered with small rocks, the pain to her feet came fresh again.

She took that glance back now. They were quite a bit ahead of their pursuers, and those in the lead were the city's guards. Their armor and all the spears they carried slowed them. There was no sign of Arshaka, the rich man who'd spoken to her; no doubt his size and age keeping him in the city. But she knew she'd see him again ... especially if the guards somehow caught up.

Nidintulugal practically pulled her now, and she stumbled when she caught her foot in an animal hole. He grabbed her up and tugged her again, a stern, fearful look on his face. She'd gotten him in trouble! They were after him now, too.

"I'm so sorry," she gushed. Shilo redoubled her efforts to keep up, her feet churning across the field. She leapt over clay pipes, realizing that they were for irrigation, which explained why the crops were doing so well in this hot land.

They ran into a section of tall crops, the stalks like corn, though there were no tassels. The tops were over Shilo's head, and Nidintulugal ducked so his head would not show either. The thrashing noise they made would give them away though.

Nidintulugal slowed, and she kept pace with him. Her feet felt like she was standing in fire, and her side ached terribly. Her chest heaved, and all over she felt feverish. She couldn't pull enough air into her lungs.

"Shhh!" He dropped her hand and gave her a stern look. He gasped for air, too.

She slowed her breathing and closed her eyes, praying for all of this to go away and for the bedroom with its high tin ceiling painted eggshell white to miraculously appear. Maybe that was the key, willing it so hard that it happened. But the pain wouldn't go away, and when she opened her eyes, she was still next to Nidintulugal and the guards were still shouting.

Back in the city the horns still sounded.

"Shhh," he repeated, so soft this time she had to strain to hear him. He crouched lower and moved to the next row, and then the next, going ever west and cocking his head, listening for the men who chased them.

Shilo followed as quietly as she could. Her breath was still ragged, and she feared that her heart was pounding so loud it might give her away.

He did not look back. Instead, he reached behind himself from time to time, fingers fluttering and touching her to make sure she was still there.

The shouts became louder, accompanied by a thrashing ruckus, as the guards hacked at the crops to clear a path and expedite their search. Shilo trembled, but didn't bolt. She noticed that Nidintulugal walked even slower now, cutting north several yards before again going west.

The water came into view when they cleared the last row of crops, and then he tugged her into the shallows, where reeds grew thick. Thankfully the bank was dry, she noted, and the earth so hard they didn't leave noticeable tracks. The water lapped around her, and she edged out deeper, still in the reeds. She watched Nidintulugal drop to his knees and tilt his face back so that only his nose protruded. The water was dark and shaded by the crops and a few trees whose roots sank into the river. She couldn't see anything else of him.

Shilo heard the shouts, and the thrashing came louder still, and so she squatted and tipped her face back, getting a mouthful of river water and sputtering it out, taking a deep breath. Only her nose stuck above the water, too, and when she had to breathe, she did so shallowly. She grabbed her robe with her hands and pulled it tight to keep it from floating up and giving her away.

Well more than an hour passed, Shilo could tell, judging by the position of the sun and the cramping in her legs. The guards continued to search through the field, grumbling to themselves, repeating the names Arshaka and Nebuchadnezzar. Several times they came to the bank farther south for a drink and to search through the reeds; she could hear them splashing. It didn't sound like any of them were going out so far in the river as she and Nidintulugal had.

What bit of fate kept them from traveling farther north? She shivered from fear, not cold. The river felt warm around her, and under other circumstances she would have enjoyed the sensation and the smell of the reeds, and the scent of wildflowers that grew just beyond the bank. The mud that cocooned her feet helped ease the ripped and blistered skin.

Finally the men moved south and east, and she and Nidintulugal stayed still for many long minutes after that. He finally stood, not straying from the reeds, and listened for the men. Shilo stood, too, and tried to hear them. But there was only the sloshing of the river and the wind twisting its way through the crops.

He didn't leave the river for quite some time more, and he gestured for her to stay until he craned his neck above the field and made sure no one was near. Then he waggled his fingers for her to join him on the bank.

She hiked her robe up and sat on the bank, pulling the sopping tennis shoes from her pockets. Her feet felt like pins had been stuck in the bottoms, and she gingerly touched them, brushing off bits of rock and mouthing *"Owh, owh, owh."*

Nidintulugal looked concerned, but he made no move to help. And when she put her shoes on, which he stared at with wide-eyed curiosity, she loosely tied them and thrust out a hand, expecting him to help her up. He didn't. He turned and faced the river, put his hands on his hips, and shook his head. His face had clouded over.

Shilo sucked in her lower lip and pushed herself to her feet. In helping her, he'd likely exiled himself from Babylon. A priest, he was recognizable, and if he returned to the city, the guards would no doubt take him.

There was no turning back.

His kindness had cost him dearly.

They were worse than lost, the both of them, Shilo thought … she impossibly far from Slade's Corners, and he denied his home and temple.

Perhaps he could return later?

Maybe explain to someone that he'd only been trying to help a stranger? But could she ever return home?

He looked north and started in that direction, walking slowly and careful not to step on twigs that would snap and make noise. Glancing over his shoulder, he gestured with his head that she should follow.

After a moment, she did. Being lost, and having company, was better than being lost alone. Besides, she couldn't stay here ... she worried that the guards might come back.

Shilo hadn't taken more than a dozen steps when she heard: "Sigurd Clawhand, heed my call."

9

NEBUCHADNEZZAR'S HAND

Arshaka paced in the courtyard, the citizens giving him space and nodding and bowing respectfully, sometimes bumping into each other as they tried to get a closer look at him. He slammed his right fist against his left palm, repeating the gesture until it hurt. He paused in his route only when one of the guards hurried from the fortress, through the Ishtar Gate, and toward him.

"She runs," the guard told Arshaka in the native tongue. "With a priest of the sun god, she runs to the north. We will catch her, Hand of Nebuchadnezzar, alive as you ordered."

"Then catch her quickly," Arshaka returned in the same language. "My patience is short and my anger is terrible. Bring her to my quarters, the faster the greater the reward."

He strode from the courtyard, along the Processional Street, two of his attendants walking shoulder-to-shoulder several yards behind. People on the street parted for him, each of them bowing, the children, too. Arshaka didn't return a single gesture, looking through them and seeing something far beyond this street and Babylon. His course took him by the Hanging Gardens, which centuries from now would be called one of the wonders of the ancient world.

His mind was seething.

He didn't register its beauty or the fragrances, or hear the water splashing down the terraces. He didn't see the people enjoying its splendor, nor any of the citizens stopping to pay their respects to him. In his mind, he saw only the girl.

News of her had reached him accidentally yesterday after the evening meal. He'd heard some of the servants talking about a scantily clad girl in the courtyard. The prattle was beneath him until one of the servants said she seemed to appear out of the air, that she talked in a strange tongue, and that with her fiery hair, she could have been a demon.

When they described her pale skin, dotted with Freckles on her cheeks, he lost all interest in the city improvements he'd been planning. He became fixated—hopefully so—on her, and he dispatched several of the guards to search. He'd said nothing of this to Nebuchadnezzar, who was making his own plans for a trip to a southern palace for a holiday with his wife. The king should not be bothered about a foreign girl, Arshaka decided, intending to keep the news and the girl all to himself.

Nebuchadnezzar did not know that Arshaka was also a distant foreigner. The king realized that his Hand, or chief counsel, was not originally from Babylon proper. But Nebuchadnezzar believed that Arshaka hailed from these lands.

Arshaka had kept his birthplace to himself; it was safer that way.

He climbed the stairs to his quarters at the eastern edge of the palace. The stairs usually winded him, but he was so angry that the guards had let the girl slip out of the city that his ire gave him energy. His rooms were simple, yet elegant, perfectly comfortable, he considered them. Nebuchadnezzar had tried to get him to move into more stately chambers in the palace itself. That way Arshaka could more readily call for servants … and could be more readily called by Nebuchadnezzar.

But Arshaka preferred the solitude and quiet of his apartments. There were fewer eyes on him here, so he could work on his plans. He dropped into a massive chair that could have passed for a throne, the deep cushion easily accepting his bulk. Putting his feet up on an ornate hassock, he closed his eyes and rubbed the bridge of his nose.

"Leave me," he told the attendants in their tongue. "Remain outside at the bottom of the stairs. And when the guards come with the girl, bring her up here immediately."

"Yes, Hand of Nebuchadnezzar," they said nearly in unison. "As you will it, so shall we oblige."

He continued rubbing at his nose until his skin felt raw and he heard the door close behind the attendants and their footsteps fade down the stairs. Arshaka guessed that they would think the girl a pleasant diversion. Arshaka was too busy to often bother with such frivolities.

Good that they think the girl a mere dalliance, he mused. That sort of gossip, he welcomed, as it would keep their tongues away from the truth—that she was valuable only for the information she could provide. Arshaka needed to know precisely where she was from, and how she got here. Georgia maybe. Probably. But when? What year had she come from? Had others come with her? If so, how many and where were they? Did she have a way to return to America? To slip between the "worlds"?

After the servants' gossip of the night before, he'd sent three of his most trusted guards roaming through the city in search of the girl. He knew it would be an exhausting search because of the city's size.

His three guards were not wearing their uniforms. He'd instructed them to dress as commoners and to divide the great city into sections, then to walk routes and listen for news of unusual foreigners. Arshaka mentioned her pale skin, and that she was said to speak a curious language they would be able to make nothing of. He ordered that if any such fair-skinned people were spotted, to detain them, with violence if necessary, but not to kill a single one.

"They are not spies, these strangers. And they are not a threat," he'd emphasized. "They are, perhaps, simply lost. We will help them find their way." He'd paid the three guards bonuses of ivory buttons, gold links, and bottles of scented ink—things that they could use to barter for something they truly wanted. "There will be more when you bring the girl, and any of her countrymen, to me. The more such strangers you find, the more you will gain."

He'd waited in his quarters through the night in this chair, fingers alternately drumming against the armrests and pulling at threads in the fabric. He expected to hear something before midnight—despite the size of the city and the few guards searching. Any strangers would stick out, unless they could barter or buy common clothes to blend in. Still, she would be noticeable by her skin and eyes.

Two hundred square miles, a most difficult search he'd presented these three men. But he knew they would rely on people they knew, asking discreet questions, and setting up a network of information-gatherers. Babylon's citizens loved gossip, Arshaka had learned in his years here. If someone had seen the girl and any friends who'd come with her, they would be more than happy to pass along the news to his guards.

"Two hundred square miles," he'd hissed after sending off the three men. Perhaps he should have sent more…but some of the others shared loyalties to Nebuchadnezzar. "People in the future will diminish this place, some will make it grander. They'll claim Babylon smaller, richer, poorer, the walls shorter, taller, thicker, easily broken…"

Arshaka knew they were all wrong—the anthropologists and archaeologists who'd studied the ruins. "Two hundred square miles...at...this...moment." He knew that the city would be growing soon. He'd been mulling over plans for improvements, which would include breaking the eastern wall and expanding the city in that direction, taking over a dozen farms and one village. The young men there would be accepted into Nebuchadnezzar's army. And when the army was large enough, Arshaka would advise the king to march on neighbors to the south.

Three hundred square miles would mark the first expansion.

Notes for those plans were neatly stacked on a low table within reach. There were refinements Arshaka needed to make, while the ideas were still reasonably fresh in his mind. But he couldn't get the girl out of his thoughts, and so he couldn't return to the papers.

He *saw* her just a short while ago in the courtyard, pale skin and red hair. Touched her and confirmed she existed. It was mere coincidence that he'd been in the courtyard at that time...fate that he'd taken a stroll and found what his guards had searched through the night for.

He *saw* her, and *touched* her, and he heard her gentle Southern accent and English words. From that moment of contact, he knew she could pave his way to glory.

Would she cooperate?

Willingly?

He knew he could be persuasive.

Arshaka planned.

He would have a lavish meal prepared for her tomorrow...she would be caught and brought to him after Nebuchadnezzar left with his wife for the southern palace. The most delicious foods Babylon had to offer would be served, and he would ply her with jewelry. She would find the place attractive and his plans interesting, and they would converse for long hours in the refined English language. She would help him, he told himself. Willingly.

But if by some chance she would have none of it...He started rubbing the bridge of his nose again.

Well, he would not give her an option.

The heat of the day and the comfort of the chair lulled Arshaka to sleep. He dreamed of an ever-expanding Babylon, with building projects to rival the greatest temples, the Esagila, and the fabled Hanging Gardens. He was mentally overseeing construction of a third wall when a knock sounded firmly on his door.

He woke, cursing himself for momentarily drifting off, then realizing he'd done more than that.

Sunlight no longer streamed through his windows, and his quarters were heavy with the shadows of early evening.

Arshaka pushed himself out of the chair and lit a large lantern on a low table. Then he trundled to the door and opened it, expecting to see his guards escorting the red-haired girl.

Instead, there was only one guard, haggard-looking and hesitant.

"Speak, Ekurzakir." Arshaka tapped his foot impatiently, but his face was a stoic mask.

The guard bowed, took Arshaka's hand, and kissed the largest ring.

"I have no good word for the Hand of Nebuchadnezzar," Ekurzakir said. His eyes danced nervously, trying to read Arshaka's expression. "Guards still search for the girl on your orders. Citizens search hoping for a reward."

Arshaka's eyes narrowed to the point he could scarcely see out of them.

"They chased her north along the Processional Way, and twice those on the wall nearly netted her. But she is fast, like the wind, Hand of Nebuchadnezzar. Like lightning. Ipqu-Aya found her trail." The guard referred to the best tracker in Babylon. "Her feet were bleeding. He followed her course into a farm field, and there he lost it."

"So many men, and they could not catch one girl." Arshaka's tone was even and silky, and it was the lack of anger in it that caused Ekurzakir to quake.

"Hand of Nebuchadnezzar, there was a priest with her, identified from his temple as Nidintulugal. He helped her escape, and..."

"Go to his family, Ekurzakir."

"He has none, Hand of Nebuchadnezzar. He was raised in the Temple of Shamash."

"And I cannot threaten any of the priests there," Arshaka said in English, smugly noting the puzzled look on Ekurzakir's face. "Keep a guard posted in the temple in the event this Nidintulugal returns. And make sure the priest is brought here."

"Yes, Hand." Ekurzakir bowed deeply and again kissed Arshaka's ring. "Guards continue to search for the girl, though the darkness makes it difficult. Ipqu-Aya thinks she and the priest escaped in the river and..."

"Set a guard, a very trusted one, at the bridge, and another near the fishing docks. They might return. Double the force searching outside the city."

"Yes, Hand."

"I will have that girl, Ekurzakir. Do you understand?"

"Yes, Hand. The foreign girl will be captured." Curiosity flickered in Ekurzakir's eyes.

"She is from a far land." Arshaka felt some explanation was in order to quell gossip that might come from Ekurzakir and the other guards. "She might hold secrets to her native land that could be useful to Babylon." After a moment, he added, "And she is beautiful. Young and beautiful."

Let the guards think Arshaka was only interested in her for pleasure.

"It would be a sad thing, Ekurzakir, if the greatest guards in Mesopotamia could not regain one barefooted girl and a boy priest."

Another bow. "Yes, Hand. I will notify you myself when we have her." Ekurzakir squared his shoulders and pivoted, walking down the stairs in rigid military posture.

10

THE TALON OF MARDUK

Nidintulugal took shilo north, keeping the river in sight on the left and walking through gaps in the tall crops. She'd not heard the call for Sigurd Clawhand for some time, and while it was a relief, it also made her angry.

"Speak to me!" Shilo finally demanded after the quiet had gotten to her. "Tease me some more, whoever you are!"

Apparently Nidintulugal had not heard the voice, though he cocked his head and listened to make sure nothing was following them.

"You think I'm nuts, don't you, Nidin?" Shilo ran her hand through her hair, knocking back her hood.

He stared at her short red hair.

"Maybe I am," she continued. "Maybe the magic puzzle melted my neurons." She poked out her bottom lip and exhaled, her breath fluttering her bangs. "I'm sorry. I'll be quiet. And I'll keep the voices in my head to myself."

The pace he set was exhausting, and more than once Shilo tugged on his arm and pantomimed that they should rest. He shook his head and spoke softly and rapidly in argument. He didn't stop until hours later when the sun started to set. Leaning against a lone tree in a field of grain, he closed his eyes. The gnats were thick here, and they stuck to his sweaty skin. Shilo was too tired to be bothered by them. She collapsed in a patch of tall grass near him, and despite the pain in her side and the terrible ache in her feet, she immediately fell asleep.

They awoke when it was dark.

Shilo stood and brushed at her robe, and cringed when she put weight on her feet again. If she was home, she'd go to a doctor, get Meemaw to take her to an all-night clinic in Milwaukee. But if she was home, she'd be sleeping in that antique four-poster bed and wouldn't have injured her feet In the first place.

Nidintulugal quietly regarded her. He tipped his face at an odd angle, and it took Shilo a moment to realize he was listening. He drew his finger to his lips…a gesture she could understand, and so she didn't say anything. After a while, he motioned to the river, and she followed him to the bank.

There was no moon, but the sky was filled with thousands of stars that reflected off the water.

Shilo stared at the field of light, not seeing for a moment where the sky ended and the river began. It was as beautiful a scene as the Ishtar Gate and the Hanging Gardens. She momentarily forgot her pain and drank it all in.

Nidintulugal scratched in the mud at the water's edge, completing his drawing before Shilo was aware of it. She strained to see it, difficult in the mud despite the brightness of the stars. He stabbed a finger at the river, then at the tree they'd slept near, then pointed to the drawing. He'd drawn hills, and there was something near the hills that Shilo couldn't make out. She shrugged when he indicated that again.

He let out an exasperated breath and cupped his hands, facing each other, fingers touching. He repeated it, then waggled his fingers and pointed at her and himself. "Here is the church, and here is the steeple," she whispered. "Open the doors and see all the people."

He tried the gesture once more.

"A village," she said. "Has to be a village you're trying to get across." She smiled and nodded to let him know she was pretty sure what he meant.

He brushed his hands on his skirt, bent and drank a few handfuls of water, then rubbed out his drawing and turned away from the river, setting a northeast course. Shilo groaned and quickly drank her fill, spitting to try to get the rest of the gnats out of her mouth. All the pain intensified in her feet in the moment she realized he intended to go to that village now. She thought about staying here at the river and dangling her feet in to let the cool water mend them. The insects weren't quite so thick here.

She didn't have to go with the priest—his plan might be no safer than something she could devise. And the village might not be safe. Besides, the guards in Babylon might have given up, and the wealthy man who'd sent them after her might have lost interest. "But somehow I doubt that," she said. Shilo lifted up the hem of her robe and followed Nidintulugal, her battered feet protesting with each step. She did not have to go with him, she told herself again, but he presented the best chance of keeping her from the guards and the rich man—and getting her to something that resembled civilization.

Shilo had trouble matching Nidintulugal's speed. She wondered if his pace helped keep the gnats from swarming... or if it was to keep her so out of breath that she couldn't complain. It was impossible for her to tell how late it was, or how many miles they'd covered. She couldn't see any trace of Babylon behind them. There wasn't even a hint of a glow from the lanterns that must be burning.

Shilo tried not to think about home.

She must have missed something in the courtyard... some clue that would point the way back to Meemaw and Wisconsin.

Her father had found his way back from the puzzle, and at a younger age. Maybe he had been cleverer.

Nidintulugal. The sacrifice he had made to help her. Would she ever be able to repay him? Perhaps he could teach her his language and then she could say "thank you" so that he would truly understand.

She drew her face forward until it was pinched. The notion of learning another language was not an agreeable one. She'd hated Spanish class her freshman year in high school. How about Babylonian instead... or whatever they called the native tongue of Mesopotamia?

"I'm in Hades," she whispered. "What did I ever do to deserve this?"

"Heed my call, Sigurd Clawhand. Time grows short."

"That's it!" Shilo stopped, standing rail straight and fuming. "I've had enough of your Sigurd Clawhand chitchat. Talking only when you've a care to invade my brain."

Nidintulugal had stopped, too, his face a mix of surprise and concern. His mouth hung open, like he was going to say something. Instead, he watched her rant.

"Sigurd Clawhand doesn't exist. Stop it! Stop it! Stop it!"

She squeezed her eyes shut and balled her fists, her nails pressing so hard into her palms it hurt. Shilo managed to keep from crying this time.

"Sigurd Clawhand was my father, and he's dead. Buried more than two thousand years from now. So why don't you just stop calling for him... whoever you are! Get out of my head."

"I am Ulbanu, and if you would open your mind, this would proceed much easier. Shut me out no longer, Child of Sigurd."

Shilo trembled.

Ulbanu. The speaker finally had a name.

Shilo clutched the sides of her head, eyes wide and staring straight at Nidintulugal, but not seeing him. Instead she saw small fields ringing a village, the homes made of glazed bricks and the roofs tiled. People milled about, weeding the crops, drawing water from the well, bathing children, playing with dogs, tanning the hide of some large animal.

In an instant she was beyond that village and into clay-colored hills, her vision suddenly so keen that she could make out the striations in sections of broken stone. There were places where dirt had gathered in bowl-shaped depressions in the rock, and stunted plants with feathery leaves grew there. She could even see thumbnail-sized green beetles that crawled on the stems.

Shilo stammered. "Nid-Nid-Nidin ... I'm scared."

Still, she didn't see him. She saw only the hill. Then her gaze traveled up it until shadows collected in thick crevices. Something stirred in the blackness, and Shilo blinked and shook her head.

"Keep your mind open, Child of Sigurd, and you will find your way to me."

"I'm not going to the hills... whoever, whatever, you are. Nidin and I have other plans, and..."

"If you want to go home, Child of Sigurd, you must find your way to me. I am the gate."

Nidintulugal gently shook Shilo's shoulders. He tugged up her left arm and used her sleeve to wipe at the sweat on her face. Her skin was warm, but she was sweating profusely like she had a fever, and she shivered all over.

"I'm fifteen years old, Nidin. Stuff like this shouldn't happen to someone my age. Stuff like this shouldn't happen to anyone."

What, exactly, had her father experienced?

Did he have visions when he went to the far, far north?

Did he hear voices in his head?

Nidintulugal looked uncertain, and Shilo thought he was having second and third thoughts about helping her.

"You think I'm nuts, don't you, Nidin?" She shook her head and wiped at her face again. "I think I'm nuts." She looked east and pointed toward the hills in the distance. "But I need to get into those hills, Nidin, I guess. And if there's something in the shadows high in those hills..." She shuddered. "I figure nuts or not, what's in the hills is probably just as bad as the guards back in the city. But at least I can communicate with what's in the hills."

She brushed by Nidintulugal and pointed herself toward the highest section. Her gait wasn't as fast as Nidintulugal's had been, but it was steady, and after a few moments he fell in behind her. Shilo stopped to rest once, sitting cross-legged amid stunted grass, brittle because the land had not been irrigated here. She closed her eyes, not wanting to meet Nidintulugal's curious stare, and listened to the insects.

Calming herself, she put her hands on her knees, trying to match the lotus position of a Hawaiian yoga instructor she'd seen a few times on television. *Clear my mind, the voice told me. Not an easy thing to do.* Impossible, she figured after a few moments. Too much to think about. There was Babylon and Slade's Corners, and...

"Child of Sigurd, there will be time to rest later."

Shilo's eyes flew open, and again she saw the village and the hills, the shadows farther up, and one wide dark shadow in particular. The darkness pulled her, and she got to her feet.

"Come on, Nidin. My destiny awaits... or something like that."

She nervously trudged on, her feet alternately burning and numb, eyes hurting from the gnats and bits of dust stirred up by the slight breeze. It was warmer the farther away from the river they traveled. Despite her stumbling a few times, and slowing, they reached the village before dawn, and Shilo skirted the fields that ringed it.

Nidintulugal pulled on her sleeve and pointed to the collection of homes. He talked rapidly, invoking the name of his god and a few other Babylonian deities Shilo vaguely recognized from his tour of the city. She shook her head and nodded to the hills.

"You can go to the village, Nidintulugal. No doubt you've family and friends there or you wouldn't be interested. You'd be better off in the village than traipsing up the hill with me... nutty me."

She waved to the village, took a deep breath, and tromped toward the hills. After several yards, she glanced over her shoulder, disappointed to see Nidintulugal heading into the village. Within moments, he was gone from view.

She sucked in her lower lip. "He's better off," she said.

Then she started to climb, humming a Wynton Marsalis tune as she went. Her legs throbbed, that pain competing with her feet and her side... and now her head, which ached because she was so hungry. There was nothing pleasant to latch on to here—no pleasing birdsong to distract her.

Instinctively she knew which cave to go to.

Shilo thought she should have been surprised to see a dragon inside of it. But like her father decades before, finding the dragon only made sense.

Her father had told Meemaw about a silver one named Fafnir. The puzzle was all about dragons, and in putting one together, she'd found the real thing.

So while she wasn't surprised to see it, she was riveted in place by the sheer size of it. The beast filled the immense cavern, its head alone larger than an adult elephant. She'd seen pictures of "Sue," the Tyrannosaurus rex skeleton on display in a Chicago museum.

As big as that was, this dragon dwarfed it.

Shilo forgot to breathe, she was so overwhelmed by its presence. It was the most beautiful and the most hideous creature she'd ever seen. Its snout was vaguely equine, silvery scales running down the center like a blaze. Bronze and gold scales covered the sides of its head, and a ridge that looked sharp and that glistened like molten metal ran from between its eyes and up over the top of its head. The eyes held her. At first she thought they were black, with no discernible pupils. But as she stared, they changed to a midnight blue, and then to a deep violet, and she saw her quivering form reflected in them. Perhaps they shifted color at the dragon's whim, she thought, blinking in disbelief when they suddenly appeared to be as green and shiny as wet emeralds.

The dragon settled on that color and edged closer, extending a leg toward her. Like the image on the puzzle box and on the gate in the city, it looked like the paw of a lion, talons longer than she was tall. Shilo felt dizzy and dropped to her knees, finally remembering to breathe and sucking in gulps of air filled with the dragon's overpowering scent. The great beast stunk, and she concentrated so she wouldn't gag and offend it. The odor was reminiscent of her father's garden in the fall when he let the tomato and bell pepper plants rot and lay there until the spring.

She could smell nothing else save the dragon … until it opened its mouth. Its breath was as strong as a gust of wind, and it was filled with the scents of scorched earth and cinnamon. The moisture of it plastered Shilo's hair to the sides of her head; it was as if she stood in a warm, misting rain.

The dragon's tongue was blood-red and slit at the end like a lizard's. It lolled out and twisted around its front fangs, then teased its lower lip and dipped down to touch the barbels that dangled from its jaw.

It moved closer still, and Shilo could see more of it now. The thing's neck was covered with scales the size of the shields carried by the guards in the city. They were a mix of metallic colors—silver, gold, bronze, brass—gleaming in a light that came from the creature itself. Plates on the underside of its neck also covered its belly, looking impossibly thick, like the armor of a tank.

Saliva spilled from its mouth and pooled on the cave floor, reflecting the dragon's scales and adding to the light of the place.

"Child of Sigurd, I am honored." The words echoed off the walls. The voice sounded sultry and whiskey-tinged, like she remembered it when she first heard it in the hallway of the antique store. *"I feared you would not come in time."*

The dragon's mouth did not move, and Shilo realized the words still came inside her head. Telepathy, she guessed, like some of the superheroes in the comic books used. *Who are you?* she thought.

The dragon did not answer.

"W-w-who…" she stammered, finding her tongue uncooperative. She could not help but be terrified in the creature's presence. "W-wh-who are you?" In fact, Shilo had never felt such a deep, heart-stopping fear. Although she shivered all over, she couldn't move, her legs like trees anchored in place. She wondered if she'd die here, perhaps of a heart attack like her father had.

But he'd made it through his dragon, watched men kill it if the tale Meemaw had recounted was true. She couldn't make it through this one, however. Her father's dragon could not have been this large. Nothing that lived was larger than this! That she wasn't dead already was a miracle. This creature could swallow her in an instant.

It would be quick, so quick she wouldn't feel a thing.

Shilo closed her eyes and waited for the end.

Would she see her father?

Was Heaven real and was he there?

"I am Ulbanu," the dragon said. *"I gave you my name before, when you walked through the fields beyond the great city of Babylon."*

Shilo's eyes flew open and she tipped her head back. The dragon had slid closer, and its head filled her vision. She nearly swooned because the stench of it was even stronger, the odors of rotting vegetation and burnt earth practically choking her.

"I sensed you," the dragon continued, oblivious to Shilo's distress, or perhaps merely ignoring it. *"Across continents and time I felt you touch the relic."*

"The puzzle," Shilo whispered.

"What your kind call the relic."

That horrible puzzle, she thought, *that wretched thing that would not let me leave it alone.*

"The sage found it on his travels and took it to your land."

"The old man who lived next to my dad." Shilo remembered that her grandmother said the boys snuck into the man's house after he died and found the puzzle. "My dad ..."

"Sigurd Clawhand," the dragon corrected.

"My dad." Despite the dragon and her hopeless situation Shilo mustered some courage. "His name was Sigmund."

The dragon cocked its head, its barbels stirring the puddle of saliva on the cave floor. "*I worried that you would not master the relic and reach me in time.*"

"You mean put the puzzle together and"—Shilo searched for the words—"activate it, the relic."

The dragon's eyes became a deeper shade of green.

"I mixed up the pieces and made a dragon that wasn't part of the puzzle, at least not what was on the cover of the box. I made a dragon that looked like you." Shilo's legs tingled, some feeling coming to them and letting her shuffle backward a handful of steps. "The dragon of the Ishtar Gate."

The creature roared then, the sound painfully deafening and causing the cave to shake as if in the throes of an earthquake. Stone dust came down like rain, and cracks appeared in the cave floor.

"Dragon of the Ishtar Gate, Talon of Marduk. Image of the God of Love and War. Guardian of Kings. Men call me all of those things, but I am none of those things. You have angered me, Child of Sigurd."

The dragon's eyes narrowed and Shilo felt her heart stop.

11

ARSHAKA'S DREAM

Arshaka padded to the river, crossing at the city's northern bridge. Babylon never wholly slept, but in the early-morning hours the fewest number of people were about. Guards always walked the streets, though not *all* the streets, and he did not see any on this trip. He'd deliberately taken the alleys through the poor quarters, where the guards rarely patrolled. Despite his jewelry and bulging pockets, and his fine clothes, he didn't fear any of the ruffians that the slums of the city engendered.

Arshaka didn't fear people.

The scents were subdued in the darkness, and so he did not have to suffer the smells of sweat and warring perfumes and oils. There were only the odors of the river and the boats. To the south he saw a light reflecting off the water, and he strained to see its source.

Nothing to concern him, he realized: a fisherman worked on his boat, perhaps had been working there throughout the night. Arshaka felt mildly sorry for the man, who would never accomplish anything great in his pitiful, and probably short, life. The fisherman might catch enough to feed his family and to sell, but would never make enough to wallow in luxury.

Arshaka craved luxury and power.

He glided into the western part of Babylon, down a narrow street made of cobblestones that had been carved to look like half-moons. Crumbled pottery and mud served as the cement between them. There were gentle sounds in this neighborhood—the soft snores of people sleeping, the chirp of crickets hiding against buildings, and still the lapping of the Euphrates reached him here.

Arshaka preferred traveling in this part of Babylon during the dark hours, when he was not likely to be noticed. Not even Ekurzakir, his most trusted guard, knew where he was at the moment. Not even Nebuchadnezzar was aware of Arshaka's little rituals. His legs protested this trip, as it was a good distance from his apartments at the northeast part of the city to this den in the west.

The shop came into view when he turned the corner. It fronted onto the narrowest street in all of Babylon, and Arshaka's shoulders rubbed the walls as he squeezed through. Three raps on a wood door halfway down—only the merchants and the wealthy in this part of the city had other than blankets and hides hanging in their doorways—then he opened it and stepped inside. The door was not locked, as he was expected.

He closed it behind himself and eased down a half-dozen brick steps, letting his eyes adjust to the dim light of a candle that lit a single sunken room. The candle had been burning for some time, as wax was pooled thickly around its base.

He wove between the tables, touching the fingers of his left hand against the gouged wood, and went to the back of the room, where he brushed aside a beaded curtain and took a longer set of stairs down to a deeper level. There was considerably better light here, ten thick candles spaced evenly on a long bench, the flickering light sending shadows dancing up the earthen walls.

There were two other occupants. The one who acknowledged Arshaka bowed stiffly. He could have been thirty or fifty, his unlined face keeping his years a secret, but his long hair and beard were shot through with streaks of silver. His hands were thin, the fingers long and decorated with tattoos where rings should be. He was a tall man for this time, well more than six feet, but his shoulders and waist were narrow, like they belonged to a smaller person.

"The Hand of Nebuchadnezzar graces our den on this Night of Portent." The man's voice was clear, each word perfectly pronounced and measured, reminding Arshaka of a practiced politician. "The gods bless you."

Arshaka extended his right hand, allowing the man to kiss his largest ring. "And the gods bless you, Belzu-Mar."

Belzu-Mar swept his hand behind him, indicating the other occupant. This one was clearly elderly, with dark, age-spotted, and deeply wrinkled skin that reminded Arshaka of a walnut shell. His hair was as thin and white as cobwebs, accenting a high forehead. He sat on a wide, low stool, humped

forward and giving his back the shape of a turtle shell. If he breathed, it was so shallowly that Arshaka could not discern it.

His eyes had been closed, but they opened at Belzu-Mar's gesture, and immediately fixed Arshaka in place. They were as pale gray as the fog that clung to the Euphrates on winter mornings, yet there was nothing gentle or soft about them. Cold and hard were the words that came to Arshaka's mind. He'd been in the Old One's presence twice before, each time getting caught by his gaze.

Arshaka did not know the Old One's true name, and though by his position in the city he could have demanded it, he'd stayed silent on the matter. Arshaka only needed the Old One's expertise. In fact, better he not learn the man's name, he decided, as that would bring him one step closer to the Old One, something the Hand of Nebuchadnezzar did not desire.

The Old One blinked and released his hold on Arshaka.

Belzu-Mar glided to a cabinet Arshaka had not noticed before and retrieved three rolled pieces of parchment that he brought to the Old One.

"The center one, Belzu-Mar. It carries the best hope for success." The pale gray eyes closed again.

Arshaka had not heard the Old One talk before, the voice sounding brittle and eerie and sending a chill through him.

Belzu-Mar returned the other two parchments to the cabinet, then retrieved four stones off a shelf and carried them in one hand. He took the parchment in front of the bench and stretched it out on the floor, using the rocks to hold the corners down. His long arms made the task easy, and when he finished, he stepped back so nothing obstructed the candlelight.

The parchment was thoroughly yellowed from age, the edges flaking off like snow. There was nothing near the margins, however, that was in danger of being lost, as the markings were in the center, and Arshaka struggled to understand them.

"The text is secondary," Belzu-Mar said.

The scrawls that twisted across the surface looked vaguely Aramaic to Arshaka. He was certain he could decipher it if he took it back to his room and studied it carefully. But the parchment would not leave this den—the Old One would not allow it, Arshaka knew, and neither did he want to have possession of such a thing. Arshaka was too important a man to be caught with evidence of dealings such as this.

"Perhaps the writing is not needed at all," Belzu-Mar continued. "In this case, it is fragments of a spell that is meant to be spoken aloud. But the ones who created such works, this one in particular, felt compelled to..."

Arshaka shut out the rest of Belzu-Mar's words and stared at the design. Images of creatures, the largest no taller than three or four inches, were scattered amid the words. Not one of them looked completely manlike, though there were pieces of each drawing that resembled humans, such as an arm or a leg, and in one case a head. Horns protruded from shoulders and chests, and extra eyes looked out from chins and palms and kneecaps. Each was grotesque, yet artfully rendered, and in vibrant colors that had not faded with the decades.

Arshaka caught himself gaping at the image closest to him. The figure had one leg, muscular and wrapped with laces from a sandal. Its torso was that of a bull, with snakes extending from its shoulders. There were hands where the snake heads should be, and wide-open eyes graced each outward-facing palm. The feminine-looking head rested atop a thick neck that was detailed with ropy veins. Scalloped marks indicated scales on its cheeks and jaw, and skin was pulled back from its forehead and tied with tendrils of inky dark hair.

"When the time is right," Belzu-Mar continued, oblivious that Arshaka had not been paying complete attention, "I will convey this pattern onto the vessel, and I or—if he favors us—the Old One will recite the necessary spell."

Arshaka blinked.

His eyes were so dry, both from this arid room and because he'd held them open for so long. He wrung his hands.

"And the others... will you use the same drawings for those?"

Belzu-Mar shook his head. "None should be alike. This parchment will be destroyed when the transcription is complete. The others will carry designs from the two parchments I also brought out. They are equally powerful, simply different than this. I believe the Old One personally knew the crafter of this, and so chose it to be the first." Arshaka glanced to his left, to the far recesses of the room where the candlelight only faintly reached.

"I am satisfied," he told Belzu-Mar.

The taller man smiled, showing teeth as yellow as the parchment. "Then I am pleased, Hand of Nebuchadnezzar."

"Twice you've called me that now." Arshaka shook his head. "That is not a title I'll accept here, for this is my business we are about. The King of Babylon is not a part of this. Understand? And so the Hand of Nebuchadnezzar has never been here."

"I understand completely." This came from the Old One. Again his eyes were open, but this time they were trained on the parchment.

Arshaka could not tell what, precisely, the Old One stared at.

"The time for this is yet to be settled," Belzu-Mar said. He, too, looked at the Old One.

"Soon," Arshaka returned. "Days, perhaps. Hopefully only a matter of days." He reached into one of his pouches and pulled out a thick, gold chain. A grape-sized topaz dangled from it. He held it out to Belzu-Mar as payment. "Send a messenger to the courtyard at sunset tomorrow. I will be there. Then I might have a more precise time for the ceremony."

Despite his bulk, Arshaka nimbly spun on the balls of his feet and climbed the stairs, his mood buoying him. He brushed aside the beaded curtain and strained to see the room beyond. The lone candle had burned down to a stub and glowed no brighter than an ember from a dying fire.

Many minutes later, Arshaka paused at the corner of a narrow street that pointed toward the Hanging Gardens.

The massive park had been one of his greatest achievements, though he knew historians—those who believed the Gardens existed—credited Nebuchadnezzar with the marvel. Arshaka had given the plans for this to the king, along with other diagrams for various buildings and devices. It curried favor and ensconced him as the Hand. Arshaka was closer to Nebuchadnezzar than all in the city, save the king's wife. The position brought him wealth and a certain amount of power, and at the same time it afforded him opportunities to pursue his own agendas... as he had in the western den.

He slipped into his apartments through a concealed entrance only a handful of his attendants knew about, climbing a curving set of stairs and easing himself into his massive chair before the first rays of the sun came up. The bath and the wine would wait, he decided, as he put his feet up on the hassock. He closed his eyes, expecting to be notified soon of the girl's capture.

Within moments he was asleep.

And moments later his mind was far from Babylon.

Arshaka stood on a curb, clutching a flag in one hand, the other hand in his pocket and clamped around his wallet. Public gatherings were rife with pickpockets, and he wasn't about to lose a single dollar to some lowlife working the crowd. Children were thick at the edge of this side of the street, and across it, where shaded by the awnings of a clothing store and a pharmacy, eight elderly women sat in lawn chairs. Each of them wore purple—a mix of dresses and pantsuits—and each had a red hat. The oldest wore a red sequined baseball hat that had a plume of purple netting hanging off one side. The Red Hat Society, they called themselves, and they wouldn't accept any members under the age of fifty. He knew there'd be more of them on a float in the parade.

His feet were tingling, falling asleep, by the time the parade finally started. The local drum and bugle corps was out front, blaring an old Sousa march that bounced off the downtown's brick storefronts. He closed his eyes and listened to the music, and when it got almost deafening he opened them again. The corps stood directly in front of him, finished the piece, then marched again, a blur of blue, black, and white, knees raising high and every member twisting at the waist so the bugles would catch the sun.

Arshaka waited for the Shriners. He liked them best, whizzing around on their miniature race cars. He'd always wanted one of the cars. Some of the Shriners were so pudgy he wondered how they were able to cram themselves into the little vehicles. If they could, he could. And a few were older than the Red Hat Society members; he figured those Shriners no longer had real driver's licenses, but were permitted to drive in the parade.

The sun was high in a cloudless sky, beating down and making almost everyone sweat. When he'd attended the parade last year, it was so hot that two of the drum corps buglers passed out; he'd watched them get smelling salts.

A little girl edged along the base of the curb in front of him, trying to get a better view. He passed her the flag so he could have his other hand free, which he used to wave to a pair of friends across the street.

They didn't see him, probably couldn't see much of anything since they were standing behind the women in the gaudy red hats. Arshaka knew he'd see them later—they would meet up for sandwiches after the parade. Nearby stood a girl with short red hair and freckles across her cheeks and the bridge of her nose. His guards would catch her soon. There were other bands, though none so good, in Arshaka's opinion, as the corps that led off the parade. Baton twirlers, one of which dropped hers a few times; dogs in ballerina outfits; floats with streamers; clowns of course, their makeup running in the heat; and fire trucks rounded it all out. The horses came at the end of the parade, and behind them the folks who picked up after the horses.

Arshaka stood on the curb while the people faded away around him, the old women in purple with their red hats melting into the sidewalk like a big chalk painting caught in the rain. Soon he was all alone, studying the buildings across from him, then turning to look at the ones behind.

The American street vanished, replaced by the Processional Way. Grandly decorated walls and buildings sprung up, and music from reed instruments floated on the air. The tune was not so impressive as the drum corps' Sousa march, but it better suited this place. He floated down street after street, alley after alley, seeing no people … as it was his dream and he didn't want anyone else here at the moment. Again he found himself on the narrow walkway between buildings on the western side of Babylon, the place where he'd physically been a few hours ago. It looked different in the daylight, so simple compared to the buildings near the Ishtar Gate.

Arshaka smiled. The simple building and its inhabitants held the key to a complex, wonderful plan.

12

No Child of Sigurd Clawhand

Shilo was surprised to still be alive.

She'd fully expected death to claim her. It would have been an escape from this cave and the monstrous dragon and a land removed by more than two thousand years from her own time. It would have been an opportunity to see her father again, and to tell him things she should have said more often in life—like that she loved and appreciated him.

Her heart skipped a couple of beats, and her chest tightened like she'd been caught in a powerful vise. She wondered if her father had felt such pain when he'd had a heart attack and died. But her heart started again, and she managed to back up a little more to gain some space from the dragon.

"Do not call me that," the dragon hissed. *"I am not the Talon of Marduk or the Dragon of the Ishtar Gate."*

Again the words came inside Shilo's head; she wasn't really hearing them.

"Ulbanu was the name given to me upon my hatching. I am not the aspect of a god, and I am not the protector of kings. Ulbanu is what I wish to be called. Only that."

Shilo finally realized the dragon was not going to kill her. It would have done that already, had that been its intent. She breathed as shallowly as possible, hoping that might cut the stench of the beast, and she circumspectly rubbed her sweating palms against her robe in an effort to dry them.

"I am merely a dragon, Child of Sigurd. Ulbanu. One more creature born to this earth, with no more right to the ground than any other."

"My name is Shilo." She was tired of the title the dragon had bestowed upon her. Sigurd didn't exist. "You say you're not the Talon of Marduk. Well, I'm no Child of Sigurd Clawhand. I'm the daughter of a man named

Sigmund, and he died less than a month ago." Again she felt her father's loss. She wished she'd have done more things with him, especially toward the end...more picnics and movies, more talk. Maybe if they'd talked more, he would have mentioned his youth and the puzzle. How had he gotten home after he'd played with the puzzle?

"*Shilo,*" the dragon pronounced.

"And I want to go back to Slade's Corners."

Neither Shilo nor the dragon spoke for several minutes. The hiss of the dragon's breath—even and sounding like a fall wind blowing piles of raked leaves across the ground—filled the uneasy interval. There was the plop of more saliva dropping on the floor, and from somewhere outside came the skree of a hawk.

Shilo's head continued pounding, from lack of food and from the intensity of her predicament. All the aches in her body magnified. *I'm fifteen. This shouldn't be happening to me.*

Fifteen!

"*I can send you home, Shilo.*"

"Thank you," she mouthed. "*Thank you. Thank you. Thank you.*"

"*Though I first require your assistance in the most important matter in the world.*"

Shilo closed her eyes. What service had her father performed to get back home? If he managed a task regarding a dragon, she could also. But what could a creature this size not accomplish that she could? What could be the "most important matter in the world"?

"Anything," she said. "I'll do anything to get out of here and back home." She brushed her hood back and raked her fingers through her hair. "And I'll never ever ever play with the magical puzzle again." *Burn it,* she thought, *spread the pieces between the garbage cans at Big Mick's Pub and the church, chop them all into tiny bits and...*

The dragon raised its lip in the approximation of a smile. "*The 'relic' is not magic, Shilo. The thing you call a puzzle is merely shards of wood and colored paper.*"

"Not magic?" She sputtered and waved her arms, surprised at her ire, and not caring that the dragon knew she was upset. "That puzzle—that relic as you call it—brought me here. The magic in it wouldn't let me leave it alone, made me hide it under my bed. Then the magic made me take it out and put a dragon together...you...put together a picture of you! I wouldn't be here if that puzzle..."

"*The relic has no magic about it, Shilo. The magic is in you.*"

The words hit Shilo like she'd been punched in the stomach, and she fell back on her rump, catching herself with her hands. *"Not possible,"* she mouthed. She quickly recovered and shook her head. "No! My father played with the puzzle, and his friends did, too. They all traveled to different times and places. It was because of the puzzle."

"Because of the magic in them." The dragon let out a great sigh that struck Shilo like a strong, hot breeze. The scents of rotting vegetation and scorched ground became unbearable, and Shilo clutched at her stomach and fought to keep from retching. The only thing that saved her was that she'd not eaten in some time.

"There is no magic in me, Ulbanu. And there was nothing magical about my father or his friends." Shilo continued fuming. "It was that puzzle. That…"

"The relic is wood and parchment, I say, and was found by the sage who I once called a friend. I will grant you that the relic is a conduit."

"A what?" Shilo picked herself up and took a few more steps back. She would have run, despite the ache in her battered feet, but the dragon had told her it could send her home, and so she couldn't leave.

"A conduit, a tool, a focus, Shilo. The relic lets you center your thoughts and relax your mind so that the magic flows within you. There are other relics in the world, all different than the thing you call a puzzle, and all in pieces that the wielder must assemble."

Shilo could not bring herself to believe the awe-inspiring dragon. *It's lying to me,* she thought. It was teasing her for some reason, a cat playing with a tiny mouse. And since it was lying to her about the puzzle, it no doubt was lying about being able to send her home.

"You are the most magical of those who touched the relic, Shilo, even more magical than the sage."

The sage? The world traveler who died and whose house her father and his friends had snuck into? The one who originally owned the puzzle?

"Only a handful of people in all the world went beyond the strictures of that relic and others. You are one of those rare people; you saw beyond the face of the relic and reached inside."

Shilo didn't understand what the dragon meant at first.

"You have an inner spark, child. It lets you see the unseen."

Her eyes widened. She'd put together the image of this dragon by combining the pieces of other dragons. This dragon was not pictured on the lid of the box, but somehow she knew there was a fifth dragon. This dragon, Ulbanu. Could the dragon be telling the truth after all?

"I can read your face, Shilo. You begin to understand."

"No. There's no magic in me."

"Then how are you here? How are you talking to me? How are you so far in time and place removed from your home?" The dragon rested its head on the cave floor, its eyes narrowing. "Your father, Sigurd Clawhand, did not travel here. His will sent him north, where my evil brother Fafnir was slain. Your will directed you here, where you are needed." The dragon paused. "Where your magic is required."

"I don't understand," Shilo mouthed. In truth she didn't. The dragon continued to expound on the relic, which it claimed it could sense because of its own inner magic. Ulbanu recounted how Shilo's father went to the time of the Vikings, and that his friends went elsewhere. The sage traveled to a realm before Babylon, and others journeyed to distant lands, too.

"But not many," Ulbanu said. "Few of your kind possess enough magic, especially in the time from which you hail."

"So I brought myself here?"

The dragon did not reply.

"The puzzle relaxed me and opened my mind so I could discover my inner magic?"

Again, no answer.

"And I suppose you will tell me that I instinctively knew I was needed here. So I came here because my magic is required?"

"Yes."

"And why is it required?"

"To save dragonkind and perhaps mankind. To save Babylon and thereby the place you call Slade's Corners. To save every good thing and every good place."

This can't be happening, Shilo thought. Please, please, God, let this all be some horrible dream. Or let me be nuts. She closed her eyes and felt tears welling in them.

"I'm not nuts, am I, Ulbanu?"

The dragon raised the ridge above its eyes in question.

When Shilo did not hear a reply, she rephrased her question: "I'm not goofy, nuts, insane, am I? I'm not a few fries short of a Happy Meal? My mind isn't lost."

"Your mind is not lost, Child of... No, your mind is whole, Shilo."

She opened her eyes and drew her lips into a fine line. "Then how about you tell me just why my magic is required? But before all of that... before any of that, you tell me what this 'magic' is that's inside of me."

Well into the night, shilo could no longer stay awake. Despite the stench of the great dragon and the aches that continued to pulse through her, she fell asleep on the hard stone of the cave floor.

Her dreams were filled with the dragon's story.

"There was great magic in the land in ages long ago," Ulbanu said. *"The energy resided in the plants and the creatures and the water. But as man grew wiser and stronger, he relied less on magic. Forgotten, the old talents settled deep into the ground, leeching away from men and creatures. Some families held on to it, though, such as yours. Dormant, the magic came only when called, like you called it when you handled the relic. There are limitations to the magic, and certain creatures are better at certain things. Your specialties and limitations are yet to be determined. And before you discover your limitations, you must first discover how to call upon your inner spark."*

The more she'd listened, the more she got confused, yet at the same time the more the dragon's story seemed plausible. Perhaps it was the beast's sultry voice, or her own hunger-caused dizziness that made the words credible. Maybe it was her desire to actually have "magic."

"I remember seeing through time and distance when your father found his magic and journeyed to Fafnir's lands. Fafnir was a powerful dragon, Shilo, and should have used that power for good. Instead he coveted treasure and embraced vile emotions. I remember watching him slain and feeling sadness not because I cared for him, but because there was one less dragon in the world."

Shilo's thoughts had drifted during part of the dragon's story. She wondered if Meemaw and Grandfather were worried about her, or if they even knew she was gone. Did time pass in the present while she was here in the past? But this wasn't the past now, was it? This was her present. She rubbed at her temples. *So terribly confused,* she thought.

"It is our magic together that lets us communicate, such different creatures. You hear my thoughts and I understand your tongue."

Shilo finally had a question. "Then why couldn't I understand the people in Babylon?" Well, she could understand one of them, the rich man with all the valuable rings. She would have to ask Ulbanu about him.

"Magic is a new concept for you, child. You can understand those in Babylon . . . you can come to understand anyone . . . if you wholly master the magic inside of you."

"And I suppose you will teach me."

"Yes."

For some reason, Shilo expected that answer.

"*But only a little now, only enough so you can move among the people of Babylon. I can teach you more later, after you have fulfilled—*"

"—my purpose in coming here," Shilo finished.

"*Yes.*"

"To save dragonkind and perhaps mankind."

"Yes."

Shilo listened to the dragon talk some more, about magic deep in the earth, and about Babylon, about dragons hiding from men and keeping to remote places so they would not be hunted. She remembered it all clearly in her dream, and she wondered that if the dragon could look through time and across distances, could she, too? If so, could she look forward and to the far, far north and see her father and his dragon Fafnir? She told herself to ask Ulbanu that when she woke up.

But when she did wake, she'd forgotten that thought. Chief in her mind was food and clean clothes. She desperately had to get something to eat and to drink.

"Or I will be of no use to you or myself," she told Ulbanu.

"I *understand.*" The dragon retreated into the recesses of its cave, returning with a thick bolt of beautiful cloth held gingerly in its teeth. It placed the bolt in front of Shilo, and she noted that though the cloth was not damaged, it was sodden from the dragon's saliva. "*The people of this world trade, Shilo, and the ones in the village beyond these hills would welcome such as this.*"

"I've got rings and earrings. I can use that to trade. I can do this on my own."

"Jewelry has little value to those people."

"Fine, I'll take your fabric."

Shilo wanted to ask Ulbanu how it came to possess cloth. But then she figured all dragons had some sort of hoard; legends and stories said so anyway.

"*Return soon, Shilo. Time grows short, and your task is terribly important. You have much work to do.*"

Shilo grabbed up the cloth, struggling under its weight. Without another word, she slipped from the cave and started down the hill.

Maybe I'll come back, Shilo thought. *If I can convince myself that a fifteen-year-old can save dragonkind and perhaps mankind because there's some magic buried inside her. If I believe only I can accomplish the "most important thing in the world." Maybe I'll...*

She froze on the hillside, looking down to the village that rested at the base of the range. It was early morning, and from her high vantage she got a good look at the land that would become Iraq. In her time it would never be this verdant. She saw crops in the distance, where she and Nidintulugal had fled through to avoid the guards and reach the river, and she saw the thriving fields of the village below her. The villagers must use wells, as she couldn't see even a stream running near the place.

Shilo was too far away to hear the sounds she expected filled the village—the chatter of the residents, the bleat of the animals, and hopefully music. But she heard the breeze stirring the dirt held in pockets in the hills, and the breathing of the dragon in the cave behind her.

Her feet were still sore, though not so fiercely as they were yesterday. And the pain in her side from running had disappeared. She picked her way down the hill, careful not to drop the heavy bolt of material. Maybe someone in the village would have some medicine she could put on her feet...and certainly lots of food to put in her belly. Appropriately, her stomach rumbled its hunger.

Maybe she'd see Nidintulugal and would be able to...Shilo stopped and swallowed hard as four soldiers appeared on a trail leading to the village, and within moments walked through the crops and disappeared between a pair of buildings.

13

Broken Barriers

Shilo perched in the hills, for what she guessed was well more than a few hours. Why hadn't she put on her watch that day she played with the puzzle? She'd put on all these rings and earrings, and the gold bracelet that she'd used to pay for this practically threadbare robe. Why hadn't she bothered to wear the watch?

She had no shade, save the little piece she found behind the rocky outcropping she hid behind. Her stomach continued to rumble and her throat demanded water, and she worried that she'd pass out here, halfway between the dragon and the village, and die without ever regaining her home.

Did the village know about the dragon?

Somehow she doubted it. Otherwise there'd be a trail to the cave, with villagers bringing up tribute. Too, no one with any sense would build a village near a dragon.

Unless the dragon protected the village. But wouldn't the beast have told her that?

The sun was almost directly overhead when she saw the four guards leave. They were talking among themselves. She could tell that by the way they occasionally turned to face each other. Two made their way down the road from the village, then to the main road that would eventually lead to Babylon. Shilo couldn't see the great city from here; it was too far away. The other two followed the road to the north. She waited quite some more time before creeping down the hill and hiding in the fields that grew on the north end of the village.

She was tempted to pluck some of the vegetables, all of which were unfamiliar to her, and eat her fill before taking the bolt of cloth inside. In fact, she could sate her appetite, find a well, and make it back to the dragon's cave, perhaps without any villagers seeing her.

But Shilo wanted a change of clothes and a bath, if possible, then food—definitely food. She made sure her hood was up so no one would see her short red hair. She struggled with the fabric as she took a back way into the village. Almost immediately she was spotted and became the center of attention. Noticed first by a boy leading a sheep, he called to his friends, who called to adults. Within minutes, she suspected everyone who lived in the village was in the circle around her.

They all looked similar to the people she saw in Babylon—the men wearing skirts to their knees or lower and sandals with laces, the women wearing robes that left one shoulder and arm bare and wrapping their long hair around their heads. The fabrics were plain, and only a few had braid around the hems. There was little jewelry save for wooden hoop earrings and bracelets.

They ogled her for a few moments, and pointed. And then they began talking in a language she couldn't understand.

"Wonderful." Shilo sat the cloth on the ground, glad to be free of its weight. It was no longer wet from the dragon's saliva, the sun and time having dried it, and the metallic threads amid the red and blue swirls gleamed.

Everything was loud—so many of the villagers talking at once, to her and to each other. It was louder than the insects had been two nights past, and certainly more annoying. She looked for Nidintulugal, but in the press of bodies, she couldn't see him. Had the guards taken him? Had she not noticed them leading the priest away? He'd been seen with her, and so certainly he could be a target. The villagers' voices continued to swirl, and she clasped her hands to her ears in an effort to blot it all out.

"Stop!" Shilo hollered when a burly man stepped toward the fabric.

He stood board straight, surprised at her outburst, and everyone in the village quieted.

"Wonderful," Shilo muttered again.

She could hear sheep bleating and the wind teasing the crops. Nearby, clothes that had been hung out to dry flapped like awkward birds. She could hear her heart beating, too, nervous. That was one thing she'd almost always been since arriving here—nervous.

This was a bad idea, she thought. *Should've just taken some of their vegetables and been done with it.*

They continued to watch her, not one of them saying anything.

Oh, why, why can't I understand them? Why can't I make them understand me? She rubbed her palms on her robe, a gesture she'd adopted recently when she didn't know what to say or do.

"Listen, I'm hungry and I need some clothes. And I've brought this to trade." She pointed to the fabric, then fingered her robe. "I want to trade. I want..."

"Trade, yes. Trade for that very fine cloth you have brought to Ibinghal." She understood every word the burly man said. 'Trade with you for robes."

"And food." She shivered that she could understand him—and that he could understand her. How? How could she do this now? And not in Babylon? *Oh, why, why can't I understand them? Why can't I make them understand me?* Had those words—that strong desire—triggered the magic the dragon claimed was inside of her?

"Food, yes," the man said, nodding vigorously. He tentatively reached for the bolt of cloth, and this time Shilo didn't stop him.

"Who is she?" a tall girl asked her mother. The girl was reed-thin and had a heart-shaped face filled with curiosity. "The skin of her hands is the color of clouds."

"Is this the one the guards sought?" Shilo couldn't see who said this.

"Her voice is music," another said. "Beautiful are her words."

"She hides her face in the heat, why?"

"Where did she come by such marvelous cloth? It is the cloth of kings!"

"Did she steal it?"

"Is she a queen?"

"Did she bring it from Babylon?"

"Did she steal it from the Hand of Nebuchadnezzar?"

"Too heavy for her to carry far. See how Draduk wheezes under it?"

"How long will she stay? Who will take her in?"

"Why would you trade such beautiful cloth? Why would you not keep it?"

"Mother, she looks young."

"What does she want to eat?"

"Anything," Shilo quickly answered that question. "I am very, very hungry."

"She likes gandos." This came from Nidintulugal. He made his way through the throng, holding out a piece of the fruit like the ones he'd traded for in Babylon. "How is it, Shilo, that you can speak our language now?" He tossed her the fruit, then crossed his arms in front of his chest, clearly a perturbed expression on his face.

"It is a long story," she told him. Then she peeled and devoured the fruit, speaking between bites. "And one you probably would not believe."

"I have a need to hear a long tale," he returned. "And I will decide what I believe."

Shilo let Nidintulugal escort her into the largest building in the center of the settlement. It was roughly round, and the few roads radiated outward from it like spokes on a wheel. A place of fellowship, it had a few long tables and low benches, a pit in the center for cooking, and something that looked like a stage. The windows were narrow and high along the walls, like in many of the buildings she'd noted in Babylon. The interior smelled of smoke and cooking spices, and it made Shilo even hungrier.

A woman wearing a dark green robe, the only one of such a color Shilo had seen so far in the village, passed her a small jug of water. Shilo drained it, and her stomach ached because she'd drunk it so quickly.

"Thank you."

The woman nodded and retreated to the fire pit, where another woman was setting coals on a fire and a third was dumping something into a pot.

Nidintulugal pointed to one of the tables, and she sat at the bench across from him.

"Thank you, Nidin, for helping me flee from the city." Finally she could thank him so that he would understand.

Still, he retained the perturbed look.

"Guards came here looking for you, Shilo. They told everyone in Ibinghal—"

"The name of this village," she interrupted.

"—that you'd stolen something valuable from the Hand of Nebuchadnezzar."

"The rich man in the courtyard?"

A nod.

"I didn't, I—"

"I explained that to everyone after the guards left. Because I'm a priest of Shamash, they believe me. I—unlike city guards—would never lie." He watched the three women at the fire pit. "Though some whisper that you stole the cloth from the Hand."

"I didn't, Nidin, I—"

"Draduk—"

"The big man who took the cloth away—"

"Proved you could not have stolen the cloth from the Hand of Nebuchadnezzar. You could not have carried that out of the city without the guards catching you. Nor could you have managed to get it this far on your own."

"I wasn't on my own, Nidin. I was with you most of the time, and—"

"I told them, Shilo. Because I'm a priest of Shamash, they believe me. I told them everything, and that I believe the Hand wanted you because you are young and from a faraway place." He stretched across the table and brushed her hood back, and the people gathered in the building gasped. "I told them about your hair of fire and your speckled face."

She tried to ignore the stares, focusing on the women at the fire pit. One was putting vegetables into the pot, another, pieces of meat. She might have been a little particular about what she ate back in Marietta and Slade's Corners, but here she didn't care what the meat was; she was that hungry. The stew added to the scents of this place, so good it made her nearly swoon.

"The guards would have taken you, had you been here, Shilo."

She decided not to tell him that she'd seen the guards from her perch on the hill.

"Why didn't they take you, Nidin?"

"I am a priest of Shamash."

So *that pretty much answered everything, huh?* she thought. Perhaps priests in this society were immune to government dictates.

"They asked you about me?"

Another nod.

"And what did you tell them?"

"The truth. That I helped you flee the city and that we escaped by hiding in the river, and that we headed toward this village, but that you went away on your own. I did not see where you went."

"And they believed you?"

"Of course. I am—"

"—a priest of Shamash. I know."

"In truth I did not see where you went. And if I'd asked you where you were going, you would have spoken gibberish. Most peculiar that I can understand you now."

"Good thing for me, huh? That you couldn't talk to me then?" Shilo decided not to ask him if he would have given her away. She didn't think she'd like the answer to that. She was spared more conversation when the woman in the green robe brought her a steaming bowl filled with the stew. There was no spoon, but the woman passed her a large piece of hard bread, which Shilo used to sop up the liquid and shovel in the pieces of meat and vegetables when she tipped the bowl.

Nidintulugal left her for a few minutes, getting himself a bowl of the stew and talking to the women at the fire pit. He returned with a stoppered gourd.

"Goat's milk." He sat across from her and ate his stew, occasionally answering villagers' questions about his time with Shilo. "Because the cloth you brought here is so fine, they served you meat. It is used sparingly otherwise in this village." Then he gestured to an older man who wore a thin skirt and a cloak, the only one in the village wearing a cloak that Shilo noticed.

"They will wonder about your sandals," Nidintulugal told her. "But if you take them off, Hre-Threndal will help you."

Shilo finished the stew and set the bowl next to her, held what was left of the bread in her mouth and turned on the bench so that her back was to the table. She raised the hem of her robe, half expecting to hear the gasps that filled the building, and unlaced her tennis shoes. She tugged them off and sat them together on the ground under the bench. She watched the people staring at them, and wondered what they would think of her shorts and tank top. A small smile played across her face.

"Sorely injured," the old man pronounced when he lifted Shilo's feet. "Cruel sandals?"

Shilo frowned. "I hurt them when I was barefoot."

He nodded in understanding and reached into a pouch, pulling out a small jar and smearing the ointment in it on the bottoms of her feet. Rising, he grabbed her ankles and turned her, so her legs were on the bench.

"Stay off your feet for a while." Then he reached under the bench and retrieved her shoes, feeling the nylon sides and inadvertently smearing some of the ointment on them. He tapped the bottoms and sniffed them, then held them up so everyone could see.

"Enough, Hre-Threndal," Nidintulugal said.

The older man replaced the shoes and left the building.

"He goes to tell the others about your extraordinary sandals. You could do well trading them."

Probably not a good idea, Shilo thought. *Be interesting if some archaeologist discovered them in a dig.* "I'm rather attached to them, Nidin."

Finished with his stew, he pushed the bowl aside and leaned across the table. "Where did you get the fine cloth?"

"I figured you'd ask me where I went after I left you."

"That is precisely what I asked."

"I am not a priest of Shamash."

"But I do not believe you will lie to me."

She lowered her voice so he had to strain to hear her. She didn't want the others to eavesdrop. "I went to visit a dragon in the hills, the one pictured on the Ishtar Gate." *See if you believe that,* she thought.

Nidintulugal didn't ask her another question. He sat quietly, sometimes watching her, sometimes looking from one face to the next in the large room. There were probably ninety people inside, a little less than half of what she guessed was the population of this place. They parted when Hre-Threndal, the old man who'd tended to her feet, came back carrying a soft brown robe trimmed near the hem and along the neck with a band of shiny white material. He held it up and looked expectantly at her.

"That will be fine. Thank you." She reached out and accepted the garment, then wondered if she should ask for another, as the bolt of cloth she'd brought here must be valuable. It would be nice to have more than one change. But before she could ask for it, a second robe was brought in, this one darker and without trim, and with no right shoulder and sleeve. "Thank you again."

A few other things followed, including a pair of sandals—real sandals—, which the old man carefully put on her feet. One wooden bracelet, and when the woman in the green robe put it on Shilo's wrist, she marveled at the rings, the plastic snake in particular.

Shilo tugged it off and gave it to her, then wished she hadn't. What about archaeologists digging in this land?

A gourd filled with goat's milk was next, and a heavy pouch filled with nuts and dried fruit. Last came a net satchel for her to carry everything in.

"No more," Shilo said, getting the attention of the woman in the green robe. "I don't need anything else." She decided not to ask for a bath. The villagers smelled pungent, like they did not bathe often, and she figured it could go badly for her if they noticed her tank top and shorts. She eased herself off the bench, careful as she put weight on her feet—not because they still hurt, they didn't, but because she didn't want to slip and slide on the ointment.

"I have to leave."

"So soon?" This from the old man.

"Stay the night." From the green-robed woman.

"You must stay. The sun sets, praise Shamash. Soon we all sleep. It is the will of Shamash."

"Tell us of your sandals, and of the red ring you gave Elru."

A girl of Shilo's age edged forward. "Tell us why your hair looks like fire and why your skin is the color of clouds."

Questions continued to swirl around Shilo as she politely gathered up her new acquisitions and left the fellowship building. "Really, I have to go." She'd spotted carvings on some of the homes, of lions and suns and half-suns, not one of a dragon. Somehow she doubted the people in this village knew about Ulbanu. There'd been not a hint of recognition in Nidintulugal's eyes when she mentioned the dragon of the Ishtar Gate. Shock was more like it. Disbelief.

Could she leave without them seeing her go into the mountains? Should she be concerned about that?

"I will stay the night," she said, turning and going back to the doorway. "May I sleep in here?" She pointed to a mat near what she guessed was the stage.

"As you wish," Hre-Trendal said.

Shilo guessed he must have some position of power in the village, like a mayor.

Everyone seemed to defer to him.

"Yes, I wish to sleep here. I do not want to trouble anyone."

"As you wish," he repeated.

A short time later, Shilo was alone. Even Nidintulugal had left her. Someone stood outside the building, not a guard, but a villager assigned to help her should she need assistance. Her bolt of cloth and her odd sandals had marked her as a person to be respected. She waited until the villager was preoccupied with carving a piece of wood. It was getting late, the stars thick on a black field, lights in the village homes burning.

Then she slipped out, as quietly as she could manage, cutting between homes and quickly reaching the northern field. She padded down a wide row, getting used to the feel of the sandals. It was easy to see with so much starlight, and so she easily avoided ruts and holes made by burrowing animals. Then she cleared the fields and headed up the closest hill, making it up about fifty feet before something grabbed her ankle.

She cried out in surprise and spun, kicking furiously and almost striking Nidintulugal in the face.

"I do not believe you would lie to me, Shilo." In the starlight, the priest's face looked stem. "But there are no such things as dragons. So I would see the demon in the hills that gave you the cloth and that you go now to meet. I would see the demon that turned your mind and gave you the image of the dragon on the gate. The demon has corrupted your heart and casts shadows on Shamash. The demon has found a way into your mind and taught you our tongue to befuddle us and put us at ease. I would see and slay this demon."

14

THE HAND OF THE HAND

Ekurzakir shopped in the southern district on the banks of the Euphrates. The Hand of Nebuchadnezzar had given him a list of oddities not found in most of the districts in Babylon. But this small assortment of shops to the south catered to unusual tastes and often featured things imported from across the sea and from the east. The list should be filled here. Rarely did Arshaka send Ekurzakir on such trivial assignments, and so the "Hand of the Hand" guessed that these requested things were of significant import.

The first was ink said to be from sea creatures and was blacker than a starless sky. He purchased all he could find and paid for the bottles with small gold links, then moved to another shop and acquired quills made from the feathers of an extinct bird. Other things on the list were more exotic still, and would have most men wondering what they would be used for.

Ekurzakir did not question a single item or worry at their purpose. It was enough that the Hand of Nebuchadnezzar wanted them—and that he wanted the gathering of them kept secret. Ekurzakir practically worshipped Arshaka; he was well aware that the most amazing improvements to Babylon were the result of the Hand's plans. Too, Ekurzakir knew that the Hand gave all the credit to King Nebuchadnezzar, and that he told no one where the designs truly came from, letting the king take full credit. Ekurzakir had found out only because he'd inadvertently overheard the Hand and the king talking one day—and had made it a point to overhear other conversations from then on.

From that first fateful eavesdropping day on, Ekurzakir had secretly sworn fealty to Arshaka, who he thought as wise as Babylon's lesser gods. Some of that greatness might come Ekurzakir's way, if he remained loyal, and if he asked no questions and continued to serve the Hand obediently.

It took him the entire morning and into the afternoon to complete Arshaka's shopping list.

There was one other stop to make before returning to Arshaka's apartments. Ekurzakir carefully picked his way down a black stone-paved street that ran parallel to the city's south wall. It was called the Street of Dreams in hushed tones, but was known on maps by another name. The vendors here dealt in expensive powders to aid in sleep, delicacies favored by Babylon's shady element, and fortunes. Ekurzakir was unaware that the greatest seers in the city operated in an unmarked shop in the western section, and that Arshaka sometimes relied on them.

Ekurzakir paid a gold link to a beggar leaning near a beaded curtain. "Will this buy me knowledge today?"

The beggar grinned, showing a row of unusually healthy teeth. "It will buy you the way to knowledge."

Ekurzakir scowled and cursed himself for giving the man one of the links. The gold he paid here would only buy him an audience; it would cost him more once inside. He thought to argue with the man, who was in truth a guard for the seer. Another time, he decided. The knowledge he sought today was valuable, and so he would meet the price. He nodded, and the guard held back the beads so Ekurzakir could pass.

The Hand of Nebuchadnezzar would not approve of this course of action; the Hand was above calling on the dark arts for aid, and possibly would have forbade their use. So he would simply not tell Arshaka of this visit or of the cost, instead saying that the ink and other goods were unexpectedly expensive and required more links than anticipated. Ekurzakir had a silky voice and could make his tales believable, even to Arshaka.

It was stifling inside the narrow building, which unlike the others on this street had no windows. The occupants used candles and lanterns for light, and did not seem to mind the infernal heat and lack of air circulation. He passed by the doorway to his right and climbed a set of stone stairs that were well worn in the middle—a testament to the numerous visitors this place had seen in the decades. There were two doorways at the top, and Ekurzakir squared his shoulders and rolled his neck before choosing the one to his left.

His eyes watered from the strong incense burning in four ceramic holders in the tiny room.

"Sarazel," Ekurzakir said, bowing slightly to the crone sitting on a frayed rug.

"Hand of the Hand," she returned without looking up. Her gaze was fixed on a collection of small bones and beads in front of her. "I sensed you would come this day."

He rested his purchases next to the doorway and sat opposite her, crossing his legs and placing his calloused hands on his knees, palms up. She reached forward and sprinkled sand in one palm and put a bit of bone and an animal tooth in the other.

"And do you also sense, Sarazel, what I have come for?"

The woman finally looked up. Her skin was almost black and was so deeply wrinkled her face looked like a shriveled prune from which tiny white eyes poked out. She might have been blind, but Ekurzakir knew she could find her way around this section of the city; in the past he'd seen her at some of the shops he'd visited today.

"Knowledge, always knowledge, Hand of the Hand." Sarazel returned to studying the bones and beads, her spindly fingers rearranging them into one pattern after the next. She continued to speak as she worked. "You have not visited me for long months, Ekurzakir. So long that I thought you dead or gone from the great city. Then yesterday I dreamed of you and a more glorious Babylon. You were dressed in the finest robes and jewels danced on your fingers."

He smiled. So tying his lot to the Hand of Nebuchadnezzar would gain him prosperity. "And you dreamed I would come here, Sarazel?"

She nodded. "You want to know about a girl who graced Babylon, but is not from the great city."

Ekurzakir did not hide his amazement. "Yes, Sarazel. With pale skin the color of the full moon, the girl speaks a language unknown to me." He leaned forward, careful not to drop the sand and the bone and tooth. "Have you seen her?"

"I saw her in a dream, Hand of the Hand. I saw her before she arrived at the Ishtar Gate."

The girl is indeed important! Ekurzakir thought. He was certain Arshaka wanted her for something other than pleasure. The rest of the guards might not suspect anything beyond Arshaka's words, but Ekurzakir had been near the Hand of Nebuchadnezzar long enough to sense when other motives were involved.

"Is she powerful, Sarazel, this girl? Is she a seer?"

The crone shook her head. "She is clouded, Ekurzakir. Most odd. It is as if she walks in the fog that clings to the river. She is difficult to understand and to locate."

"But you see her?"

"I see her running from the city guards."

"That is the past. They have not yet caught her."

"With a priest I see her running."

"Nidintulugal, a minor priest of Shamash. He is—"

"Water surrounds her and covers her."

"The guards believe they escaped in the river."

Sarazel said nothing else, continuing to move the bones and beads.

"Did she drown in the river, Sarazel?"

The crone pulled a few bones to the side of her design.

"Is she dead?"

She rearranged more of the beads.

"What is the girl?"

"Trouble to you, Ekurzakir, and to the Hand of Nebuchadnezzar. She is not powerful now, but she will be—if she is not stopped."

"I must find her."

"She is not an evil thing, Ekurzakir. But neither is she a tool for any great good. I hesitate to reveal her, for I've no desire to bring about the demise of a young one who is not tainted. That could anger the fates and attract the unwanted attention of a demon. It could blemish my soul."

"I will make it worth your while, Sarazel."

"Material wealth will not enrich my path beyond this life, Ekurzakir."

Ekurzakir considered a threat, but the furrowing of the crone's brow hinted that she knew what he was thinking. Physical threats were meaningless anyway, he suspected.

"This is very important to me, old woman." He tried unsuccessfully to keep the ire out of his voice. "I need to know where the girl is. I need to know—quickly."

Sarazel brushed the bones and beads from in front of her and splayed her wrinkled hands flat against the rug, thumbs touching. "She is in darkness, Hand of the Hand, inside the earth."

"Dead? Buried?"

The crone shook her head. "I told you she is trouble to you, and the dead do not trouble the living. She breathes, Ekurzakir, well outside Babylon and near the ridge. There is a village there, of farmers and shepherds."

"Ibinghal. I know of it."

"Her precise location is masked, Ekurzakir, by something more powerful than I. An art neither dark nor light wraps her in its cloak. But she breathes near all of that."

He brushed the sand from his palm and placed the bit of bone and the animal tooth with the rest, stood and bowed again. Then he reached into his pocket and retrieved another gold link.

"I'll accept no payment," Sarazel said. "And you will not come here again."

15

Secrets Shared

Shilo was exhausted by the time she found the opening to the dragon's cave. In the end, she closed her eyes in exasperation and prayed to find it. The dragon was her way home, and therefore she had to find the dragon. The cave, oddly, was near a rocky outcropping she'd passed by several times in her searching. Why hadn't she noticed it before?

She'd tried to get Nidintulugal to return to the village, but he dogged her steps, determined that what she sought was a demon, and equally determined to slay it. He had even brought a knife with him, tucked in his belt.

"There's no such thing as a demon," she told him. But her words held more conviction than her thoughts. If there were dragons and magic and time travel, there could be demons. Couldn't there? "Ulbanu is a dragon, not a demon."

"The dragon of the Ishtar Gate?"

"Yes, but no." Shilo had shaken her head, certain Nidintulugal could see her well in all the starlight. "Ulbanu looks like that, but the dragon'll get mad if you call it that. It says it's just a dragon, not an aspect of a god or—"

"It is a demon, Shilo, and I will slay it with the power of Shamash."

"And that knife? Hah!" She groaned and didn't speak to him again until after she'd found the cave. The stench of the dragon didn't reach outside, something she'd noticed when she left to go to the village. Perhaps that was part of the dragon's magic, and helped it to go undiscovered, stopping its stink at the cave mouth. Perhaps she would not have discovered the cave opening were it not for her own magic.

"This is going to smell bad," she told Nidintulugal. "Worse than I smell for sweating so much and not taking a bath for days. The dragon smells horrible."

"Demons reek," he replied.

"And you know this? You've met a demon before?"

He shook his head. "I have studied about them, Shilo, at the feet of the elder priests of Shamash in the great city of Babylon."

"And they've met demons before?"

Nidintulugal didn't answer.

Shilo was just as struck by the dragon's size and presence as she had been the first time. Again she was trembling and weak-kneed, though she got over it faster this time. The smell was just as odious, and the dragon still gave off enough light so they could see it and the enormous cave.

"Ulbanu, this is Nidintulugal. He is the priest of Shamash who helped me escape from Babylon. I didn't want to bring him here."

The dragon's narrowed eyes told Shilo it hadn't wanted Nidintulugal here either.

"But he is persistent," she continued. "And he did save my life." She paused.

"Nidintulugal, this is the dragon Ulbanu." She turned to gesture to the priest so she could formally and properly introduce them, but Nidintulugal had passed out in one of the pools of the dragon's saliva.

"He thought you were a demon," Shilo said, turning back to face Ulbanu. She would deal with Nidintulugal later; he was breathing strongly and didn't look hurt.

The dragon growled, the rumble racing through the cave floor and causing Shilo to lose her balance. She picked herself up and brushed at her robe and decided not to complain about it.

"There are demons in this world, Shilo. Creatures smaller, but far more powerful than I—powerful because they use their magic to foul ends, and do not worry of the consequences."

Again the dragon's words came in Shilo's head.

Shilo shuddered, more because she feared the dragon was angry with her for bringing Nidintulugal than because she'd mentioned a demon.

"Child, you are here to fight such demons. To save dragonkind—"

"—and perhaps mankind," Shilo finished. She suddenly felt chilled in this very warm cave.

So you're going to tell me now just what i'm supposed to do, right?" Shilo sat a few yards back from the dragon in a chamber deeper in the hills.

It was a larger chamber than the one she'd met Ulbanu in, and so for the first time she could see all of the dragon. She put it at two hundred feet or more from nose to tail tip, and it curled around a natural stone wall, looking peculiarly catlike. The floor was wet, either from the dragon's saliva or its condensed breath or both, and she took care not to slip.

"Do you ever leave this cave?" Shilo had meant to press the dragon on the matter of teaching her about magic and pursuing demons, but the question came out. "You're … huge. How could you leave this place and someone not see you?"

"Some nights I leave. To hunt and fly."

Shilo noticed the dragon lacked wings. But she supposed its magic let it fly.

"Though rarely do I leave, else I would risk discovery and bring about my doom faster than the years bring it upon me. My magic cloaks me, and it well hides the entrance to my cave. But there are those who can see through the enchantment."

"Like me? I found my way here."

Ulbanu tapped a claw against the cave floor in what seemed an impatient gesture.

"Back to the demons, huh? And saving dragonkind and perhaps mankind." She settled herself on the cave floor, not minding if this robe got damp. She had the two she'd traded for in the village, and she intended to put one of those on after she discovered a way to take a bath. Shilo looked at the dragon—there had to be water deeper in the cave; a creature of such size would need a water source. There was at least another chamber beyond this; she could see a wide, black slash in the rocks that was the opening. Maybe there was some water there, and she could wash herself.

"Bad enough that you were gone so long to the village, Shilo. Can you not grasp the importance and urgency in this?"

Shilo quickly told the dragon about seeing the guards and waiting until they left before going into the village.

"The rich man," the dragon began, *"he wants you badly, Shilo. Perhaps he has discerned that you threaten him. He will send more than guards soon."*

Shilo sucked in a breath. "I've threatened no one!"

"But you will, child, him in particular, if you are to—"

"—save dragonkind—"

"—and perhaps mankind."

Shilo let out a great sigh. "Please tell me what this is all about."

The dragon's expression changed, and were the face human, Shilo would have called it sad. The huge eyes darkened, and the light that emanated from its hide dimmed.

"I said I leave my cave, though rarely." The dragon shifted so that its head was directly across from Shilo. It set its jaw against the cave floor, sending ripples in a pool of saliva.

"I sensed a herd of wild camels to the north, and so I flew to hunt. I require little food, Shilo, magic largely sustains me. But from time to time a hunger comes, and so I went after the camels."

Shilo patiently listened, curious how camels were going to tie into Babylon and demons and her needing to save dragons and men.

"I feasted, leaving not a drop of blood or a piece of fur behind to mark my passage. I gorged myself on their sweet meat. They were easy prey, locked to the ground in their terror of me."

Shilo wrinkled her nose, picturing Ulbanu swooping down on the camels and swallowing them right and left.

"Drunk in my fullness, I took to the sky and soared, staying too long away from my lair."

Shilo rested back on her hands. This had nothing to do with demons and the rich man in Babylon, and were Ulbanu not a frighteningly huge dragon, she would have voiced her boredom at the tale.

"When I returned to this cave, my eggs were gone."

Shilo's eyes snapped wide. "Eggs?" Ulbanu was a she.

"Four perfect eggs, Shilo." The dragon's visage registered more than sadness, Shilo realized; it was etched with despair and utter loss. *"There are few dragons in the world in this time, and none in yours unless you aid me. Men have hunted us to near-extinction, and perhaps rightly so. Many of my brethren were filled with darkness and preyed upon men and other creatures. They brought about their own demise, as the men banded together and changed the tide of the hunt. But my eggs, they hold a promise of a future."*

Ulbanu paused and closed her eyes, opening them and seeing past Shilo to another time.

"Not all of my brethren were cruel and so voracious, yet most of the men could not distinguish us, and so pursued us all. We few who are left live in remote places. I thought only a scattering of men knew I laired here. I thought myself safe. And I thought my offspring would flourish."

"The sage," Shilo whispered. "The one who had the puzzle. He knew you lived here."

"Yes, the sage was one. But there must have been others I was unaware of. When I feasted on the camels—a trap that was well planned for me—I left my eggs vulnerable. And I paid the highest price for my foolishness."

"Why would anyone want your eggs?" The moment after Shilo asked the question, she realized the answer. To tame a dragon—dragons—to have them under your control, would make you powerful. Like a man in modern times having possession of a nuclear bomb. "So you need me to find your eggs, right?"

"Not find them. I know where they are, Shilo."

Shilo sputtered and shook her head in disbelief. "Then why do you need me? Why is my magic required? Never mind that I don't understand what my magic is and what I can do with it. If you know where your eggs are, why not just swoop right in and take them? Swallow the men who stole them and …"

The dragon's growl was low and sent a soft tremor through the floor. *"The common citizens of Babylon, even the great King Nebuchadnezzar, do not know I exist. My image is on their gate, but so too are the images of lions and bulls and suns. I cannot risk showing myself. In doing so I would risk my life, my eggs, and the lives of other dragons who lair elsewhere."*

"Because everyone would know for certain that dragons exist." Shilo scratched her head. "But won't they know dragons exist anyway if your eggs hatch and someone controls your offspring?"

"Not if you are successful, Child of Sigurd."

This time Shilo did not tell the dragon that she hated that title.

"So I'm supposed to use my magic to rescue your eggs." She stuck out her lower lip and exhaled, her breath cool against her sweat-dotted face. Shilo pushed back her hood, wriggled out of the robe, and sat on it. The heat was only a little more bearable in her shorts and tank top. "I don't even know how to use my magic, beyond finding your cave and finding my way to ancient Babylon."

"I will teach you a little, Child of Sigurd, just enough, as our time is short. You must discover the extent of your magic on your own. My eggs will hatch before ten days pass. You must be successful."

"I realize that." Shilo was angry with herself for tarrying in the village— she should have left as soon as she'd made her trade for the clothes, shouldn't have gone there to begin with. But without the clothes, she'd be easily recognized in Babylon, and perhaps easily caught. "I have to find your eggs and bring them back here." She pursed her lips. "I understand how important this is to you and to dragonkind. But how is this going to save mankind?" There, she'd asked it—what's in it for her?

"The men who have my eggs will use them for ill, Shilo. Look." Ulbana scratched her talon across the stone floor, making a deep groove that shimmered in the pale light cast by the dragon.

The shimmering spread to the rest of the stone, and within heartbeats the floor resembled a frozen-over lake. Shilo had not personally seen one, but her father had pictures of Wisconsin lakes in the winter in an old album. She wished it felt cold like ice, but it felt no different than the stone that had been there moments before. The surface sparkled and became as clear as glass, and then an image formed in the space between her and the dragon.

'That's Babylon?" Shilo gasped.

Shilo recognized part of it, from her tour with Nidintulugal. The view the dragon presented in the magical vision was top-down, like she was a bird hovering over the city and trying to take it all in.

The Hanging Gardens seemed larger and more amazing than when she'd walked by them. She stared—they were larger. There were more tiers, stretching up and up like a skyscraper, and the shades of green were amazing. She saw trees from distant parts of the world—birch trees that she knew weren't found anywhere near Mesopotamia or Iraq, massive weeping willows laced with kudzu, cypress trees found in swampy lands, pinyon pines, and more.

"How did they?" She let the question hang as she continued to ogle the city. Three waterfalls graced the gardens, in addition to the water conveyor that siphoned from the Euphrates to keep this place verdant. Colorful parrots flitted here and there, macaws from South America, toucans, and African grays. Spider monkeys scampered in the branches, and she had a hard time pulling her eyes away from it. "It's like Busch Gardens in Florida, but better."

She looked to the Processional Way, which was longer and wider, the walls and buildings rising on either side of it more spectacular than before. More images of dragons, lions, and bulls were displayed, some carved, some molded and glazed. The Ishtar Gate was still there, but there were three more gates beyond it, each taller and more impressive than the one before.

"When is this?" Shilo continued to study the gates, and the palace that was easily three times the size as before. The temples were still there, and she located the Temple of Shamash by the river. It was no longer in the southern part of the city—Babylon had expanded that much. Now the temple sat roughly in the middle.

"Not quite one hundred years from now," Ulbanu answered.

"A long time," Shilo said. But not so long considering how much the city had grown. She couldn't spot the poor quarters she'd traipsed through. All the buildings were shiny and fine, and all had doors and wide windows, many of glass. The roofs were glazed tiles, some with decorations on them. It was all so incredibly beautiful. *How could this be a bad thing?* she wondered. *How could this upset the dragon?*

The image shifted to the south, so all she could see was the outer wall now, ten feet thick and patrolled by guards with bows and spears. The land beyond looked blasted, as if bombs had been dropped on it.

Scrub grass grew here and there, near the banks of the Euphrates. Once more she remembered her father reading the Bible, and that the "great river Euphrates" had been mentioned in connection with apocryphal events. One such event had certainly happened in those hundred years.

"Show me more, Ulbanu."

The image shifted farther south, and Shilo saw the remains of village after village, all looking like they'd been bombed. Everything was in ruins. Farther south she saw small clusters of people, living in tents and keeping camels and sheep, but the people and animals looked emaciated and hopeless. The image turned to the north now, finding the land parched where once irrigated fields had thrived. The village Shilo had traded with was gone, only scattered bricks and chunks of tile hinted that something had been there. The hills beyond, where Ulbanu laired, had been flattened, as if some great earthquake had leveled everything.

"Was there an earthquake, Ulbanu?" Shilo hoped something natural and beyond anyone's ability to prevent had been responsible. "Or was it your offspring?"

"Neither," Ulbanu rasped. The word was audible this time and sent a tremor through the floor.

Farther north and to the east was another city, where Shilo guessed Baghdad would sit in modern-day Iraq. It looked like a miniature version of Babylon, and there were similar images of lions, bulls, and the Ishtar dragon on walls and towers. Again the land around the city looked bleak and blasted, and farther out were the ruins of more villages. The only crops she'd seen were within the walled cities.

"Beautiful and horrible at the same time," Shilo said. "How did this happen?"

The dragon tapped a claw and the image quavered, like a camera going out of focus and coming back in. This time it was night, or perhaps Shilo looked into some dark cavern or cellar. Tiny red flames flickered, but they didn't produce enough light to reveal anything of the surroundings. The flames were set in pairs, and as Shilo stared, she saw twisted faces, some with scales and bulging lips, some with no lips, all of it too shadowy to make out many details.

"They're not lights," she said after a moment. "They're eyes." The red flames flickering were eyes blinking. "Demons."

"Yes, those are demons." The voice came from behind Shilo. Standing a few feet back, sweat-soaked and trembling, was Nidintulugal.

16

BABYLON BADLY REBORN

The red eyes and shadowy shapes became a swirling mass of dark fire that spread like a surging wave across the land, moving so frenetically that Shilo and Nidintulugal could not see the actual forms of the demons. They could tell that the malicious creatures devoured everything in their path—buildings, pens, animals, trees, and people.

Shilo stared as the swarm circled a well in a prosperous village, the stones of it withered to dust and the water boiled up and turned to steam that scalded birds that had been flying overhead.

The swarm of demons seemed to be selective, passing by some villages and nomadic bands and leveling others into ruins. There was not enough left of the victims to bury.

"There are always a few survivors so they can relate the horrible tale," Ulbanu supplied.

The dragon continued to speak aloud, the power of her voice sending stone dust down from the ceiling.

"Others need to be told of the terror so others could be afraid. Fear makes it easier to conquer people."

The swath of red came to a sizable city, which Nidintulugal said was southeast of Babylon. "It is a place King Nebuchadnezzar hopes to take under his influence. For years they have resisted the king's attempts."

Red flowed up the city walls, which melted beneath the highly corrosive demons. Sound came with the image, a chittering, hissing, cackling cacophony that caused both the people in the city under siege and Nidintulugal and Shilo in the cave to cover their ears. Man upon man fell to the swarm, and no woman or child was spared. Then the demon hoard melted into the ground, turning the earth blood-red and sending the city into ruins. The chittering subsided, replaced by the moans of the dying.

Clouds raced across the sky, and the sun rose and set in rapid succession indicating the passage of time. A city grew up in place of the devastated one, this looking like another miniature Babylon. It was swiftly populated with hundreds who migrated there.

"Loyal to the King of Babylon," Nidintulugal guessed. "Loyal because they fear his demon army. Fear makes the conquering easy."

"I thought demons were all made-up," Shilo said. "The stuff of Stephen King stories and bad horror movies."

"At least as real as dragons," Ulbanu said. "More powerful than dragons because of their numbers and their intent."

"Are they in my time, the demons?" Shilo didn't want to think about such a hoard sweeping across the face of Wisconsin.

The dragon scratched a talon on the cave floor. "Hidden, like dragons are now. But far less in their numbers and strength if you are successful, Shilo. Never to be wholly destroyed, but they can be crippled."

So she could save dragonkind and perhaps mankind by saving Ulbanu's eggs.

"But what do your eggs have to do with all of these demons? I see demons ruining cities and killing people. I don't see a single dragon or any of your eggs. Your eggs don't hatch into demons, do they?"

"No." The dragon let out a great sigh that gusted across the cavern and evaporated the sweat off Shilo. "My magic is not absolute, Shilo. I only know that my offspring will play a role in the coming catastrophe. And I know that only you have a chance to stop it. Only you, Child of Sigurd. My magic has divined that in all of the world, in all of the times, you are the one."

Shilo stood and shook out her arms, still keeping her gaze on the image of the reborn city. "I'm fifteen years old."

"And I am nearly fifteen hundred."

The dragon's age did not surprise Shilo.

"Look, I understand that you don't want to swoop down on Babylon, reveal yourself and thereby let the world know dragons still exist. But I would think you'd risk all of that to stop all of this." She stabbed a finger at the image. The scene had shifted once more, showing demons sweeping at the front of an army, heading to the east.

The chittering resumed.

The dragon sighed again, the force of the breath nearly knocking Shilo over. "I would risk all of that, Shilo, and more if I knew I would be successful. But I have divined the fate of a direct approach by me as a failure. The world will know of dragons, my eggs will be lost, and the demons will still be loosed. I would accomplish nothing good."

Nidintulugal stepped up to Shilo's side. He quivered, though not as pronounced as a few minutes earlier. He swallowed hard and looked up to stare into one of the dragon's eyes. "How can this one girl succeed when a creature as powerful as yourself is destined to fail?" He shook his head to emphasize his disbelief. "This makes no sense to me."

The cave floor trembled when the dragon growled. More stone dust filtered down, and a crack appeared at Nidintulugal's feet.

"Because she is magic," the dragon said. "Powerful, even though she does not realize to what extent. And above all of that, she is small."

"Small?" Shilo raised her head from the image. "What's small got to do with it?"

"My eggs are beneath the earth, Shilo, hidden from me and from men, in a horrid warren twisted by the foulest of men. Beneath Babylon. They are below a place beautiful and green."

"Tunnels below the Hanging Gardens?"

"I do not know what men call the place. But my divinations show it to be the greenest land in all of Babylon. The tunnels below, though, are dark and hidden from my magical prying. Narrow and—"

"You're saying that you're too big to go get the eggs?"

"Shilo, do not ask why I cannot dig for them."

Shilo was going to ask just that. "Because in doing that, you'd probably collapse something and break your eggs."

"Yes."

"Dragon eggs are fragile, huh?"

"All life is fragile," the dragon returned.

Shilo sagged against Nidintulugal. "So I need to sneak into Babylon, which I can do because I have new clothes, find my way beneath the city, retrieve the eggs, and bring them back here?"

"Yes."

"Oh, that'll be a piece of cake."

The dragon gave her a quizzical look.

"How heavy is one of these eggs?"

"You carried the bolt of cloth to the village."

Shilo realized the trip to the village was a test. If she could carry the fabric to the village, she could carry a dragon egg.

"But there are four eggs." Shilo was talking to herself now, and had leaned away from Nidintulugal. "Four trips from somewhere under Babylon. I'd have to get a wagon to get them out of the city. They have wagons, don't they?" She remembered seeing one on the street. "Does the village down the hill have a wagon?" She could take that into Babylon. "Four trips."

"You will be risking your life, Child of Sigurd. And you will need help." The dragon looked at Nidintulugal.

A profound silence settled in the cave.

Deep in the hill, no sounds from outside could be heard. There was just the rhythmic breath of the dragon, echoing against the walls, its force stirring Shilo's hair like a strong breeze.

"I will aid Shilo. It is the will of Shamash that—"

"Accepted, priest. But your help alone will not be enough," Ulbanu interjected. "Four eggs, four people, four hearts and minds, four wills, four with courage."

Four, Shilo thought, *like the four dragons pictured on the lid of the puzzle box.*

"More priests of Shamash?" Shilo looked to Nidintulugal.

"Perhaps." He rubbed his chin and shifted forward on the balls of his feet. "They must be made to understand about dragons and the threat of demons. Priests would believe me."

Unless they think you're mad, Shilo thought. *Then they'll try to lock you up.*

"Priests, they would stay silent on this matter if I asked them."

"I guess it's settled then," Shilo said. "This is all pretty dangerous, Mission Impossible skullduggery, and no Tom Cruise in sight. But if I want to get home, I'll give it a shot. We'll sneak into the city and—"

"No." Ulbanu had closed her eyes. "Priests of Shamash are not the answer. They believe in their god, but not in magic. They will think you a demon, Shilo, or touched by one. There is too much risk in approaching them. Besides, the temple is watched."

"I did not believe in magic," Nidintulugal whispered. Louder: "I will convince them, great dragon. I will find a way to reach the priests and—"

"There is another way." The dragon's lips quivered, sending ripples in the pool of saliva beneath her jaw. The image of a devastated land shattered, the chittering of demons receded, and the floor's stony appearance returned. "I sense two others who will aid you, Shilo, priest. I call them even now, and they will come. You will soon find them in the courtyard."

"In Babylon?" Shilo didn't like the sound of this.

"Where you appeared in the city," Ulbanu continued. "They believe in magic and dragons, and if you are convincing they will follow your instructions."

"Wh-who?"

The dragon didn't answer this, as she started humming, a dissonant tune that Shilo instinctively knew was some sort of spell. "Ulbanu, you said you'd teach me how to use my magic, you said—"

The humming continued for several moments more, growing louder and causing the cavern to shake.

Nidintulugal looked on wide-eyed, and Shilo wondered just how much of all of this he really believed. Spiderweb-fine cracks appeared in the cavern floor, and Shilo worried that the hill would come down on top of them. But then the humming stopped and the cavern settled. Ulbanu opened her eyes.

"You gained things in the village, Shilo. Bring them."

Shilo decided against repeating the question, and retreated to the other chamber and brought in the net bag. She started to pull out the clothes, looking for a dry spot on the cavern floor to place them.

"No, the nuts."

"Nuts?" How did the dragon know what she'd traded for? She shook her head; the dragon seemed to know a lot about a lot of things. She reached for the bag of nuts.

"Sit."

Shilo likened herself to a dog in obedience school, but complied.

"The nuts…"

Shilo put them in her hands, turning them over, feeling the smoothness of some of the shells, and the wrinkled roughness of others. "I need a better disguise than just the clothes, don't I, Ulbanu?"

'Yes." The dragon seemed pleased that Shilo comprehended the point of this lesson.

"But how? What's nuts got to do with—" *Sherwood Forest!* Shilo thought. She'd read a story about Robin Hood and his Merry Men, and how one of them needed a disguise and so made a dye from walnut shells. "I need to have darker skin, don't I?"

"As will your new companions," the dragon said.

111

"How can I—" Shilo juggled the nuts so she could take off all of her rings. Then she cupped the nuts close to her, stared at them, and concentrated. Like ice cubes, they melted in her hands and turned into a paste that she rubbed on her arms and face and legs and feet. There was just enough to cover her entirely, and when she was done she looked into one of the pools of saliva, using it as a mirror. "Wow. It worked."

"Your magic, Shilo, is to manipulate things. You altered the nuts because you willed it. Use your newfound skill well."

"Wow," she said again. She replaced her rings, careful not to spread the nut dye on them.

Nidintulugal gaped at her, his gaze alternating from her hands to her face, his lips moving, but no sound coming out.

"But my hair. I don't think nut shells will work on that."

Nidintulugal shook his head to clear his senses and retrieved Shilo's net bag. He fumbled with it for a few moments, then cinched the tie cord and placed it on Shilo's head like an odd-looking hat. It was similar to some of the head coverings she'd seen women in Babylon wear.

"Your companions come, Shilo, priest. Though the journey will take most of a day, it would be best that you be in the courtyard to meet them. Pity if they would draw the attention of Babylon's guards."

Shilo selected the brown robe and put it on. *No time for that bath,* she glumly decided.

Wouldn't want one now anyway; it would only wash off her new skin. For a brief moment she thought about the tennis shoes, much more comfortable than these sandals. She grabbed up her old robe, and the other one she'd traded for in the village. She figured she might need them for the two others the dragon had summoned.

"I don't suppose my magic will let me fly or run really fast to whisk us back to Babylon?"

Ulbanu gave a disconcerted sigh. 'Your magic, Shilo—"

"—allows me to manipulate materials. I know." She offered the dragon a weak smile.

"Wish me luck, huh?"

"I wish you well," the dragon returned.

It was still dark when they reached the village, though the sky was lightening ever so faintly in the east.

"I will need something different to wear," Nidintulugal said. "A ... disguise ... as you name it. And you will need more nuts for the people we are to meet in the courtyard."

On the trip down he'd asked her how she would notice the two who would help them. Shilo merely raised her eyebrows and gave him a "how do you think" look.

"They will look out of place," Nidintulugal said to himself.

"Like a fish pedaling a bicycle."

It was his turn to raise his eyebrows.

Shilo had expected him to find the village elder or mayor, the old gentleman who'd tended to her feet. Instead, he crept around to the eastern edge of the village, plucked a man's robe off a line, reached in through a few windows to gather bowls of nuts, and then scuttled to what passed for a barn. Every few minutes he held his finger to his lip to make sure Shilo stayed quiet. *Like I'm going to make a racket now,* she thought.

Inside the barn he pointed to a four-wheeled wagon and a large, two-wheeled cart. He selected the latter, which looked sturdier and less worn, and pulled it outside, cringing when the wheels creaked as they moved. He did his best to silently hitch it to an ox, and to put the small bowls of nuts in it. The village had one ox and a big horse. Shilo had gestured to the horse, but he shook his head and led the ox through a pair of buildings and down the widest village street. A few people were stirring; hushed conversations and the clanking of pots drifted out of windows. Shilo took off a pair of her silver earrings and placed them on the windowsill of one of the homes where he'd appropriated the nuts. She breathed a sigh of relief that no one had stopped them.

He turned the ox north and started in that direction away from the village. Shilo tugged on his belt.

"What do you think you're doing?"

Nidintulugal gestured with his head toward the village. "Gehud watches us out his front door. And Nurthar saw us out his window. Let them think we go to the north."

Shilo fell in beside him, deciding not to stay with this ruse long. She didn't have to. As soon as they'd passed out of sight of the village, by following a curve in the road, Nidintulugal put on the borrowed robe, and took the ox off the road and started southwest.

The land sloped down, and so they would not be spotted by any villagers—unless they came out onto the road and purposely looked in this direction.

113

A mile later, they made their way through tall grass, the stalks so high it hid them at times.

"Now you have me confused, Nidin." Shilo reached over and scratched at the ox's neck.

She was walking on the opposite side of the ox now, talking across it to Nidintulugal.

"You stole that robe and this cart, this ox, bowls of nuts. *Stole* them." She had put her two spare robes in the cart, glad to have her hands free.

"Borrowed them, Shilo."

"Not very priestly, whatever you want to call it. And there's no borrowing—the nuts."

Her brow furrowed, and she opened her mouth to press the matter.

"I will return these things, Shilo, if I am able. And pay them for the nuts."

"Able?"

"If demons become involved, I...we...may not live through this. But if we do, I will return these things and compensate the people for their use." Nidintulugal's face was lined with worry. "I could not simply ask to use these things, though my friends in that place would have allowed it. They would have wanted to know what I needed these things for."

"And a priest of Shamash does not lie."

"I would have told them, yes. Though I would not have mentioned the dragon."

"Just dragon eggs."

"Eggs. Just eggs."

Shilo smiled at that. While the priest wouldn't lie, he wouldn't necessarily tell the complete truth. "You would make a good politician in my time, Nidin."

"I do not understand the word. Politician."

"That's all right. I don't understand politicians either."

The banter ended, Nidintulugal tugged the ox into a reasonably fast pace. Shilo thought the horse would have been the better option, but as she watched the animal's muscles ripple in the growing light, she realized the ox was stronger, maybe younger, and should have little trouble pulling a cart filled with four heavy dragon eggs. They could have traveled faster without the ox and cart, but then they would have to deal with acquiring something similar in Babylon. Perhaps Nidintulugal didn't have anyone to borrow these things from in the city, Shilo thought.

They traveled through what was left of the night, staying off the road and not seeing the squad of guards that marched toward the village, led by the Hand of the Hand.

17

IBINGHAL'S DISRUPTION

Ekurzakir stood before the hand of nebuchadnezzar, face glowing with pride. He'd presented the items on the shopping list, which made Arshaka smile. Ekurzakir had not seen Arshaka smile in many days, and so he decided to reveal the rest of his information, rather than save it—to make his employer supremely pleased.

"There are people in this city, Hand of Nebuchadnezzar, who deal in rumors and secrets."

Arshaka nodded as he sniffed the special ink. "And they gave some of their secrets to you." It was not a question.

"Yes, Hand."

Arshaka looked up and waited. He did not press Ekurzakir. His expression admitted that Ekurzakir had something promising to disclose and would relish the telling.

"The girl traveled to a village north of here, a place of farmers and shepherds."

"Ibinghal?"

"Yes. I do not know if she is still there, but I have assembled a dozen guards to accompany me. If she is hiding in Ibinghal, we will take her and bring her back to the city. If she is not there, we will discover where she is."

Arshaka was obviously pleased and disturbed by the news.

"While I want this girl, Ekurzakir, I wanted as few as possible involved in her capture. One dozen guards...I would have chosen three or four of my closest men. Still, my men have come up empty-handed so far." King

Nebuchadnezzar would be away for weeks, and had left Babylon in Arshaka's more than capable hands. On his return, the king might learn nothing of the girl, and certainly nothing of Arshaka's plan. "Until it is too late."

"Your pardon, Hand of Nebuchadnezzar?"

"Nothing, Ekurzakir. You brighten my day with this information."

Ekurzakir did not try to hide his smile.

"I was going to keep this information to myself for a time," he admitted. "I wished to come by the girl and bring her here to surprise you."

"Surprises are not always good." Arshaka's eyes narrowed almost imperceptibly. "Better that you told me. Better that you keep no secrets, Ekurzakir."

"Yes, Hand of Nebuchadnezzar. By your will, I go to lead the men to the village of Ibinghal."

"You have my leave," Arshaka said. He reached out and clamped his hand on Ekurzakir's shoulder, applying a little pressure, which could be taken either as friendship or a warning. Arshaka meant it as both. "Hurry, and be successful."

Ekurzakir rushed from Arshaka's apartments, wishing he'd not told the Hand of the girl's possible whereabouts. If for some reason he was not successful, things would not go well for him.

"Then I simply must be successful," he said to himself, racing through the streets and down the Processional Way, where the dozen were gathered. He had a horse waiting for him, and was quickly on it and through the tunnel that led out of Babylon. He prayed to Ishtar, Marduk, and Shamash as he went. "Please let me succeed. My prosperity is tied to the Hand of Nebuchadnezzar."

He pushed the guards to a brutal march, his mind churning with the possibilities of his reward. He recalled the crone Sarazel's words of his riches and power to come, and he drew that notion into his heart. He'd assembled the men shortly after he left her den, ordering supplies to last them three days, which should be more than enough. If the men needed more, they would trade with the village or with herders; he had more gold links in his pocket. But they should not need more. They would reach the village by the following morning, allowing only for a brief stop to rest his horse and for the guards to nap.

This endeavor would have been easier had they waited for the morning. The men would have been well rested. To leave in the late afternoon drew the attention of people in the courtyard.

They marched without speaking, the only sound that of their sandals scuffing on the road and the measured clop of the horse's hooves. He didn't stop until deep in the evening, and then the noise was the buzz of insects and his men's snores. Ekurzakir could not sleep.

They resumed the march earlier than he'd planned, but he noted that his horse was still in reasonable condition, and he desperately wanted to gain the girl.

Sarazel's words still hung strong in his mind.

Ekurzakir was so intent on the journey and reaching Ibinghal as soon as possible that he did not look to the field to the west of the road. Had he done so, or had the sky been a little lighter, he would have noticed an ox pulling a cart, and a young couple setting an equally determined pace. He would have questioned them, as he would have considered it suspicious that they did not use the road. And he might have discovered his prize right there.

But Ekurzakir did not see them, his eyes fixed on Ibinghal.

The guards came into the village as everyone was stirring. Ekurzakir was quick to find Ibinghal's spokesman, the elderly man named Hre-Threndal.

"Honored one of Ibingbhal ..." Ekurzakir began. His tone was silky, copying the manner he'd heard the Hand of Nebuchadnezzar use when trying to exact information or favors. "It is with sadness that I disrupt your fine community. But as the sun rises, so arises the need for your cooperation."

Hre-Threndal stood straighter. Guards from Babylon had visited Ibinghal before, when bringing goods to trade for crops or sheep or when wanting water from the well during a long march. But this was something different; the old man could tell it from Ekurzakir's bearing.

"How can we of Ibinghal assist the men of King Nebuchadnezzar?" Hre-Threndal tried to sound formal.

As when Shilo had appeared in the streets, all the villagers had turned out of their homes to be part of the assembly. Whispers filled the air.

"We humble people are loyal to the great king of the great city." Hre-Threndal added a slight bow, which a few children in the throng mimicked.

Ekurzakir slid from his horse and passed the reins to a broad-shouldered young man. "Water for her, please, and brush her if you will." The horse's nostrils and lips were flecked with foam. The man obligingly tugged her toward the barn and paid attention to her front leg, which she favored.

Standing on his toes, Ekurzakir scanned the crowd. Ibinghal was a good-sized village, with nearly two hundred residents. He looked for the pale-skinned girl the Hand of Nebuchadnezzar had carefully described.

"You harbor a foreigner," Ekurzakir said. "She is a young woman, about the age of her." He pointed to one of the taller girls toward the front of the crowd. She giggled and hid her face in her hands. "But she has pale skin."

"And spots on her face." This came from the woman in the green robe. She shifted her gaze from Ekurzakir to the red snake ring on her index finger.

"Yes, fetch her for me." He added, "Please," and smiled.

No one in the assembly moved, and none spoke.

Ekurzakir cleared his throat and fixed a stern gaze on the woman. "We mean her no harm, but she must be brought back to Babylon. She stole from one of King Nebuchadnezzar's most trusted men, and she must be made to answer for that."

Still nothing from the villagers.

"I said she will not come to harm, will likely be ordered to clean stables and floors, simply made an example of." Ekurzakir could tell there were doubters in the assembly, and he immediately wished he'd brought half this number of men. Why would a dozen armed and armored guards be required to capture one young woman? Arshaka had been correct; fewer men would have been better.

"She stole something valuable," he added, thinking that would serve as a reasonable explanation for the force.

"Cloth?" This from the woman again.

"Yes." Ekurzakir wondered if he had hesitated in answering.

"This cloth?" She held up a shawl that had already been cut from it.

"Yes." Ekurzakir saw the disappointment in the woman's eyes. "But you can keep the cloth." He added, "all of it," when he saw another piece of the material with another woman. "We desire only the girl, not what she stole."

Hre-Threndal waggled his fingers, trying to disperse the villagers.

"She is not here," he said, turning back to face Ekurzakir. "She was here, though how you know of that so soon is a wonder. She was here only yesterday, and she left during the night." He crossed his arms in front of his chest and scowled at a group of young men who were standing firm and not returning to their chores.

"Where did she go, sir?" Ekurzakir stepped toward the elder. He did not try to hide the menace growing in his eyes. "And when in the night did she leave?" Again he raised up on his toes and scanned the villagers, most of whom were returning to their homes.

Hre-Threndal shrugged his shoulders.

"I know of that, of the girl and the priest who was with her." A stoop-shouldered man with a careworn face came to stand behind Hre-Threndal.

"And you are—"

"Nurthar, brother of Kuth, son of

"Good meeting, Nurthar." Ekurzakir returned to his silky tone. "You saw the girl leave?"

Nurthar shook his head briskly. "Not the girl, but the Shamash priest. He was with a different woman. It was a dark, still night. I could not sleep, my stomach ailing me." He patted his stomach for emphasis. "I stood by my window and looked to the south, thinking the stars would ease my discomfort."

Ekurzakir tapped his foot, but forced himself to be patient. "And the girl—"

"Not the pale-skinned one. But another one was with Nidintulugal."

Ekurzakir's lips tightened. He remembered the name of the Shamash priest who'd helped the girl flee the city. Two guards he'd met on the road had been coming from Ibinghal and mentioned seeing the priest there, but not the girl.

"And—"

"They took my brother's ox and cart. I thought my brother must have given his permission. Nidintulugal is known to us, a friend to Hre-Threndal. Nidintulugal would never steal."

"But I did not give my permission." A man looking similar to Nurthar shouldered his way to the front. "Nidintulugal took the ox and cart without permission."

"You must be Kuth. So the priest stole—"

"Borrowed," Kuth corrected. "A priest of Shamash would not steal."

Nurthar nodded. "I watched Nidintulugal and a young woman, but not the pale-skinned one with the spots on her face, take the ox and cart down the road to the north. I'd not seen the woman before. She was not from the village, and I do not know where she came from. In any event, the two of them must be traveling to the village Knarr. There is a shrine to Shamash there."

"I will get my ox and cart back." Kuth glowered at his brother. "And the priest had best provide a gift."

Ekurzakir growled softly. "Hre-Threndal, elder, I would speak with you and Nurthar alone."

Hre-Threndal appeared surprised, but nodded, turning and inviting Ekurzakir and Nurthar into his small home. Ekurzakir gestured to four guards, who followed. Once inside, Ekurzakir grabbed the elder by the throat and shoved him up against a wall. The guards made certain Nurthar did not interfere.

"Old man, I have no patience left for this. The girl who left the village in the night…she must be the same one who left with the priest. Disguised, wearing different clothes, I see no other explanation."

Hre-Threndal tried to speak, but Ekurzakir gripped him tighter.

"Sh-sh-she might have been the same one, she could have been." This came from Nurthar. Visibly shaken, he looked back and forth between Ekurzakir and the four guards. "She traded in the village for clothes. It was dark when I looked out the window. She could have been wearing one of the robes she traded for. In the darkness, I might not have seen her pale skin." He swallowed hard. "Indeed, as dark as it was, I could not have seen her pale skin."

"And they traveled north?"

Hre-Threndal made a gagging sound and Ekurzakir loosened his grip.

"Y-y-yes," Nurthar said. "There are other villages to the north, but I thought they might go to a Shamash shrine."

"Because of the priest Nidintulugal?" Ekurzakir hissed.

"Y-y-yes." Nurthar directed his full attention to Ekurzakir now. "Why so much worry over a girl with sore feet and pale skin? Why so many guards? Why—"

"Why do you ask so many questions?" Ekurzakir indicated that two of the guards should leave. "Get my horse, we leave for the north immediately. Tell Ipqu-Aya to search for wagon and ox tracks." Ekurzakir had included the expert tracker in the dozen guards.

"Elder, describe the garments she traded for." Ekurzakir pressed his face against the old man's. "Describe them very precisely." He turned to Nurthar. "And you supply any information this one leaves out."

Ekurzakir again grabbed his throat. "This one's tongue," he hissed to the two guards. "He doesn't need it anymore." He gestured with his head to indicate Nurthar. "And he can do without his as well." Ekurzakir shoved the old man to the ground. "Make sure neither of them screams too loudly. And be quick to join me on the road."

Ekurzakir had not ordered such violence in a long while, but did not want the men telling the villagers and other visitors about his interrogation.

This girl, he had come to believe, was very important.

Gaining her for the Hand of Nebuchadnezzar might do more than insure his own prosperity.

18

TO SAVE DRAGONKIND

Shilo had expected Nidintulugal to ask her plenty of questions: about magic—since he'd admitted he hadn't believed in it, and about where she had come from, and what she intended to do.

"It has to be possible," she whispered.

As they made their way toward Babylon, she kept turning over various answers in her mind: that magic was new to her, too, and that a part of her was excited by it; that she came from this world, but not this time or place; and that she wanted to go home, even if she didn't like Wisconsin. The more she played with the answers, the more disconcerted she got that Nidintulugal didn't ask her about anything.

"Penny for your thoughts, Nidin."

"Pardon?"

"What are you thinking about?"

"This," he said, waving an arm to indicate the fields. "This dryness is typical of this time of year. But Babylonia is not always like this. Much of the year the land north of the great city is marshy, which is why the crops flourish, such as in the village of Ibinghal."

"You're thinking about the weather." She shook her head.

"The heavy rains should start within a few weeks, making irrigation unnecessary. Wheat, barley, sesame, flax, vegetables, fruits. All grow tall and plump in Babylonia because of the seasonal rains. The heat of summer will remain once they start, but the ground will be soggy. In the mornings, fog, like steam, will hover around the stalks."

The weather, Shilo groaned to herself. *Leave it to someone to avoid all the important topics by talking about the weather. Barley and flax and rain. Lovely.*

"The great city itself is dryer, rarely seeing the rain that this land to the north enjoys. It is as if a line has been drawn, and foul weather not permitted beyond that point."

"I see," Shilo said.

"The river is down along its banks now, but still there is plenty of it to irrigate the fields north of the great city and to supply the Hanging Gardens with enough to keep everything beautiful and green. In a few weeks, the river will flood its banks, and the Gardens will grow wild. The heat and the rain make Babylon lush. In the Gardens, I try to stand in the shade of the weeping trees every few days. Through their branches the sun shines at me in patterns. I try to read the play of light and see if Shamash is sending me messages."

Shilo had nothing to add to that monologue, and so after a while said: "I'm used to it being hot." *I'm also used to taking a shower once in a while,* she added to herself, sniffing at her armpits and wrinkling her nose.

When they were several miles south of Ibinghal, they led the ox back onto the road. Nidintulugal did not want the ox and cart to damage the irrigated fields any more than necessary.

"The friggin' weather." Shilo decided if he wasn't going to ask her anything pertinent, she'd politely badger him. "Nidin, will you return to the Temple of Shamash if we manage to escape with the eggs?"

He shrugged.

"Can you return?" Though sounding similar, Shilo knew it was a different question.

He shrugged again.

"Because you helped me? The priests at your temple can't be mad at you for that."

"Shilo, I do not know if I can return...to the only home I have known. The priests are forgiving, but they have no real power in the city. If I have angered those in power by helping you, I will cast shadows on the Temple of Shamash with my presence."

"And shadows in the sun god's place probably aren't welcomed," Shilo said.

"Not shadows of a human sort. Perhaps I will have to test just how much of a shadow I cast."

They rested late in the afternoon, to the east side of the road this time. The ox made it plain he was tired. Nidintulugal gathered grasses for the beast arid emptied one of the nut bowls, filling it with water from one of the irrigation pipes, and letting the ox drink before either Shilo or himself.

Shilo nearly complained at that, but knew she'd diagnosed used Nidintulugal well more than enough grief. Besides, she was so thirsty that she didn't care who or what she drank after. She dozed with her back against a wheel, finding it uncomfortable, but not so bad that she wasn't able to catch a little sleep. *And to think that I grumbled about the mattress in my room at Meemaw's,* she thought.

Nidintulugal leaned up against the wheel on the other side. Shilo figured he kept his distance so he wouldn't have to answer any more of her questions…a priest of Shamash, he wouldn't duck them once asked. But if he could avoid them in the first place…

No need for an alarm clock. Shilo knew if the ox decided to stir, taking the cart with it, she and Nidintulugal would wake up. She listened to it snort, and to the grass rustling in the warm breeze, and she tried to remember the Wynton Marsalis tune, "Thick in the South," that had been playing on Big Mick's jukebox some nights past.

She finally drifted off, seeing her father's face, then seeing him in the casket at the funeral home, seeing the faces of his friends and coworkers who had come to pay their respects. What would her father think of her adventure? she wondered. He probably would have been envious, she decided. And he probably wouldn't have needed a huge silvery-gold dragon to send him home.

She was still tired when the ox moved and woke them up. The breeze had vanished and a cloud of flies had gathered, biting and annoying the ox. Her neck was stiff and her back a little sore from sleeping sitting up—probably feeling a little like the stagecoach passengers who had passed the night on the third floor of the antique store once upon a time.

Nidintulugal swatted the flies while Shilo led the ox back onto the road. She retrieved a small handful of nuts from the cart, held them in her hand and concentrated, pleased when they quickly turned into a brown paste. Some of the dye had streaked on her feet and fingers, and she applied enough of the new mixture to cover the patches of pale skin. Nidintulugal gently pointed to the soft hollows beneath her eyes and the skin just under her lips, and she spread the rest of the paste there.

Then without a word, he started toward Babylon again, his pace fast but tolerable, Shilo easily keeping up, her feet no longer aching.

They neared the city the following afternoon, just before Shilo applied one more handful of nut dye to her skin.

"What's our cover story, Nidin?"

Nidintulugal gave her his perturbed look.

"You know, our story. If someone asks us why we're in the city with an ox and a cart, a couple of bowls of nuts, and two spare robes, what do we tell them?"

"We will hope that they ask you and not me."

Because you are a priest of Shamash and will not lie, she thought. "Do you know how to get beneath the Hanging Gardens?"

"No." He nodded to a pair of middle-aged men leaving the city. When they had passed, he said, "They are priests of Marduk, on a pilgrimage to the villages to the north. Today is Akitu, the festival of the House Where the Goddess Temporarily Dwells in Babylon. Akitu honors the mother goddess, and so only a few Marduk priests will leave. It is the month of Tashritu, the barley harvested two months past, and so a good month for bringing brides into homes."

"Excuse me?"

"The Marduk priests go to perform marriage ceremonies in the villages, I said. Other Marduk priests go to the south. We priests of Shamash prefer to perform such ceremonies in Arakhsamna, Sabatu, and Adaru."

"You have months for weddings?"

Nidintulugal looked surprised. "I know the names of months vary from place to place, but certainly you understand of what I speak."

Shilo raised a hand to scratch her head, then stopped herself, not wanting to smear any of the nut dye. "Uhm, no. I don't understand."

Nidintulugal let out a deep sigh. "I know you are from far away, Shilo, but do you not have a calendar?"

"Of course I have a calendar." *My favorite is the Far Side cartoon-a-day calendar, and I keep it on my desk.*

"And does it not have alternating twenty-nine-and thirty-day months? And does not your king add a month three times every eight years, or more if the calendar falls too far from the seasons? And do you not have dates for festivals, such as the Festival of the Carnelian Statue of Su-Sin? The Festival for the Chariot of Nergal? Dates for offerings to Lugalasal and Lugalbanda? The Day of Anointing the Throne of Shamash? Do you not have lucky days?"

"Ummm ..."

"We have two hundred and forty-two. And half lucky days? We have thirty. Do you not set aside days twenty-six and twenty-seven of each month for penance in preparation for the moon disappearing on the twenty-eighth?"

"Ummm...you really have months for marriage?" Shilo tried to change the subject without altering it too much. *I think I liked it better when he was quiet.*

"There are months for all manner of things. King Nebuchadnezzar recites penitential psalms in the months of Nisannu, Simanu, Arakhsamna, Tashritu, and Abu. He cleans his robes and skirts in Nisannu, Ajaru, Abu, and Tashritu. You may move out of your dwelling in Simanu, Abu, Sabatu, and Adaru, and into a dwelling in Nisannu, Ajaru, Adaru, and Arakhsamna: A palace can be founded in ..."

"Wow, where I come from we only have to worry about the first and last of a month for rents and mortgages, bills and such. And I don't have to worry about any of those things because I'm only fifteen."

He shook his head, exasperated that she didn't seem to understand the simple matter of days, and directed his full attention on the road.

So *he considers the discussion ended.* Shilo, however needed a little more information.

"I should have asked this earlier, Nidin, but does Babylon have hotels? Motels? Super 8s of Mesopotamia?"

"So many of your words sound pleasing to my ears, Shilo, but they are as cryptic as when we first met." His face looked stern, but his eyes glimmered with amusement.

"Look, I'm very sorry. When I'm nervous I tend to babble on—" She put her hand over her mouth. "Oh, I made a pun."

He raised his eyebrows.

"I talk when I'm nervous."

"Then try not to be so nervous, Shilo."

"You like my company, don't you, Nidin?"

He drew his lips tight and shook his head again. "I find you interesting, Shilo. And I think Shamash put you in my path as a test."

"A test of what?"

"I have not yet figured that out."

They passed into the city, Shilo shivering and drawing herself into her robe. *Act natural,* she told herself. *Walk casual.* She held her breath when she passed by a guard. All of this notion to save dragon eggs had seemed intimidating but doable when Ulbanu had spelled it out in the cave. Shilo knew roughly how heavy an egg was because she'd carried the bolt of cloth, and she knew they were in tunnels or chambers somewhere below the Hanging Gardens.

Perhaps it had sounded doable earlier because she wanted to return to No-wheres-ville, Wisconsin ... and because she wanted to save dragonkind and mankind.

But now—in this city—guards and buildings all around, and her more than two thousand years out of sync, everything seemed suddenly impossible. She gasped for air.

"What is wrong?"

"Nidin, I'm hyperventilating."

A look of horror appeared on his face. "You are what?"

"Not dying," she quickly added. "I'm just real nervous, having trouble breathing. Happens every once in a while. Freshman year before a swim meet, speech team competition, before my first date." She waved a hand in front of her mouth. "Is there someplace to stash the ox and cart? Near the Hanging Gardens?"

With a nod, he pulled the animal in that direction.

She slowed her breathing a little. *It's all right,* she told herself. *Everything's fine. No one's stopped us and asked questions, we look just like the locals. Heck, Nidin is a local. Slow it down. Slow it down, or someone will look too closely at me.*

They went down a road so narrow there were only inches on each side of the cart.

"The courtyard, Nidin. We passed through the courtyard and through the Ishtar Gate. I didn't look for two strangers. We have to turn around and—"

"We will stable the ox first, Shilo, else we will be looked badly upon."

"What?"

"Standing with an ox in the courtyard that could sully the ground with its—"

"I understand, we ditch the ox and ... we stable the ox and cart, take the nuts and robes, and go back to the courtyard."

"And hope that the dragon's allies have not already come and gone."

The stable was about a block to the south of the Hanging Gardens, and while Nidintulugal bartered with the stable master—settling on the other pair of Shilo's silver earrings—she scanned the edge of the garden, trying to find a way below it.

"It's not going to be so easy as looking for a manhole cover on a city street," she whispered. "No such things here, it seems."

The stable master inspected the earrings. "How long will you be in the city—"

"Ulbanu," Shilo cut in, fearful Nidintulugal would supply his name. She figured Ulbanu was a female name, since it belonged to a female dragon, and so would serve as hers.

"We will be here a few days at most, good sir. Those earrings should cover that."

"And if you are here longer, Ulbanu—"

"Then I will pay you more. But we should not be here long, I say."

"Visiting relatives?"

Nosey, she thought. *People are the same all over.* "Yes, relatives. We are here for a wedding. It is the month for it, you know." *One of the months anyway.*

He nodded and smiled, accepting the answer and apparently pleased to have a tidbit of information.

When they left, they walked along the southern edge of the Hanging Gardens, both of them looking for a way beneath it, and Shilo avoiding Nidintulugal's gaze. She expected him to berate her for lying.

"The river," Shilo said finally, "as a last resort the river."

"I do not—"

"As a way to get below the Hanging Gardens. Whoever designed the machine that pulls water from the river did it by bringing the water under the ground. There are no pipes running on the surface. Not that I can see."

Nidintulugal smiled. "You are wise, Shilo."

And still terribly, terribly nervous, she thought. And wanting very much for Mission Impossible to be finished so she would be forced to come up with another excuse for missing Big Mick's fish boil.

"Remember that hotel I asked you about, Nidin? Babylon has places like that, right? Places for visitors to sleep?"

"An inn?"

She nodded. "We'll need one, near the Gardens if we can."

'To the north of it, yes, another near the courtyard, one near the Temple of Shamash and the Temple of—"

"North of the Hanging Gardens. We'll need a place to stay."

"My temple, I can—"

"Not a chance. Nidin, we don't want anyone to know you're here…just in case they're looking for you. The guards might be looking for you just so they can find me. And we need a place to think, to—"

"I will arrange a room, Shilo." He looked at her hands and pointed to one of her silver rings. Fortunately it was not her favorite. "The inn master would prefer food or drink for barter, but silver is acceptable."

"I'll bet it is." She tugged it off, then smudged some of the dye around her finger to even the color. "I will meet you in the courtyard, Nidin. Please don't be long."

131

"When I have gained our lodgings, I will carry the nuts and the garments to the courtyard." He cradled them in his arms, then turned down a side street by the Gardens, disappearing in the growing shadows cast by weeping willows.

Shilo felt her heart speed up. Alone again in Babylon shouldn't be so bad, especially since she looked like she fit in here. But the importance of her mission weighed her down and added to her edginess. "Don't hyperventilate again," she whispered. "Don't cry, don't—" Her father had survived his trip through the puzzle and lived to tell Meemaw about it. He was younger than her then.

"I can do this. I have to do this." She fixed her gaze forward, head tilted slightly down, grateful that it was nearing sunset and that the shadows cast by the taller buildings both cooled her and helped conceal her features.

The city's odors pleasantly surrounded her—the scents of evening meals being cooked, the fragrances of the flowers blooming in the Gardens, the sweat and perfumes of passersby. She tried to concentrate on those things to keep her mind off what was to come. The sounds were the same as before, music and laughter, and conversations that she could understand this time. Babylon was a lot like any big city in Georgia, or probably in Wisconsin, too.

Do *the people here have the same concerns as in Slade's Corners?* she wondered. *Do mothers worry about the health of their children? Do men fret over their family's wealth or lack of it? Are they happy? Bored? Excited about an upcoming marriage? Angry over an unexpected death? Do they look forward to someone's birthday or visit? Are they planning a vacation? Do they love as fiercely? Do they get as depressed as often?*

She passed a young man and woman engrossed in each other's company. They stood beneath a large balcony, leaning on one of the thick support columns. The woman was smiling and blushing, dipping her head and giggling softly. The man held a loaf of bread in one hand and reached up with his free hand to stroke the woman's face.

Shilo moved on, pleased that she recognized buildings and statues. She'd paid attention to their trip to the stables and the Hanging Gardens, and she'd remembered from the tapestry map in the Temple of Shamash that the roads were laid out like a grid—much the way roads in many American cities were. She wasn't lost.

So far no one had paid her more attention than a passing, polite nod. Of course, she'd not tarried anywhere to draw attention to herself. She recalled the advice her father gave her when they went to Atlanta two summers past:

"In big cities, walk like you know where you're going, even if you don't know. Don't look like a stranger or a tourist, it makes you easy pickings." Shilo doubted there were many pickpockets or muggers in Babylon, not like in Atlanta. This city seemed simpler and cleaner, a place she thought she could live in if it had indoor plumbing and air-conditioning,

Minutes later, she saw walls and building trim displaying lions, suns, bulls, and the Ishtar dragon. She knew the courtyard was just around the corner, and the gate she'd appeared in front of days ago was near.

Don't hyperventilate, she thought. *Keep it slow, relax.*

There were more guards in the courtyard today than on her previous visit. She had spotted them when she and Nidintulugal came through with the ox and cart. She scanned the courtyard and the balconies on buildings to the south and west of the open area. There were thick columns she could stand behind, which supported railed balconies, and the shadows would help conceal her while she waited.

Waited for whom?

And waited for how long?

Would she have to stay in the courtyard all through the night and the next day before the two the dragon picked to help arrived?

Might the dragon's two other pairs of hands not arrive at all?

And would Nidintulugal find her if she hid herself behind a post where the shadows were the thickest?

Would...

She heard someone call for the guards. A horn blatted once, then again. She grasped her robe and held it up just high enough so her feet wouldn't become entangled in it. Then she ran toward the ruckus for all she was worth.

The dragon's helpers had indeed arrived.

19

DEMON BOWLS

Arshaka sat in his comfortable chair, feet propped up and a small, wheel-thrown earthenware bowl on his lap.

He was alone, having dismissed two of his attendants, who had brought him news that King Nebuchadnezzar was safely ensconced in his vacation palace.

The bowl he inspected was unique, not in its design, but in its inscription—similar in form to the ones on the shelf in the den he'd visited the other night, and to a larger one in his own collection. By necessity, each inscription was different, the Old One had said.

Arshaka had already known that. An archaeologist by trade—at least in his previous occupation and residence—he'd studied bowls such as this. They were a good part of the reason he'd come to Babylon.

He ran his fingers around the edge. It was smooth and felt pleasant to his touch, but there was a slight chip in it. Still, a marvelous specimen. Centuries from now, Arshaka knew such specimens would be found at digs in Iran and Iraq, and that his peers had dated them to sixth, seventh, and eighth centuries A. D.

Nowhere else in the world had such bowls been uncovered, and the ones that archaeologists had found in Iran and Iraq had inscriptions in Pahlavi, or Persian, and in three Aramaic dialects: Mandaean, Syriac, and Jewish-Aramaic. Like the bowl on his lap, and on most of those on the shelf in the den, the inscriptions were written in spirals that started at the rim and moved toward the center. Some bowls were also inscribed on the outside. He had only two of those.

Arshaka had been fascinated by the bowls in his other "life," as he liked to think of it. And now he had come to be obsessed with them. The bowls, the eggs, and the red-haired girl he was confident the guards would find, all would bring him inestimable power.

He had translated pieces of the most ancient script on some of the bowls he'd collected. Dark words of hope and hopelessness that rolled off his tongue as if he were a native speaker. With time he could translate anything; such was one of his gifts.

The bowl in his lap was achingly easy to decipher, though words were missing because the ink had smudged. It read: *Gemekaa, daughter of Apuulluunideeszu, with her twin male sons, has heard the voice of the weak. Gemekaa has heard men fighting and women raging, women who are cursed and afflicted because their descendants are tainted. Gemekaa has become cursed herself, and this vessel offers a cure. Yazdun, Ruphael, Yaqrun, Sahtiel, Prael, Dudu, and Laquip have seized Gemekaa and the raging women by the tufts of their hair and broke off their hidden horns. Yazdun and Laquip tied Gemekaa and the raging women by their braids and shouted at the demons in their heads: "Leave these women and end the bitterness of the curse. In the names of Azdai and Prael and Sahtiel, we release you. End the curse, you idol demons, surrender now and embrace the sickness you have wrought. In the names of Denday and Negray we heal these women and annul the demons' work. Upon an unsplit stone, upon this new bowl of clay, we send back the evil."*

The text was Mandaean, an Eastern Aramaic dialect, and had been composed on the bowl in three wedge-shaped panels. Arshaka recognized the ramblings as a spell and counterspell, both intended to protect the owners of the bowl, in this case Gemekaa and two nameless cursed women, against the demons being cast out.

The archaeologists Arshaka had associated with in his previous life did not believe in demons, but they recognized that the people who once lived in Babylon believed in them.

"They were fools, my so-called peers," Arshaka said, using the Aramaic language on the bowl. He liked the sounds of the words, and more than that, he liked the fact that he could speak it fluently. "Fools not to believe in demons. And fools to think these bowls had but one purpose."

Some of the bowls Arshaka and his colleagues had uncovered in the largest Iranian dig were decorated with names of Babylonian gods and symbols, called ouroboros, and magical motifs. A few of the bowls, the most intact that were removed from the site, had been discovered facedown, and in one case two bowls had been cemented together with pitch. They'd carefully pried them apart in a restoration room at the East Azerbaijan Archaeological Museum. Inside were fragments of a human skull and crushed eggshells. Arshaka's colleagues were confident that based on the positions of the bowls in the digs that they were intended as traps for demons.

"The one thing my so-called peers were correct about," he mused.

The bowls indeed were designed to protect individuals and places from the most malevolent of demons, and most often were put upside-down in the corner of a room. The Old One had told Arshaka that corners are the most vulnerable for demon intrusion, as where the floor, ceiling, and walls meet creates an opening to another plane of existence.

There, demons find it easier to enter this world.

So the bowls lured the demons to them, trapped them underneath, and held them there because of the protection spells. Trapped, the demons could not hurt the humans who lived in the home, nor could they damage anything else there.

Bowls with certain incantations inscribed on them were found in cemeteries—where the Babylonians believed demons were plentiful. Sometimes such bowls were placed near the intended victim's house. In almost all cases, these bowls were filled with eggshells. The archaeologists had no clue about the significance of the shells.

At the time, Arshaka hadn't either. But after spending a few decades in Babylon, he understood it well.

The egg was the beginning of life, a powerful and precious symbol that could also mean the beginning of a relationship between entities, the start of a new era.

"The beginning of the reign of Arshaka," he hushed.

Arshaka had four very special eggs that he would use in his bid to control first Babylon, and then a good chunk of the world.

20

A Dog and a Mustang

"Neato-keeno!"

Shilo heard the odd exclamation as she hurtled around the corner, nearly catching her robe on a wood post.

"Neato-keeno!" repeated an Asian boy. He was at the south end of the courtyard, where she'd appeared days before. She immediately recognized him as the boy from her dream who talked about courage. He was wearing cutoffs and a white T-shirt that was smudged with dirt. He wore a catcher's mitt on his left hand and held a softball in his right.

The horn blatted again, and she saw a pair of guards rush toward the boy.

"Oooops," she heard him say.

Her mind raced as her feet churned. She was closer to the boy than the guards, and so she grabbed him and rushed under one of the balconies in the south before they could do anything. With her free hand, she reached out and grabbed a thick pillar, slamming her eyes shut and concentrating.

If my gift is to manipulate material, then let me manipulate this, she thought. *Please, please, please let this work.* If it didn't, she and the boy would be caught, and who knew what would happen to dragonkind and mankind.

The post was wood and flowed like butter, and as a result the balcony above collapsed. Shilo tugged on the boy's arm and hurried around the corner just as the entire balcony came down. He fought against her, but she was strong in her desperation. She prayed there'd not been anyone standing on the balcony; she'd not had time to look.

"Hey! Who are you? What are you doing?" The boy's wide eyes were defiant, not frightened.

"Trying to save you," she said. "Shut up and run!"

She pulled him around the next corner, darting behind a wide, two-story building and into a narrow alley. There was no one here, and so she pulled down a curtain that served as someone's doorway, praying no one was inside. She wrapped it around the boy and pushed him to the end of the alley. It was dark here, the shadows from the buildings made long by the setting sun.

"Who are you?" he repeated, almond eyes narrowing.

"Shilo." She pressed him up against the building. He wasn't much shorter than she was, and she put him at ten or eleven. "Listen, I haven't the time to explain everything to you. I expected someone older to show up." She let out an exasperated sigh. "The dragon had no right to ..."

"Dragon?" The boy brightened.

"Yes, the dragon. She had no right to pull someone so young into this."

"I'm not that young. I'm almost twelve."

Close, she'd guessed close.

"Listen ..."

"Kim."

"Listen, Kim, there's a dragon that needs help. But before we can help her, we have to get you out of here. You're in danger, just 'cause you look different. I'm in danger for the same reason, I think. I don't understand all of it, but you'll just have to trust me."

"Okay." He nodded. "Where are we going?"

She didn't know. "I've a friend getting us a room in an inn. We'll hide there, I'll explain everything, and then ... oh, the dragon had no right. You're too young."

"I'm almost—"

"Twelve. I know."

"What about my friend?"

"Friend?"

"He was in the courtyard with me. Didn't you see him?"

She grabbed his shoulders and squeezed. "Kim, stay here. Stay hidden. Don't talk. Don't move. Understand?"

"Geez, lady. Cool down. I'll be here when you get back."

She couldn't see his expression; the curtain was over his head like a hood. "Don't ... go ... anywhere. ' Then she sped away to the east, intending to circle the building and come into the courtyard from another direction. *Hurry,* she told herself. *Don't get lost, don't draw attention… too much attention… to yourself. Cool down. Sheesh? What kind of an expression was that, cool down?*

The horn had stopped blatting, and Shilo didn't hear a commotion coming from the courtyard by the time she'd found her way back to it. Maybe Kim's friend had been caught already. There were plenty of guards, however. Eight of them were picking through the rubble of the collapsed balcony, and there were plenty of onlookers. Another half-dozen guards were stationed at the main streets that led west from the courtyard—the direction she'd initially tugged Kim.

Kim. She recalled her dream more vividly now. Why was the name familiar?

"There are three kinds of courage," the boy had said in that dream. *"Courage in the blood."* A face appeared in the air above him, becoming red with anger. *"Courage in the veins."* The face turned blue and lost some of its ire. *"And courage in the spirit."* The face did not change color this time, but its eyes sparkled intensely, and the boy's voice became stronger. *7 have the three kinds of courage, the virtues of a hero. You'll have to find them, too."*

The boy had knelt and combed the sand around his feet with his fingers, drawing a curled foot with long claws.

"Empty is the clear path to Heaven, crowded the dark road to Hades. When the mantis hunts the locust he forgets the shrike hunts him. Take care what hunts you, Shilo."

She shivered again, as she had in her dream.

"My dragon was the First Minister and General in Chief to Emperor Liu Pei." The boy gestured and a sword appeared in his hands. *"The Slumbering Dragon mine was called. Yours can never sleep, Shilo, at least not unless you help. And yet if you value your life and want to hold on to your father's memories—if you don't want to risk everything you know, you must never heed her call."*

Kim … that was the name of her father's friend. Meemaw had talked about him. Kim … "Omigod!" Shilo said. Her knees gave out and she fell. Hiding in the shadows, by a northwest wall in the courtyard, she spotted a boy in a T-shirt and jeans. "Omigod. Omigod. Omigod."

Clinging to the sides of buildings and the walls, fingers brushing the ceramic images of lions and bulls, Shilo trotted around to the other side of the courtyard, trying to make it over to him. She was panicked, her breath coming fast, as she worried that the guards might see him before she could get there. That they hadn't noticed him already was a miracle, but then they had the collapsed balcony to contend with. That they hadn't noticed her was another wonder, but then she looked like a local.

"Please don't let my skin run."

His blue jeans were patched at the knees, his dark high-top tennis shoes had untied, frayed laces, and his gray T-shirt had a design on it. Focusing on it, she made out the details as she got closer. It was a car, draped in an American flag, or painted to look like a flag, and beneath it were the words in cherry red: *Mushing Mach 1.*

"Oh, please don't let this be happening. By all that's holy, don't let this be real." She recognized the T-shirt from an old photograph.

It took her a few minutes to reach the boy, and a moment more to grab his arm and pull him down a side street.

"Hey!"

"Shut up. Just shut up." Immediately she regretted the words. *God, I just talked terrible to my father!*

"Hey!" He shouted it this time, as if trying to attract someone's attention. "What are you—"

"I'm trying to save you," she said, her voice soft but stern. "Don't make this difficult. If you call for what amounts to the cops around here, we're both screwed."

That calmed him a little. "Save me, huh? So where are we goin'?"

"You've got a friend named Kim?"

"Yeah. He's here! I thought I saw him. Wild. The puzzle brought us both here? At the same time? What about Ras and—"

"Just you and Kim." She didn't think the dragon would bring more than two.

"Wild. At least this place is warmer than—"

"Shush." She noticed two men and a girl watching them, and she turned south down an alley. It was so dark here from the shadows of the buildings that she had a hard time seeing.

"You're not going to mug me or somethin', are you, lady?"

"I ... said ... I ... am ... trying ... to ... save ... you."

There was a corner where a building jutted out, and she pressed her back against it, drawing him close, still disbelieving this. She sucked lungfuls of hot air in, nearly gagging on the scent of garbage that lay near her feet.

Oh, God, please don't let this be happening. Let this be some horrible dream. Oh, please.

Oh, please. Oh—

"So where's Kim?"

At least he whispered this time.

She glanced to the end of the alley, looking north and hoping the two men and the girl were not there. Nothing. A glance to the south. People walked by on the street, but they didn't look in the alley. A guard hurried past, carrying a catcher's mitt. *Arrrgh!* When she'd grabbed Kim it must have fallen off, and she didn't think to pick it up. What would an archaeologist make of that? What would whoever is in charge of the guards think of it? What if they took it to the rich man who knew about Georgia?

"Kim's not far from here. We've got to sneak through a few alleys to find him. You're not exactly dressed for this place, so we'll have to be careful."

"What place?"

"Babylon."

"Babylon. Wow. What's the circa?"

"Huh?"

"The date. What year is it?" Still he whispered, his voice so soft she had a hard time hearing him.

"I don't know. About twenty-five hundred years ago, I guess. Nebuchadnezzar's the king."

"Cool. Very cool. So you're not from around here either, huh? I can tell by your accent. Where you from? You get here with a puzzle, too? What's your name?"

"Shilo." She regretted answering that immediately.

"Shilo? Wild, a great name. Parents must like Neil Diamond a lot, huh? Or dogs?"

"Dogs?" Shilo clamped her teeth tight.

"Don't you know nothin' about music, lady? Neil Diamond wrote a song with that name. It was about a favorite dog he had when he was a kid. Song came out in 'sixty-eight, but it didn't hit the charts until almost two years ago."

'Two years?"

"Nineteen seventy, you doofus. Made it into Billboard's top one hundred. Anyway, great name. Mine's—"

"Sigmund."

"How'd you know that?"

"She has magic." This came from Nidintulugal. He'd appeared behind them, moving so silently neither had heard him approach. "Put this on." He passed Sigmund a robe, the one Shilo had appropriated when she was in the city, and the one she gestured to.

143

"Phew!" The boy wrinkled his nose, but hesitated only a moment before putting it on.

"Why can't I have that other one?" He pointed to the one draped on Nidintulugal's shoulder.

"It is longer," Shilo said. 'Your friend, Kim, he's taller than you. He gets the longer robe."

Sigmund was shorter than Shilo by about a head, and so he gathered the robe up at the waist and tucked it into the waistband of his blue jeans so it wouldn't drag. Then he pulled the hood up and wrinkled his nose at the smell again.

Nidintulugal retrieved a handful of nuts from his pocket and gave them to Shilo. She closed her eyes and felt the smoothness and the roughness of them, and envisioned them melting.

"So who are you?" Sigmund asked.

"Nidintulugal."

"Definitely not a song title," Sigmund said. "You sound like a native, Niddy."

Nidintulugal frowned at the nickname and rolled up Sigmund's sleeves. Shilo started rubbing the dye on his arms and hands, then his face, carefully smearing it around his eyes and mouth.

"Your robe is too high," she whispered. "They can't see your tennis shoes. Everyone wears sandals here."

"My ... oh." He was about to tug the robe down a little, but Nidintulugal stopped him and did it for him.

"You do not want to smear your skin. " Nidintulugal stared at him. "I only brought enough nuts for two."

"For Kim, huh?" Sigmund said. "Gotta find him." He started to move, but Nidintulugal shoved him back against the wall. "Hey, watch it, Niddy!"

"Nidintulugal," Shilo corrected. "This is serious, okay, Sigmund? There are people looking for me, and probably for Nidintulugal, and you and your friend Kim will stick out like proverbial sore thumbs. And so they'll be looking for you, too. Maybe they saw both of you in the courtyard and are looking already."

"Why? What'd we do to anybody?"

Nidintulugal shook his head.

"You don't know, Niddy?"

"We're not sure," Shilo said, again dropping her voice to a whisper. "Maybe 'cause I'm different. There's a guy, a rich one, who knows I'm from Georgia."

Sigmund smiled. "I'm from Georgia, too. Kennesaw."

"I know," Shilo whispered. "Stay here." She padded to the south end of the alley, watching people pass by on the street. Behind her, she heard Sigmund—her father—jabbering to Nidintulugal.

How could Ulbanu have done this to her?

She leaned against the corner of the building at the end, a residence, she guessed, for someone who was a little well-to-do. How could the dragon have reached through time and across the miles and grabbed her father...when he was eleven or twelve? Her father! Maybe the dragon could touch her father because he'd touched the puzzle, the conduit as Ulbanu had called it. Maybe that's why the dragon grabbed Kim, too.

The dragon had no right!

That she was here from the future was evidence that traveling through time was possible. So if she could be here, her father and his friend—at younger ages—could be here, too. But her father! A great part of her was furious that Ulbanu would do this. Shilo was having a hard enough time dealing with his death as it was.

Now she had to deal with his life...before he moved to Wisconsin, before he grew up, before he moved back to Georgia and met her mother. Before she was born and named after Neil Diamond's dog.

But a small part of her—a part she couldn't deny—was terribly happy to see young Sigmund. At least in Babylon her father wasn't dead.

Tears threatened at the corners of her eyes.

"No more crying," she hissed. "No more crying ever." She sucked in a deep breath and straightened her back. "Find the eggs, save the eggs, and get out of this Hades." She motioned to Nidintulugal and Sigmund.

The boy—her father—still chattered to the priest.

"Niddy, I've time-traveled before. When the puzzle took me to the far north, I got to help with this huge forge. I just appeared there, but in nice warm clothes that looked pretty much like what everyone else was wearing. Too bad that didn't happen this trip. I wouldn't have to wear this smelly thing. Anyway, this dragon came...actually, this was just a couple of days ago...and—"

"Shush. Walk casual," she whispered to Sigmund as she returned. "Follow me. Walk like you live here, like you know where you're going. Don't do anything to draw attention to yourself."

"Same advice my maw gave me when we went to Atlanta last year," he whispered back.

Then she stepped to the end of the alley again, then out into the street, and turned to the east, turning south minutes later when she reached the courtyard. Guards were still helping people clean up the bricks and wood from the balcony, but they were almost finished with the work. She didn't see anyone injured, nor any sign of blood, so she figured no one had been standing on it when she made it collapse.

"Whew," she said as she lengthened her stride and heard Sigmund's and Nidintulugal's footsteps behind her.

"What are we doing here?" Sigmund asked the priest.

Shilo was amazed that he could communicate in the native tongue. It was magic, she knew, magic that came easier to a boy three or four years younger than she. And was there magic in her because she'd inherited it from her father? Like one inherits physical features and propensities for some diseases?

"I don't need to be thinking about stuff like this." She turned east again, remembering the alley she'd shuffled Kim down. "I need to get us all together and to that inn." *Nidintulugal had gotten them all a room, hadn't he?* "Kim. Where did I put him?" The sun had set quickly, and the alley was darker than when she'd been here several minutes before.

"Niddy, are you going to tell me what this is all about?"

"Later." Nidintulugal's voice took on a hardness Shilo had not heard before. "When we are away from here and safe, across from the Gardens, boy."

"Sigmund."

"Sigmund, then."

"What gardens?"

"Later." The severe tone ended Sigmund's questions.

"I can't find him, the boy Kim." Shilo whirled to face them, her eyes locked on Nidintulugal's, as she didn't want to look at her father right now. "I left him here—right here—wrapped in a blanket." She pointed to the very spot where she'd told him to stand. "I told him not to move."

Shilo swore it felt like her stomach had risen into her throat. She could hardly breathe. "*I told him not to move,*" she mouthed. Her eyes were wide with worry.

Nidintulugal stepped past Sigmund and Shilo. At the edge of a building, a run-down place that looked empty, he bent and picked up a blanket.

"Did you wrap him in this, Shilo?"

She turned and stared at the cloth in his hand. She swallowed and nodded.

21

DIIPANII

The old one rarely stood or walked, let alone left his den. But this was a momentous day, and so he did all of those things.

Today was Akitu, the festival of the House Where the Goddess Temporarily Dwells in Babylon, one of the longer-named festivals in the city. If the Old One's memory served, this day was Ishtar's. Goddess of Goddesses, Shepherdess of the Lands, Righteous Judge, Forgiver of Sins... could she forgive his?

He shuffled along the street alone, ignoring the stares of children who had not yet scurried inside for the evening meal.

Rarely did the Old One eat.

The scents of fish and bread held no interest.

The sun had set, and the last twinkling bits of bronze it had painted on the Euphrates disappeared as he crossed the bridge and entered the eastern half of the great city.

The Old One used to revere the goddess, and the gods Marduk and Shamash and Anu, too... But that was when he was younger and without power, when he believed in something divine and something beyond himself. He was called Diipanii then, a name his mother, Tattannu, had given him. He could not recall the name of his father. Neither could he remember the man's face, though the visage of his mother still flitted in his memory from time to time.

Those years were so very long ago that he should not be expected to recall them.

No one living knew his birth name. The souls who did were bits of bone and hanks of hair lying beneath the earth. How many souls rested beneath Babylon? When he stepped off the bridge and found himself looking up at the

Esagila, the imposing Temple of Marduk, he wondered if he stood on anyone who had been significant.

Where would his bones rest? He shook his head. As old as he was, he had decades left, perhaps centuries; his magic would see to that. The herbs and compounds he mixed and ingested would help. He would not be able to stave off death indefinitely, but all those now living in the city, save perhaps the Hand of Nebuchadnezzar, would be dust before he breathed his last.

A most momentous day, this!

He passed a fisherman bringing his catch to a buyer's hovel. The fisherman talked rapidly, wanting to move along to the temple, and not wanting to lose time in bartering.

"It is the festival," the fisherman told the buyer. "Do not make this difficult."

The Old One's face bore a rare smile. This was a momentous day, but not because of a festival to honor a goddess that likely would never forgive his innumerable transgressions. The day—what was left of it—was significant because he would view what the Hand of Nebuchadnezzar had managed to acquire.

The Old One could have waited until Arshaka summoned him.

Or the Old One could have demanded that the eggs be brought to him. (He was, after all, the most respected crafter of demon bowls anywhere, and so was entitled to make such stipulations.)

But he did not want to wait.

He wanted to see the eggs now.

No common chicken or duck eggs, these that would be crumbled and buried in a demon bowl. No skull-sized eggs of exotic flightless birds.

Dragon eggs!

What energy and magic must reside in them!

He'd sent word ahead to Zuuth, a seer in the old quarter near the Temple of Marduk, and he would stop there before going to the Hanging Gardens. The Old One had visited Zuuth years past, and considered his counsel acceptable. The Old One had not sought the wisdom of another in quite some time, but this was indeed a momentous occasion, and so he made another exception.

No one was on this street, everyone either eating dinner or praying to Ishtar. Zuuth's shop was in the middle, made of baked bricks laced with straw and reinforced with lead slats. The Old One entered without knocking; Zuuth's shop had no door or curtain.

His senses dulled from the decades, the Old One barely registered the smell of the sheep tied in the corner, or the dung it had dropped. He nodded to Zuuth, then shuffled to a wide stool in front of a low table made of some dark wood.

Zuuth, stoop-shouldered and wrinkled, but a child compared to the Old One, moved only a little faster than his esteemed client. He drew a knife and went to the sheep, slit its throat in a quick motion, then stretched it out along the wall and drew the blade across its belly, stepping back so not to sully his skirt. He used the knife to separate the organs that spilled out, then reached in and withdrew the liver. This he carried to the table and placed almost reverently in the center.

He cut the liver into four roughly-equal pieces and studied them. After a few moments he turned the pieces over, then rubbed his fingers on them.

"What you plan will stretch through the ages." These were the first words spoken since the Old One's arrival. "What you plan will rival any spells cast before. I see that the world will shake and that Babylon will be reborn."

Zuuth's fingers trembled.

"I see death."

"But not mine," the Old One said.

"Never yours."

"You see success?"

Zuuth nodded. His fingers hovered over one of the quarters. "Horrid success, provided ..." He closed his eyes and picked up the piece, squeezed it into a pulpy mass. "You must keep the future from touching the past. You must keep away the father and daughter who will try to interfere."

"What father?"

Zuuth shook his head. "This is all I have."

"It is enough." The Old One put his hands on the edge of the table and pushed himself up. "You see success and the world shaking. It is more than enough."

The Old One left the shop, his gait a little slower, as he was growing fatigued. He shut out the sounds of prayers spilling from open windows and the clink of dishes and mugs. He turned north, peering through the shadows and picking his way carefully and deliberately toward the Hanging Gardens.

22

THE HISTORY LESSON

They have him, the guards." Shilo shook from fear for the almost twelve-year-old kim. She was angry at herself for leaving him, though she'd thought she had no choice; angry that he'd left this spot when she insisted he not move; furious that the dragon would pull a boy through time and throw him into what could be a deadly situation.

"How do you know this?" Nidintulugal shared her concern: "I saw no guards carrying a boy."

Sigmund looked around for his friend, but stayed close to Nidintulugal.

'They have him. I know because I saw a guard with a catcher's mitt, not that you know what one of those are. But Kim had one, and I bet he dropped it when I hid him. And I bet he went looking for it. So they have him, and I don't know where they would take him or how we can get him back."

"If the guards have him, then we cannot get him back." Nidintulugal put on a stoic expression. "I grieve for the absence of the one you call Kim, but we do not have the time to worry over this. I take the dragon's vision seriously."

"Dragon? You talk about a dragon again." Sigmund stopped looking into corners and shadows and turned his attention to the priest. "What dragon? Not Fafnir, he's dead. The red one on the box? No, that was Pendragon, Artie said. And not the gold or the blue. So what dragon?"

"This talk is for another place…a place we should retreat to now. Yes, Shilo?"

She chewed on her lower lip, still glancing this way and that, wringing her hands together and inadvertently smearing the dye. "I suppose." *Is this my fault? Should I have done something differently? Not left him? I'm fifteen years old! Fifteen!*

"The room you wanted, Shilo. Let's talk there."

She turned to follow him, scuffing her sandals against the street, feeling defeated before they'd even started after the eggs.

"Wait for me!"

Shilo whirled. Kim rushed toward them, arms flailing at his sides. Where he'd come from she hadn't a clue. His T-shirt was off and turned inside-out, wrapped around him like a skirt. His attempt at looking like a native was laughable, and Nidintulugal was quick to throw the robe on him.

"No time for your dye, Shilo," the priest said, grabbing Kim's hand and pulling him along. Nidintulugal gestured with his head at a woman leaning out a second-floor window, watching them. "Gossip is popular here, as you know, and seeing a pale-skinned boy with such hair and odd-looking eyes will set lips moving."

"We had best move fast."

Several minutes later, the four of them were winded and looking out their own window of the rented room Nidintulugal had arranged. Shilo stayed at the sill, commanding the middle of it and propping her elbows on it. She purposely took up most of the space, and so the priest and the two boys backed away.

This isn't happening, she thought. She was relieved to have Kim with them; she didn't want to think how they would have managed to retrieve four eggs with only three people. But she still had a hard time accepting the presence of her father.

"So what's going on? What's this all about?" Sigmund sat on one of two mats in the small room, arms crossed in front of his chest, and robe pulled up to his waist. "It's nice to have company this time. When I was way far north, it was just me and some Norsemen. Hey, can I take this off? It's hot as Kennesaw in here."

Kim didn't give Nidintulugal the opportunity to answer any of Sigmund's questions. "Tell me about the dragon!" Kim's eyes were wide. "Is it the one on the box lid?" He'd hiked his robe up and plopped down next to Sigmund. "Wish we had a fan or a big glass of lemonade. It's hotter than ..."

"About the dragon ..." Sigmund prompted. "Tell us about it."

"Which one on the lid?" Kim pressed.

"A different dragon," Shilo said. "I thought I'd told you it's a different dragon." She leaned out the window and looked down at the street. There was an oil lamp in the room, but they'd not lit it, relying on the emerging starlight. A block away the Hanging Gardens loomed, looking like a black mountain in the twilight.

"So...about this dragon," Sigmund insisted.

Nidintulugal began to describe it, and Shilo shoved all of his words to the back of her mind.

She watched three men walk shoulder-to-shoulder to the west, and she guessed they might be priests. They must be praying, since it was a holy day for Ishtar. She thought Nidintulugal, though a priest of Shamash, would also be praying were he not occupied with Kim and her father.

She stared at the trio, no longer seeing them. Instead she saw the image of her father in the casket in the Marietta funeral home. She'd a mind to catch some sleep, then walk all the way back to Ulbanu's lair and tell the dragon to send her father back, that the dragon had made an unconscionable mistake, and that there must be someone else in the world who could help in retrieving the eggs.

But there might not be time for that, as the dragon had impressed her with the need for speed. The image of her father's face melted and she saw the wave of demons crashing over the land and melting walls and buildings.

Still, the dragon knew that Sigmund was Sigurd Clawhand, and had repeatedly called her Child of Sigurd. So the dragon knew she'd pulled Shilo's father back through time to Babylon.

Taunting Shilo perhaps?

No, Shilo shook her head. Ulbanu would not taunt, she wanted her eggs too badly.

Shilo grabbed the sill and dug her fingernails into the wood. *Why? Why? Why?* If Ulbanu had to bring someone who'd touched the puzzle or dealt with dragons, why couldn't she have brought one of her father's other childhood friends. Meemaw had mentioned Artie and Ras. Why not them? Why her father?

It was a cruel thing, foisting a young Sigmund on her. Torturous. Her stomach churned, she was so upset. She didn't want to look at Sigmund. Every time she looked at the boy, she saw an older version in the back of her mind— the one who had taken her to fish frys and Disney World, who had gotten her interested in history, who had held her close the day the attorney served the divorce papers, who had died too young and relegated her to No-wheres-ville, Wisconsin.

When tears threatened her eyes this time, she did nothing to stop them.

Why had the dragon done this? How could Ulbanu, who needed her help, be so horribly, horribly cruel...And yet, that small part of her was pleased to have her father back—even if he was eleven or twelve years old.

Maybe that was it. She brought a hand up and wiped at the tears. Maybe Ulbanu hadn't meant to be cruel, maybe she'd meant it as a gift. Maybe the dragon was giving Shilo a chance to say the things to young Sigmund that she hadn't said to her father.

She turned away from the window, and so she did not see a very old man shuffling down the street. His back was rounded like a turtle shell, and his eyes glimmered merrily. Shilo sat on the floor, the back of her head bumping against the sill. Enough starlight spilled in through the window that she could watch the boys and Nidintulugal.

I owe the priest a lot, she thought. *More than I will ever be able to repay.* He was patiently talking about the dragon and the stolen eggs, that they needed to find a way below the Hanging Gardens to find the eggs, that this would most likely be dangerous and that demons could be involved.

"Babylon, wild. It's still hard to believe," Sigmund said. "Not impossible, I realize. After all, I already saw one dragon."

"But not a demon," Kim said, making a face like he had eaten something sour.

"So tell me about Babylon. Ancient history's not my favorite subject," Sigmund said. "Yeah, Niddy, I've heard of King Nebuckets, but that's about it."

It was Nidintulugal's turn to make a face when Sigmund butchered the king's name. "History?"

Sigmund threw his hand over his mouth, realizing the priest might not know about time travel. "Uhm, geography actually. I'm not from around here, you can tell. I really don't know nothing..."

"Anything," Kim corrected.

"Yeah, I don't know anything about Babylon."

Nidintulugal closed his eyes and sighed, his breath hissing out between clenched teeth.

A lot, Shilo thought again. *I owe him an awful lot.*

"The great city is the capital of Babylonia, the great country that rests between the Euphrates and the Tigris. King Nebuchadnezzar"—he spoke the name drawn out and with emphasis—"is responsible for the most beautiful buildings, including the Ishtar Gate. The name, Babylon, means the gate of the gods. This place is the most important city in the world."

154

Shilo could tell from Sigmund's expression that he did not believe that. Kim, however, was being more respectful and nodded as the priest continued.

"These lands have seen many kings, some of them foolish and unthinking toward the people. But a Babylonian soldier named Nabopolassar changed that. He had fought the Assyrian army and claimed this kingdom as his own. Nabopolassar was Nebuchadnezzar's father. Nebuchadnezzar is in his twentieth year of ruling."

The longer the priest talked about Shamash, then about kings and the land and all the impressive temples and other structures, the more Sigmund became interested. He leaned forward, making sure now that he caught every word, and asking questions when he missed something.

Nidintulugal spoke with such passion that even Shilo was caught up in his history lesson. He discussed the land around the city and events that stretched a few centuries into the past.

"History's pretty wild, huh, Kim?" Sigmund stifled a yawn. "Tell us more, Niddy. '

Shilo grimaced. Niddy was worse than Nidin, which she'd sometimes been calling him.

"Yeah, tell us more. This'll make a great report at school in the fall," Kim said.

"I'm going to the library when we get home." Sigmund beamed, the heat forgotten. "I'm gonna check out some history books."

Nidintulugal talked about the Hanging Gardens now, and Shilo let her mind wander. Was it possible her father's love of history started here, by listening to the Shamash priest? Was it possible that his visit to Babylon shaped him into the man she knew?

A shiver raced down her spine. What if they couldn't save the eggs, let alone find them? Would they all be stuck in Mesopotamia? And if her father didn't get back home, he'd never grow up to meet her mother, so she wouldn't be born. And if she wasn't born … she rocked forward and held her head with her hands. This was all too much to contemplate.

"Tell us more, Niddy. About…"

"It is time to sleep," he said, stretching out on the floor and leaving the mats for the boys.

"Sleep quickly," Shilo said. She closed her eyes. "As soon as there's enough light, we look for a way under that mountain of green." She'd thought about leaving now. But the starlight wouldn't be enough, and someone might think it suspicious that four people were searching along the ground for something when practically everyone else was sleeping.

They would find the way down in the early morning—blending in with nut paste. Shilo did not doubt that they would find the way; they would have to or they wouldn't be going home. And then later, under the cover of shadows and darkness, they would use that way to go beneath the city in search of Ulbanu's eggs.

"I'm in Hades," she whispered.

23

WEEPING TREES

Shilo used all but a few handfuls of nuts to dye their skin, Nidintulugal carefully helping spread the paste on their eyelids.

"Do not scratch," he told them. "Do not wipe off sweat."

"Yeah, we get it, Niddy," Sigmund said. "Don't smear the color." The boy sniffed at the robe again, wrinkling his nose and pantomiming gagging. "Hope the other folks in the city don't believe in baths, or no amount of that nut dye is gonna camouflage me."

Kim sniffed at his armpits and his robe. "I'm not so bad as you, Sigmund."

"Enough talk." Shilo was at the window, looking out and adjusting the net bag that helped hide her red hair. "The sun's up, and I see people moving. We should've been out of here a while ago."

She turned toward the door, noticing that the boys looked serious. Maybe they understood the importance of this endeavor. "You sure you want to help us?" Shilo asked Nidintulugal.

"I must find out what Shamash's test is about," he said. He patted the knife still tucked in his belt. It looked like he intended to say something else. Instead, he gave the others one final inspection, then led them from the inn.

They walked along the river, pretending to be interested in the fishing boats that were just leaving, but actually trying to find something like an irrigation pipe through which river water could be pulled to the Gardens. They found nothing.

"And going in the river to look isn't an option, huh?"

The others shook their heads at Kim.

"Then why not look at the other end?" Kim suggested, lowering his voice when a Marduk priest and two elderly women stopped nearby at the bank. "Why not find where the water comes out in the Gardens, then try to backtrack and find our way in?"

Nidintulugal patted Kim on the head, then pointed down a street. "What wisdom you bring from your faraway place." He paused. "Take care, there will be more people in the Gardens than along this river."

Shilo had only seen the Hanging Gardens from the outside, and was unprepared for the intensity of the fragrances when she started up the steps behind Sigmund. The scent of the earth was strong because it was so damp, and the riot of flowers warred for her attention. She likened it to going into one of the big department stores in the mall and trying on all the perfumes at the cosmetic counter. *At least it cuts my stink*, she thought. Nidintulugal was in the lead, and they'd put both boys between them, wanting to keep a close watch on them. The priest had suggested leaving the boys in the room, but quickly discarded the notion, recalling how desperate Shilo got when looking for Kim.

She had been to botanical gardens before, once when she was so young she barely remembered it, to some gardens in St. Louis. Shilo thought she might have been in the first or second grade, and that she'd had her picture taken with koi—a sea of color—as she stood on a little bridge in the Japanese section. She recalled the day because in the picture there was an ice cream stain on her pink shirt, and her mother had gotten very angry with her. Her mother's tirade blotted out whatever fun she'd had in the park.

The king must love his wife very much, she thought, shaking off the bad memory and focusing on the whorls in a thick trunk, the pattern looking like an owl. Nidintulugal had said Nebuchadnezzar's bride came from a verdant land and missed it so terribly that he arranged for the construction of this place. It had pained him to see her so homesick, and she was brightened by the Hanging Gardens not so much because of their beauty, but that all the people of Babylon could enjoy something so marvelous.

To be so loved would he amazing, Shilo thought.

Some of the trees here were old, and Nidintulugal told her they had been brought by barge along the Euphrates from the north and south, and carefully planted here. Vines overhung the brick terraces, and more vines hung from the branches of the tallest trees.

The green would have been overwhelming, but flowers interjected other colors here and there, as did flocks of parrots that Nidintulugal said came

from the south. Occasionally one of the parrots would fly close and squawk, a blue and yellow one saying "Marduk" repeatedly.

"You might think them magic birds, Shilo," the priest said. "But there is no magic in their speech. Those birds with curved bills are capable of repeating our words."

"Parroting them," Shilo said.

She let herself truly relax for a few minutes and focus on everything around her. Despite the number of people going up and down the stairs, it was quiet. There was the soft "shushing" sound everyone's sandals made against the bricks and the dirt paths that cut through the Gardens, and the chirps of parrots and other birds, the occasional screech of a monkey, but there was little talking.

Toward the top, statues were placed between some of the trees, serving as anchors for small trunks. She recognized an image of Shamash, and she saw Nidintulugal bow to it, his lips working, she suspected, in prayer. Beyond the Shamash idol, between gaps in veils of leaves, a thin waterfall splashed. She touched Sigmund's shoulder, startling him, and nodded to a trail that led away from the stairs and toward the waterfall. Sigmund, in turn, tugged on Kim's robe, and Kim interrupted the priest's prayer.

As Shilo passed under the branches of something that resembled a weeping willow, she looked out and up. Light came through the leaves like light shining through a lacy window curtain, and she held up her dyed hands to see patterns on her skin. Shilo found no message in the play of sunlight, and wondered why Nidintulugal could possibly think Shamash was sending him messages here. But Shamash was the sun god, and so maybe the priest could read things in the light that others couldn't see.

Sigmund prodded her to move along, clearly uninterested in the light patterns. She turned her thoughts reluctantly away from the flowers and trees and the priest and back to business. Moments later, she was at the edge of the waterfall's basin, looking up at the falls and keeping her distance so the water wouldn't splash her and ruin her skin.

"Let's try up there." Sigmund referred to a narrow set of steps, each one a brick baked with straw in it, leading up to the terrace where the waterfall started.

Shilo shook her head no, and pointed to another path that led higher, to where she spotted a bucket dumping water, part of the conveyor system Nidintulugal had mentioned.

Sigmund either hadn't seen her or wasn't paying attention, and scrambled up the steps. Before she could call to him, Kim cut in front of her, following his friend while deftly avoiding tripping on the hem of his robe.

'The dragon, perhaps, does not know the exuberance of youth," Nidintulugal observed as he followed Kim.

"I guess we're going this way," she said.

Shilo stuck out her bottom lip and exhaled, cooling her face. She glanced around before heading up, wanting to make sure no one was paying them any undue attention. She supposed the four of them could have looked like a family on an early-morning outing.

Shilo had managed to carry the heavy bolt of cloth down from the dragon's cave to the village, so she supposed she could carry an egg down this mountain and to the stable where the ox and cart waited. The boys were young, but they looked as strong as her, maybe stronger. But there was the matter of finding the eggs first, and before that could be accomplished, they needed to find a way in. Backtrack to the river, Sigmund had suggested. At the time, Shilo had thought it a good idea. Now, however, she hoped to find a way in through the Gardens itself. She wanted this over and done with.

But carrying the eggs out during the day would be a bad idea.

Out of the corner of her eye, she saw a young woman and a bare-chested man, perhaps her husband, embracing beneath a weeping veil of leaves.

The king must love his queen very much to have built these Gardens for her, Shilo thought again.

The waterfall was surprisingly loud for being so narrow. But the drop was a fair distance, and she found herself enjoying the roar of the water. She couldn't hear the whispered conversation Sigmund and Kim were sharing, and she could barely hear herself call to get Nidintulugal's attention. He'd been studying where the water originated—not from a stream or river, or any source such a feature would normally flow from. The waterfall was born out of a fissure in a rock, too narrow to fit through.

Told you, she thought. *We should be looking over there.*

Shilo pointed to the west, where from their higher vantage point it was easier to see the bucket and pulley mechanism that brought water up the man-made mountain and sent it down irrigation ditches and streams that fed all the plants. Kim saw her gesture and yanked on Sigmund's robe. The two boys headed toward the machine.

She and Nidintulugal sighed in unison and hurried to catch up. There were two men near the mechanism, but they moved on by the time the boys reached it. More people were interested in the trees and flowers than the device that watered them. The view from up here, the very top of the Hanging Gardens, caught Shilo's breath.

It was dizzying, looking down the slope at what was essentially a small rain forest. Babylon spread out below that, the city looking clean and impressive in the early-morning sun. The temples she could see, including the Temple of Shamash, shone in places where gold had been applied to cornices and columns. South of the Gardens, down a street Shilo had not walked, a statue of a rearing lion looked as if it were catching a beam of sunlight in its outstretched claws.

Everything she'd thought bad about this place and her predicament vanished in that instant. This magical journey that had made her feet and head ache and made her long for Wisconsin was suddenly all worth it. To see something so splendid as ancient Babylon, when the city was at its height, was worth everything she'd been through.

"Wow." Sigmund was taking it all in, too. "Double wow." She heard the boy suck in a breath and hold it.

She wanted to hold this moment in her heart forever, treasuring it and thanking God for this opportunity. This was Heaven, not Hades, and there was nothing more beautiful in the world than the panorama she couldn't pull her eyes from.

"Triple wow," she mouthed.

Shilo wasn't sure how long she stood there, Sigmund at her side and neither blinking, scarcely breathing. Nidintulugal had been saying something to her, but the words were like the buzz of a cloud of gnats, an annoyance. Finally, he clamped a hand on her shoulder.

"Shilo—"

He broke the trance and she sadly turned toward him.

"What?"

"Kim has disappeared. I looked away from him for just an instant."

"He does that," Sigmund said. "I suppose we'd better start looking for him." His shoulders slumped, sad that he couldn't stare out at the city anymore. "Can't find the eggs until we find Kim." He brightened slightly. "Hey, Niddy, which came first, the Kimmy or the egg?"

24

UNDER THE GARDENS

Nidintulugal found the way below. There was a gap between buckets that were affixed to a primitive conveyor belt of leather and metal links. He saw that Shilo and Sigmund were watching him, and that there appeared to be cover. Without a word, he clambered onto the belt and disappeared into the mountain, grateful no guards had been posted next to the machine.

Sigmund was quick to follow him, grinning broadly as if this was all a big adventure.

Shilo hesitated. She was worried someone was watching them and would alert the city's guards. *There could be laws against this*, she thought. Too, she was afraid Kim hadn't taken this route and that he had wandered off elsewhere. If they guessed wrong about Kim's path, they might never see him again.

"But I can't spend all of my time chasing him," she said. "There's a world to save." After another quick glance to see if anyone was nearby or paying attention to her, she grabbed the chain between buckets with a hand, held her breath, and jumped into the hole.

It felt like her arm was pulling out of the socket, but she held tight with aching fingers and gritted her teeth so she wouldn't whimper. Her side banged against the chain and a bucket, and she set all the buckets nearby to clanking and thunking, and spilling the water out of some of the ones coming up the other side. Her feet dangled free, and she flailed about with them, trying to find a bucket lip to stand on or a way to hook her knees around the chain. She couldn't manage either, as her robe was too long and kept tangling around her legs.

How had the others done this without making so much noise? Was she that clumsy? Just last week Meemaw had suggested dance lessons, and now Shilo wondered if she should have agreed.

She reached up with her free hand and grabbed on to the chain. The extra feeling of security helped, and though her right arm still throbbed, it no longer felt like it was going to pull out.

She looked up while she continued her ride down. The only light came from the hole above her, streaming around the buckets and chain, bright in her eyes and making her blink.

She couldn't hear herself, though she knew she was breathing raggedly. The groaning of the chain moving along whatever mechanism drove it, and the clunking of the buckets, echoed in the shaft. Too, there was the gurgle of water. From somewhere below she heard the *plash* of bucket after bucket striking the water supply, and the *slosh* of the water as it was drawn up on the other side of the belt, passing her by on its trip to the top.

Shilo hadn't thought ancient people capable of such an engineering feat, but then they had managed the magnificent Ishtar Gate and the towering temples she'd walked by, the glazed bricks displaying bulls, lions, and the Ishtar dragon, and no doubt many other marvels she'd not yet seen. The Hanging Gardens themselves were perhaps the most amazing. Were the circumstances different, she thought she might like to hang around in Babylon a while longer, and see more of the city and all its wonders and discover what other fascinating things these people had crafted.

But as she descended farther into the mountain, she discovered that the only thing she really wanted to do was find her way back out and get home. She worried that if Kim hadn't gone down this conveyor belt, he'd be on his own and would have to find his own way home, which she doubted was possible without the dragon's help.

Suddenly hands clamped around her waist, and she squealed in surprise, released her grip, and found herself pulled away from the belt. A hand pressed firmly over her mouth.

"Hush, Shilo, there are men below and they might hear us."

It was Nidintulugal.

He released her, and she sagged back against him, blinking furiously and trying to see her surroundings in the dim light.

"Shhhhh." This came from Kim.

So he had come down here! She wanted to grab his shoulders and shake him, tell him not to run off ever again. Instead, she just stood there, her vision adjusting and separating the shadows. Sigmund was next to Kim, shaking a stern finger at him. *Great minds think alike,* Shilo mused. *It must run in the family.*

They stood on a wide ledge that ringed the shaft. She got a better look at the conveyor mechanism by watching the buckets pass by at eye level. The chain was big, the links thick, like those she'd seen attached to drawbridges in pictures of castles. She didn't know the people of ancient Babylon had forges, but they had knives and spears, and she'd seen metal plates in the guards' armor, so there had to be blacksmiths or something like them. ... But the links looked more complicated than fashioning something flat like weapons. They all looked so uniform, like they had been poured in molds.

The buckets were wood, held together with metal bands and things that looked like rivets, the handles thick leather straps, and lined in either leather or cloth—she wasn't certain which. They were affixed to the chain with a link extending from a metal bar, which kept the buckets from spilling until they got to the top and were tipped by another mechanism, causing them to spill their contents into a trough. From there the water would flow down the mountain and into various parts of the Gardens.

"Pretty amazing, huh?" Sigmund whispered. "I hadn't thought people this long ago were capable of something like this. It seems way too modem. I gotta get me some history books when I get home."

Shilo didn't see the curious look Nidintulugal gave Sigmund.

"Look down there." Sigmund stabbed a finger over the edge.

Shilo steadied herself against Nidintulugal and peered over the ledge. The shaft continued down into darkness. "I don't see anything." She kept her voice low.

"Just keep watching."

She did, and a moment later she saw a light flicker below, moving in a circle, then passing out of sight. She caught a glimpse of a bare arm and a head, then nothing.

"See, there's someone down there," Sigmund continued. "Niddy heard 'em first." His whispers echoed off the shaft wall across from them. "Wonder what they're doing? Think they're making all these buckets move? I bet they operate this whole contraption."

Shilo shrugged. "No, don't you dare." She grabbed at Kim. He was reaching for the chain, obviously intending to go down farther. "Don't be an idiot."

The boy looked hurt and confused. "I thought we were—"

"Hush," Nidintulugal said. "All of you hush." He edged away from Shilo, circling the shaft with his back to the wall. He made an exaggerated beckoning motion so they could see him in the dim light. There was a slash in the wall behind him, and he ducked inside.

Shilo kept a hold of Kim. "Listen, you." She kept herself from being too nasty as she whispered, "This mission we're on...it's more important than you. This isn't just about you. If you paid attention to Nidin last night, you'd know it's about our future, about a whole lot of people's futures. We need your help, your hands and strength. We don't need you running off again."

She felt him tremble under her grip.

"Sorry," he said.

She couldn't see his expression, his face tipped down, but she was pretty sure he'd stay in line now.

"I really am sorry," he said. "I guess I just got...I dunno...excited."

Shilo couldn't stay mad at him; he was only eleven years old and filled with a youthful fascination for what was essentially an unknown world. She doubted that he knew to be afraid. He hadn't been pursued by guards and wanted by a rich man who knew about Georgia, or at least about the United States. He hadn't come face-to-face with a dragon. Or had he? He'd traveled because of the puzzle before. But his dragon couldn't have been as big as Ulbanu.

Nothing living was as big as Ulbanu.

"We should catch up with them, Shilo. They're gonna get too far ahead." Kim whispered softly, and he cast his gaze even farther down so he wouldn't have to look her in the eyes. "Don't want to lose them, do we?"

"No running off," she repeated, raising her voice ever so slightly. Then she nudged Kim toward the slash in the shaft, wishing she had a leash to put around his neck, just to be certain he didn't stray again.

"Can't see where I'm going." Kim had stopped in front of her.

She squeezed by him. "Hold on to my robe," she told him. "And don't..."

"I know, don't let go."

Shilo cursed herself for not immediately following Nidintulugal. Maybe a priest of the sun god had better vision, and so could find his way in the dark. She raised her hands and found the wall on each side of her, making this tunnel, she guessed, about a yard or so wide. She ran her fingertips along it, discovering a mix of earth and bricks that had straw baked in them. A man-made tunnel then, she knew. She went slow, too slow for Kim she could tell, as he bumped into her a couple of times.

She couldn't see *anything*, and was afraid to move faster. It was like being in a cave. She'd done that before with her father in Georgia, went in one of those caves on a tour with a bunch of elderly folks who were from out of state. They'd followed a path that had a rope along one side to keep people from wandering off. At one point in the tour the guide flipped the light switch, plunging the cave into blackest black. The guide was demonstrating what it was like to be caught in a cave without a lantern.

Shilo hadn't enjoyed that part of the tour, just like she certainly wasn't enjoying this. Here she was in a cave again, and with her father again—but he was somewhere ahead of her. And he was younger than her and oblivious to the fact that they were related.

This wasn't the way they had planned to get under the Hanging Gardens. In fact, she thought that the point of this morning's exercise was to find a way into the mountain—which they had—but by the Euphrates, by backtracking the water and finding a way in via the river. They were supposed to come back at night when it was dark.

Well, it was plenty dark here.

This should have been planned better, she thought, *maybe with diagrams and certainly more discussion.* Certainly with candles or a lantern—they would have brought those at night. Maybe if she'd been older, if all of them were older, they would have approached this differently, certainly not so unprepared.

There was a scraping sound ahead, regular and soft, and Shilo guessed it was Nidintulugal's sandals hitting the floor. She reached behind, her hand closing on Kim's arm.

"Wait," she told him, squatting, and feeling that he squatted with her. She placed her free hand flat against the floor, feeling straw-laced bricks. "All of this is man-made," she whispered.

"I don't like this," the boy admitted.

"I don't either,"

She stood and moved forward again, a little faster now that she realized the floor was even and not likely to trip her up.

Shilo kept her right hand against the wall and her left arm thrust out in front of her, hoping she would feel Sigmund's or Nidintulugal's back. The wall was wet, and she slowed her pace slightly, fingers dancing over the mud and bricks. She guessed one of the troughs or basins in the Hanging Gardens was leaking.

"Shilo..."

"Nidin!"

"Hush," he told her.

A heartbeat later, Shilo's fingers brushed Sigmund's back, and she came to an abrupt stop, Kim bumping soundly into her.

"Listen," Nidintulugal said. The priest was directly in front of Sigmund. "Do you hear it?"

Shilo heard voices, two of them, and by concentrating she turned their tongue into words she could understand. They were speaking a language similar to Nidintulugal's, but there were differences.

"Water comes down this wall," one man said.

"It is a leak that we must trace to its source." This voice was deeper and had a rasp to it. "Climb the east tunnel and see if the problem is there. We repaired the east pipe a few days ago. It is likely the source of the problem again."

"Are we in the east tunnel?" Sigmund asked.

Shilo could tell Sigmund was trembling. At least he well understood the danger in what they were doing.

"I don't know," Nidintulugal said. "I really don't know where we are."

Then Shilo felt Sigmund move away and heard the priest's soft footfalls.

"We're moving again," she whispered to Kim. Again she kept her right hand on the wall and her left reaching out, trying to touch Sigmund's back. After a few moments, she heard the voice with the rasp, the unseen man complaining about being forced to look for the leak. At the same time, her right hand lost contact with the wall, indicating a turn in the passage. She located the corner and took the turn, Kim following her.

A few moments after that she saw a glow in front of her, growing brighter with each heartbeat. She likened herself to a deer frozen in the headlights of a car. For an instant she didn't know what to do.

A man held out a lantern, spotted Shilo, and stopped.

"Who?" he asked.

Shilo could hardly see him, the light coming forward and revealing everything in front of him, while keeping him in shadows. However, she could tell he was short and broad-shouldered, almost stocky—she could tell nothing beyond that. The lantern illuminated the walls. The dirt was hard-packed, serving as mortar between the baked clay bricks. Many of the bricks were etched or glazed with images of lions and bulls. The brickwork curved up to make an arch of the ceiling, and all of the bricks there were glazed and shiny-looking, as if they were wet.

Shilo didn't have time to figure out if they really were wet, as the man held the lantern higher and closer so he could better see her.

"I'm lost," she said. "I-I-I fell down some hole and—"

The man growled. "One more thing to worry over today." He sighed and lowered the lantern, giving Shilo a better look at him.

He wore a skirt that came to about his knees. The fabric probably had been close to white at one time, but there were gray and black streaks in it, like the soiled shirt an auto mechanic might wear. His legs, arms, and chest gleamed with sweat, and his face was unlined and smudged with dirt, his hair oiled and pulled back into a ponytail.

Nidintulugal had not come this way, and had probably kept going straight. This side passage had been a bad mistake. *Great,* she thought. *Great, great, great.*

"I'm lost," Shilo repeated. "I don't know where I am." The truth. "I am so hopelessly lost." The truth again. She relaxed when she saw him offer her a faint smile, the tightness of his face easing. "I'm glad you found us, really. It was so dark, we couldn't see anything. I don't know what we would have done if you hadn't come by."

"I will take you outside." He held out his free hand. "Come, let us be away from here."

So they would be able to get out of here without hitching a ride on the water conveyor! But Shilo didn't want to leave just yet. There was her father to consider, and Nidintulugal and the eggs. Now what was she going to do?

Suddenly he pulled his hand back, his eyes widening and mouth opening. "Who are you?"

Not how did you get down here. That would've been the question Shilo would have asked. She followed his gaze. He was looking at her right hand. She'd been running it along the wall, and where the wall had been wet—it had smeared the dye. Her fingers and palm were pale, and the skin from the back of her hand to a few inches past her wrist was horribly streaked.

"Skin condition," she said, thinking quickly. "A terrible rash."

She might have been able to convince him of that. But as she watched, the dye ran in a brown blob down her arm.

"Ooops."

25

NIDINTULUGAL'S QUANDRY

Nidintulugal wondered just how many more tests shamash was going to put him through. Clearly meeting Shilo that morning in the temple was the first test. Had he passed it by scurrying with her out into the city? And helping her escape from the Hand of Nebuchadnezzar and the guards?

Or had he failed that first test? And because of it, failed the rest?

Though Nidintulugal supported King Nebuchadnezzar and appreciated all the fine things he had brought to Babylon, the young priest was not especially fond of some of the king's representatives, including the Hand. So while it might have been a favorable thing to keep the girl out of the Hand's clutches, perhaps it had not been the right thing to take her from the Temple of Shamash that morning.

Maybe he should have sought the counsel of the elder priests. Maybe Shamash had wanted the girl turned over to them for safekeeping. Nidintulugal had been handed over to the temple as a child, having lost his parents to an illness.

Was Shilo to have shared the same destiny?

But Shilo had not been able to speak their tongue at the time, and so who knew what the elders would have decided to do with her. If he had turned her over, would she have discovered the dragon in the cave? Would she have learned of the demon threat?

She came from far away, that was certain. Her skin and hair and accent were like none he'd ever encountered. But just where exactly had she come from?

"Where are you from, Sigmund?" Nidintulugal had resisted asking Shilo that question before. In truth, though he'd wanted to know, he hadn't wanted to possess that knowledge. Priests of Shamash were utterly truthful, and if someone had asked him where the girl came from, he would have told them. Would that bit of knowledge have mattered?

Now, walking in the pitch-black inside the Hanging Gardens, the priest's curiosity finally won.

"Whatdya mean, Niddy?"

Nidintulugal had come to accept Shilo calling him "Nidin" once in a while, and almost found the shortened version of his name endearing. But he did not like "Niddy." Somehow it felt demeaning.

"I mean … *Sigmund* … from what land do you hail?" Nidintulugal kept his voice to a whisper. "Certainly not Babylonia."

Sigmund made a funny noise with his mouth, striking his tongue against his teeth. "I probably shouldn't tell you where I'm from, not that you'd understand if I told you. But then I'd have to explain just how I got here, and why it should be impossible for me to be here, and then—"

"Never mind, Sigmund. It was wrong of me to ask."

The priest wondered what Shilo thought of his question, as following so close behind she would have heard. Sigmund and she came from the same land—he knew that much—as their accent was similar, and they shared the fair complexion and dusting of dots on their faces. The boy, Kim, looked nothing like them and certainly claimed a different homeland.

"Among other things, Shamash tests my patience." Nidintulugal wondered what lesson Shamash expected him to learn by helping the girl and now shepherding her and these two boys through midnight black tunnels.

"Shamash? Who's Shamash?"

"Never mind." Sigmund definitely was from very far away.

Was Nidintulugal to learn that it was folly to help foreigners?

Or was it good to help strangers—no matter how *strange* they were?

He was helping them to the best of his ability—and helping a dragon and perhaps all of mankind in the process. Was this what Shamash intended for him?

Was he to take that leap of faith and go against society's strictures? Risk the wrath of the city officials? Perhaps risk the wrath of the elder priests? He'd certainly gone against the Hand of Nebuchadnezzar, who was in charge of Babylon in the king's absence. He'd been going against the Hand every minute of each day since in Shilo's company.

Avoiding the guards, not returning to his temple, "borrowing" an ox and cart and a robe from the villagers in Ibinghal.

Maybe Shamash's test was to accomplish something important, putting himself last and risking his life. He was doing that, too—every effort had been for this mysterious girl, and now for the even more mysterious dragon.

Nidintulugal picked up the pace, shoving thoughts of the girl to the back of his mind. *Concentrate on the eggs,* he told himself, *and pray to find a way into Shamash's light.*

He didn't know that Shilo and Kim had found a side passage and taken it. He thought them still behind Sigmund. He wasn't listening for their footfalls; he was too focused on what might be ahead.

"Georgia." Sigmund said the word a little too loud for Nidintulugal's liking.

"What?"

"I'm from Georgia, Niddy." Sigmund wisely dropped his voice back to a whisper. "I figure I might as well come clean and tell you, since you're being so good to help us and the dragon and all, and because we might die here by stepping in some big pit since we can't see anything. I figure if we die, you knowing I'm from Georgia ain't gonna make a difference. And I figure if we don't die, you knowing about Georgia ain't gonna make a difference either."

"Georgia." Nidintulugal liked the sound of the word. "Does it sit to the south?"

Sigmund chuckled. "Yeah, it's in the south, but not to the south of here. It's in the United States of America, a place that won't exist for at least two thousand more years. It's all magic, Niddy. I don't know if you—"

"I understand the concept of magic, *Sigmund.*" Nidintulugal emphasized the boy's name, hoping that the show of respect might get the boy to stop calling him Niddy. "The dragon—"

"The dragon that I didn't get to see, but you and Shilo saw?"

"Yes." Nidintulugal regretted bringing up the question, as he feared they were whispering too much and someone might notice them. Whispers sometimes carried far too well.

"I think Shilo's from Georgia, too. Sounds like it anyway. Maybe South Carolina. Kim—Kim Stevens—was originally from Hong Kong. You couldn't have heard of that place either. It doesn't exist in this time. But then he moved to Kennesaw—Georgia. He doesn't live too far from me." Sigmund made the noise with his tongue and teeth again.

"Anyway, magic brought me here—across time and space—Kim, too. Neato-keeno, huh? Georgia's across an ocean, and in my time we have botanical gardens like this one, but I bet you can't climb around underneath 'em. Oh, and we don't have dragons. At least, I don't think we do anymore, Niddy."

"We had best be quiet, Siggy. Lest someone hear us." Nidintulugal initially dismissed the boy's words of Georgia as ramblings meant to tease him. But the more he thought about it, the more likely it was that the boy told some fashion of the truth. But the future … was it possible?

He'd not thought of dragons as real, but he'd seen one.

He'd not thought he'd ever make a significant difference in the world, but here he was, trying to do just that by this venture.

If magic was possible, he supposed it was possible these two boys and Shilo came from another place, as well as another time.

It was all very difficult—practically impossible—to comprehend.

"Shamash," he whispered, the words so faint he knew Sigmund and the others could not hear, "have I lost my way? Do I continue this? Or do I retrace my steps and return to your temple? Have I gone mad?" "Nuts" was the word Shilo had used for it.

A part of him wished he were mad, as it would explain all the odd happenings, or wished he were sleeping somewhere and dreaming all of this. But even as he said it, he knew he was sane and awake. A pale light ahead ended his musings.

He reached behind himself and touched Sigmund.

"I see it, Niddy."

"Tell Shilo … quietly."

Nidintulugal took a step forward, and then another, pressing himself against the wall as he went. The light was steady, and so it came from a lantern on a table or hanging from a hook. He hoped no one was there; he wanted the opportunity to see Shilo and discuss what to do next. Find the eggs, certainly. Get the eggs and themselves out, if they could. But where …

"Shilo's not there." In his surprise, Sigmund spoke too loud. "Kim's not there either."

"Hush," Nidintulugal warned. "Are you certain? They might be farther back. We might have walked too quickly.

"They're not behind us. Shilo's missing!"

"Shilo?" The word came from in front of the priest and Sigmund.

The light flared brighter, then was blotted out as a shape moved in front of it.

"Did I hear someone mention Shilo? That's the name of the girl I seek."

Nidintulugal recognized the voice.

It belonged to the Hand of Nebuchadnezzar.

"Move back, Sigmund." The priest spit the words out through clenched teeth. "Be quick." Nidintulugal pushed Sigmund to speed him. "Hurry."

"I can't see, Niddy. I can't—" Sigmund tripped, either on his own feet or because the priest pushed him too hard.

Nidintulugal bent and groped in the darkness, hands closing on the boy's robe and tugging him up. At the same time, the light flared brighter still and was accompanied by the hurried slap of sandals against the brick floor.

"Take them!"

Nidintulugal could not make out any of the details, just that there were four men; a fifth and larger one behind them carried the light.

"Take them quickly, I say!"

Nidintulugal and Sigmund were grabbed by strong hands and thrust up against the wall. Two men held each of them. The men were dressed uniformly, but not as guards. Each wore a coal gray skirt that hung to just below their knees. Their chests and heads had been shaved, and their muscles gleamed in the light from the lantern.

Nidintulugal could have struggled against his captors, possibly breaking free and thus able to run. But Sigmund wouldn't be able to get away, he could tell, and so the priest did not resist.

"Hand of Nebuchadnezzar," Nidintulugal said.

Arshaka nodded as he approached, carrying a lantern in his right hand and a cloth in his left. He was dressed more simply than usual: a long brown robe that brushed the ground, a long left sleeve, and a bare right arm. A swath of yellow cloth draped around his neck to add a little color. The Hand dabbed the cloth on his forehead and neck; he'd been sweating profusely, even though it was cooler inside the Gardens.

"You are the priest..."

"Nidintulugal of Shamash."

"I saw you with the girl called Shilo in front of the Ishtar Gate a few days past. All I wanted was to talk to her, and you helped her run from me. I meant her no harm."

Nidintulugal smelled the man. His clothes stank of sweat and of a perfume he'd used to help cover that smell.

"How could you think that the Hand of Nebuchadnezzar meant to harm a child?"

The priest opened his mouth to offer a reply, then thought better of it.

"I only wanted to talk, priest of Shamash. Like I want to talk now. Where ... is ... she?"

In the lantern light Nidintulugal saw Arshaka's face redden. "Is she with you? Did you lose her in the darkness?"

"Yeah, she was with us."

Arshaka turned and dropped his gaze to the boy.

As quickly as it had turned red, the color drained from Arshaka's face. His jaw worked, but no words came out, and his eyes grew wide.

"The hood, push it back. Do it."

One of the men holding Sigmund released one hand, brushed aside the hood, then regained the grip. The boy struggled a little, and so the man squeezed the caught arm tighter.

"Hey, that's not necessary!" Sigmund snapped. "I didn't do nothin' wrong, honest, and ..."

Arshaka coughed and wiped at his mouth with the cloth. "Sigmund?"

"Yeah, my name's Sigmund. What's it to you, huh?" Sigmund tried to act tough, but his lips quivered, and he tried one more time to pull out of the men's grips.

Arshaka stared at the boy, holding the cloth in front of his mouth now.

"What do I want done with them?" Arshaka mused aloud.

He kept staring, as if he were looking into Sigmund and measuring him. The lantern nearly slipped from his fingers, the light jumping and sending him into action.

He stepped close to Sigmund and brought his face within an inch of the boy's. He held the lantern close, too, so that the light and the heat were bothersome.

"Shilo, Sigmund. Where is she?"

Sigmund blinked furiously and wrinkled his nose. "Don't know," he said after a moment. "Haven't seen her since yesterday."

"You were talking about her, Sigmund. Calling to her maybe."

Nidintulugal watched the exchange, his hands forming fists and arm muscles working beneath the men's grips. He liked the Hand of Nebuchadnezzar even less now. Again he thought about lashing out and trying to escape. He could return to the temple and relate the entire story to the elder priests, convince them to come here and help find the dragon's eggs ... but then Sigmund might be alone, unable to break free. And Nidintulugal could not leave the boy.

"I said I haven't seen her since yesterday. But, yeah, we were talking about her. She's kind of cute, for a girl. Pushy, though. I think she left the city. Said something about going home."

"To Georgia?"

Sigmund's eyes grew impossibly wide. "H-h-how do you know about Georgia?"

"And the good old U.S. of A.?"

Sigmund nodded. "How do you ..."

"The girl, Sigmund. Where is she?"

"You deaf?" Sigmund taunted. His tone was filled with false bravery. "I said I haven't seen her."

Arshaka stepped back from the boy and turned to Nidintulugal. "How about you, priest?"

Nidintulugal cocked his head, like he didn't know what Arshaka referred to.

"I heard you mention Shilo, too. Your voice is easy to distinguish. Where is she?"

"I do not know." It was the truth. Priests of Shamash only told the truth.

Arshaka shook his head. "You really don't know, do you?"

"No, Hand of Nebuchadnezzar. I really do not know."

Arshaka's eyes narrowed, and he used the cloth to again wipe his forehead. "When and where did you last see her, priest?" Arshaka smiled. "Ever truthful priest of Shamash."

Nidintulugal swallowed hard and met Arshaka's gaze. "I last saw her yesterday, Hand of Nebuchadnezzar. In the courtyard before the Ishtar Gate. It was exactly as Sigmund says. She mentioned something about going home."

The priest felt his heart seize, and he struggled to keep from gasping and showing an outward sign of his lie. He'd never lied before—not that he could remember. Perhaps in his first years of life, before he'd been taken in by the Temple of Shamash. But not since then.

Never since then.

It was clear that the Hand of Nebuchadnezzar believed him. The Hand knew that priests of Shamash did not lie.

And so Nidintulugal had kept Shilo safe. But he'd damned himself and just failed the greatest test Shamash had put before him.

"It was before sunset," Nidintulugal added, continuing the falsehood. "I've not seen her since."

"Pity," Arshaka said. "I was looking forward to chatting with her."

26

DEEP TROUBLE

"We're in trouble, ain't we?" Kim tugged on shilo's robe. "Deep trouble."

"Deep pucky," Shilo said. It was an expression she'd remembered her father using. "Very deep pucky."

"Pucky," Kim repeated.

The man holding the lantern stared at her, his gaze flitting from her right arm, where the nut dye was running, to her face, squinting and perhaps seeing more dye running. It was clear he didn't know what to make of her, or the boy who poked his head out to better see what was going on.

"Skin condition," Shilo repeated. "I told you I've a problem. Uhm, I'm sick. So you don't want to get too close to me. It could be contagious. Your skin could get all runny, too. Just show us the way out of here." *But I don't want to get out of here,* she thought. *I need to find Nidin and Sigmund and Ulbanu's eggs.* She was desperately worried about Sigmund. But she didn't know what else to say to the man.

"Shilo, you stink at bluffing," Kim whispered.

The man stood indecisive one moment more, then reached out again with his free hand, not in the beckoning gesture he'd used before, but trying to grab her.

Shilo jumped back, bumping into Kim and sending him to the floor. He cursed at her in a language she guessed was Chinese—she understood each word and was amazed an eleven-year-old would know such atrocious phrases. She nearly fell, too, but she caught herself on the wall, scraping her bare arm in the process.

"Ouch. We don't mean any trouble," Shilo said. "Just show us how to get out of here. That's all we need." *Just to get out. And then back in another way after dark.*

"I think I need to take you to Juvaii," the man said. "He will know what to do. Come here." He reached forward again, and this time Shilo darted under the sweep of his arm and spun around behind him.

"Don't touch me. I'm contagious," she tried again.

He turned, too, and the play of the light from the lantern in his hand sent shadows skittering across the floor and wall. The light struck the glazed images of animals, and it looked like some of them were moving. Shilo knew it was a trick of the light, but the man saw it, and it held his gaze for one moment too long.

Shilo reached out with both hands and grabbed the lantern. She yanked hard and pulled it from his fingers. She ducked below the swing of his left arm. His fist was balled, and she heard the air whoosh around it. She knew that if it had connected it would have hurt. She crouched and set the lantern on the ground, then leapt up and to her right, again narrowly avoiding a swing.

He lunged at her now, arms wide and intending to scoop her in, eyes flaring with anger. 'You're the one the Hand wants. I know it! I've heard the whispers about you."

He would have grabbed her, but she fell backward, unexpectedly pulled off her feet when Kim yanked on the back of her robe.

She hit hard, the air rushing from her lungs, and a flash of pain racing up her spine.

Kim slid past her and drove his hand into the man's stomach, raised a leg and kicked at his knee.

Keeping his leg up and bent, Kim kicked at the man again and again, Shilo hearing a snap and a groan of pain. Kim had broken the man's leg. He fell, and Kim plastered himself against the wall. Shilo managed to skitter back just in time. The man sagged first to his knees, crying out when he landed on the broken one, then pitched forward and started groaning.

Kim didn't stop. The boy drove his heel into the man's back and made a chopping motion twice to his neck. Then Kim grabbed the lantern with one hand and held his other out to Shilo. She shook her head and got up on her own.

"Is he dead?" Shilo worried that Kim might have killed him. She couldn't tell if he was breathing.

"I don't want to know." The boy moved down the tunnel, taking the light with him, clearly not wanting to learn the man's condition.

Shilo caught up and took the lantern. This was her expedition, and she'd not have her father's eleven-year-old friend take over. "Stop. We can't just let him sprawl there. Dead or alive, someone will find him."

Kim thrust out his lower lip. "Sure someone'll find him—but we don't have any place to stash him, do we?"

She regarded him silently for a moment, troubled thoughts whirling in her head. *This was all so wrong! They were supposed to sneak in at night, all of them staying together, find the eggs and get out.* Now someone might be dead, and she was separated from her father and Nidintulugal.

"Ulbanu, help me." She'd not heard the dragon's voice since the cave. When she was hearing the voice, she hadn't wanted to. Now, she begged the dragon to reach in her head and communicate. "Open my mind," she whispered. "Make it easy."

"Where should we go?" Kim tugged on her robe. "Down that way, I think. The guy came from there. Might be something interesting, huh?"

Shilo tried to shut him out, searching her head for Ulbanu's voice. But the dragon wasn't intruding. *Maybe the dragon couldn't,* she thought after a moment. The dragon couldn't determine just where under the Hanging Gardens her eggs were. Maybe something about the mountain blocked her magical senses.

"Let's go this way." Kim was intent on retracing the man's steps.

Shilo thought it likely that Kim didn't want to pass by the man he'd beaten up.

"If you hadn't attacked that man, Kim, he would have caught me … us. I don't know what would have happened if he'd caught us. But I think it would have been 'game over.'"

He cocked his head.

The expression was a few decades beyond him, she realized. *Who will you grow up to be, Kim? Will you have a family like my father did?* She shifted the lantern to her other hand, finding the leather strip rough and too wide to comfortably fit in her palm. *But you won't grow up to be anything if we don't get back to the dragon.* Again she fumed that Ulbanu had pulled two children from the future to help.

Kim started down the tunnel. "Your skin is all smeared, Shilo. Hope mine doesn't look that bad. Doesn't look like no skin condition, no rash. Looks like paint running." He looked over his shoulder at her. "I'm going this way, Shilo. I ain't going back that way. No reason to go back that way."

Every reason to go back that way, she thought. *My dad's back there... somewhere. And Nidin's there, too. Somewhere.*

"Sigmund's there, Kim," she said aloud. "We can't leave him." *I won't leave him.* "We're going this way instead." She turned to prove her point and took a few steps, the lantern's light reaching the man on the floor. She stared at his back. It wasn't rising and falling, and his head was turned at a sickening angle. Kim had killed him, using some sort of martial art form.

"C'mon, Kim. It'll be easy to retrace our steps now that we have a light." She wished she would have brought the last of the nuts with her so she could reapply the dye. But maybe she could find something else down here that would work. Maybe Nidintulugal had nuts with him.

"C'mon, Kim. We have to find them." She turned and saw that the way behind her was empty. Kim had disappeared again. "He promised." *Well, let him wander off that way... in the utter darkness,* she thought. Shilo's father came first, and Nidintulugal. Kim was little more than a stranger, an acquaintance the dragon selected.

Her father's friend.

She knew where Kim was, or rather where he was going. But she couldn't say the same for her father and Nidintulugal. Who knew where they were right now? Shifting the lamp again, she hurried after Kim, gritting her teeth in dismay that her sandals made slap-slapping sounds against the floor.

The light made everything easier, yet at the same time more frightening. The animals on the bricks kept appearing to move in the play of the lantern. The darkness, though scary, had hidden the details of her surroundings— that the tunnel was so confining. She likened it to being swallowed by some big beast, slipping down its throat and heading toward the oblivion of its belly.

She saw Kim just ahead. He'd been copying her, right hand along the wall and left hand in front, moving slow enough so it was easy tor her to catch up. Once more she wanted to throttle him, wanted to grab him by the shoulders and spin him around, push him back the other way.

Maybe they really should do just that, go back the way they'd come. But... ahead of Kim the tunnel forked, the right-hand side going up. There were steps, a way out.

"Stop." Shilo didn't say it loudly, but her word had an edge to it. Kim stopped. He didn't turn to face her, though, clearly not wanting to look her in the eye.

She padded up to him, the lantern light dancing faintly. Touching the bricks near the ascending stairway, she settled on a lion and concentrated.

"I can manipulate things," she said. She was talking to herself. "I can mark our way." This would be better than leaving a trail of bread crumbs. She felt the glazed brick soften, and she sculpted it like clay, turning the lion into an odd-looking creature. She wasn't about to take the time to try to make it into something artful. She changed the image of a bull and another lion on nearby bricks, making their heads melt.

"We can come back this way, get out of here later."

She melted a few more farther down. When she was finished, she stepped past Kim, not saying a word. She wanted to scold him; she had a string of venomous sentences running through her head. But she didn't say a word.

She walked at a steady pace, eyes trained on the tunnel ahead, ears straining to hear something other than the slap-slapping of her sandals.

"Sorry," Kim offered. "I just thought—"

She waved her free hand behind her, silencing him. She thought she heard something ahead, though it was soft and she couldn't quite distinguish what it was. It might have been something dripping, maybe a trough leaking. She slowed and held the light low now.

Maybe her father and Nidintulugal were in front of them. It was likely these tunnels connected ... they had to connect. Whoever built this place had to have planned it. *Better than we planned this rescue operation,* she mused. The corridors had to make sense, like Disney World. Her father had a friend who worked there. And during their vacation, he'd taken them below the Magic Kingdom. It was like a city beneath the place, and workers scurried from one end of the park to another.

They didn't get to explore long, though, as her father's friend didn't want to get in trouble. Shilo hadn't liked being down there anyway.

The Hanging Gardens, though large and impressive, weren't nearly as big as Disney World. So this particular corridor couldn't go on forever.

Shilo told herself she'd have just as good a chance of finding her father and Nidintulugal by going this way, perhaps a better chance, as the corridor curved back the way they'd come. The dripping sound got louder as she pressed on. She didn't look back; she knew Kim was there, hearing the occasional squeak of his tennis shoes against the brick floor. She suspected he knew that he'd killed the man—a terrible burden for an eleven-year-old. If ... when ... they got out of here, she'd tell him again how he likely saved both of their lives. Maybe she'd tell him before they got out. But right now, she wanted quiet. She wanted to focus on the dripping sound, and any other sounds she might pick up.

She desperately wanted to hear Sigmund and Nidintulugal talking, maybe calling for her. They had to be worried, had to know they'd gotten separated. They were probably searching for her, though without a light they'd be just stumbling around.

"We have to find them." She walked faster again, praying that she wouldn't come across any other workers down here, but knowing that it was inevitable.

After a few minutes they came to another fork in the tunnel, one curving farther toward where Shilo suspected her father might be. The other was narrower, at best two feet wide, and sloped down. The walls and floor were earth, not a single brick that she could see, and she could stick her fingers in the walls; they weren't hard-packed by time.

"That's where we gotta go, ain't it?" Kim brushed at one of the sides and watched the dirt fall away. "This's all new, Shilo. Dug not long ago."

"Yes, I think this is where we need to go." Shilo tipped her head, listening down the narrow tunnel. It was where the dripping sound came from.

"Bet Sigmund ain't down there, though." Kim sniffed at the air. "Kinda stinky. Bet Nidin ain't down there either."

Shilo took a deep whiff. It was a fusty smell that reminded her of some of the old things in the antique store's attic. But there was a dampness to it, and a tinge of rottenness, like something had spoiled and had never been cleaned up.

The dripping sound persisted.

"I don't like it," Kim said.

"Neither do I."

"But that's the right way. I can feel it." He squared his shoulders and thrust his chin forward. "It'll just take a little bit of courage is all."

"There are three kinds of courage," Shilo whispered.

Kim looked up at her, mouth open. "How did you know that? Did you meet my dragon?"

You told me about courage of the blood, she thought, *in a dream more than two thousand years from now.*

"I don't know how I knew that." Shilo shrugged. "Sounded good," she said. "Three kinds of courage."

"So what sounds good now, Shilo? Going down there, maybe, where we're probably supposed to go? Or going after Sigmund?"

My father, she thought. *Going after my father sounds like the best thing to do.*

"Going down there, Kim." *To save dragonkind, and perhaps mankind, too.*

27

GEORGIA ON HIS MIND

Arshaka spun away from Sigmund and Nidintulugal, raising his free hand and making a circling motion with his index fingers. "Bring them. Since Sigmund has joined us, I no longer require the girl. Sigmund will likely suit my needs better anyway."

Nidintulugal did not put up a struggle, though Arshaka's men thought he would, tightening their grips so their fingernails dug painfully into the priest's arms as they pushed him along. He no longer thought about escaping; he'd lied, committed a sin in the eyes of his god and his temple, and so decided to accept whatever punishment was in his future.

Sigmund fought, however, spitting and kicking, and getting picked up by the men when he planted his feet and resisted with all his strength.

The boy reminded Nidintulugal of Shilo—determined and defiant. He'd come to admire those traits. Perhaps all the natives from the land called Georgia were so strong of character. *Or perhaps it is indicative of all the natives from that time,* the priest thought. Sigmund had told him they were from the future. He believed the boy, though he still had difficulty comprehending it.

The men half dragged, half carried Sigmund, and Nidintulugal listened sadly to the boy's cursing.

"Don't hurt the boy," Arshaka said over his shoulder. "Not yet, in any event." After a pause, "The priest, either. I'll not sully any of our souls by causing harm to one of Shamash's own."

Shamash's no longer, Nidintulugal thought. *A priest no longer. I've lied ... twice. Can I possibly repent and find redemption? Perhaps in saving the boy from whatever the Hand of Nebuchadnezzar has planned, I might be delivered. And if I can save the boy,*

187

maybe I can still entertain the notion of saving the dragon's eggs. I must do something to save my spirit from the endless abyss.

Arshaka trundled down the corridor, which sloped sharply and then opened into an oval room, the walls of which were covered with glazed bricks decorated with lions and bulls. A wide, arched door led from it, and Nidintulugal could barely make out brick stairs going down—the Hand's light did not reach far enough to see beyond the first few steps. There were two benches in this room, both carved from dark wood and polished so they gleamed, the legs resembling lions' legs and ending in black stone talons. A table near them held a diorama of sorts, and after staring at it a moment, Nidintulugal realized it was a miniature representation of the Hanging Gardens. It was flat, as if someone had peeled off the greenery and stretched it across the table.

A lit oil lamp hung above the table, casting its soft light everywhere. There were small flags across the diorama, and squinting, Nidintulugal read a few names of trees. Blue ribbons curled here and there, apparently representing the troughs and streams that watered all the plants. In the very center was a tiny bucket on a post, this being the conveyor machine that brought water up from the river.

Were he not a prisoner, Nidintulugal would have asked to examine the map, and he would have asked how the wondrous conveyor machine worked. He would have asked where the most exotic of the plants and trees came from, and how the king's representatives had managed to put all of this together. Despite his predicament, he couldn't take his eyes off the diorama. Did it show ways out from under the mountain?

And was there another table somewhere, with a diorama that showed the tunnels that twisted beneath the Hanging Gardens?

"I do not understand." Nidintulugal finally spoke. "I do not understand, Hand of Nebuchadnezzar, why the girl was important to you. And now why this boy has caught your interest."

Arshaka went to the table, put his lantern on the floor, and leaned over the diorama. "A curious priest. Of Babylon's gods, I favor Marduk. Not because I believe in him, or because I like what is ascribed to him, or because his priests are not so inquisitive. But because his temple is the largest. I've not been inside the Temple of Shamash in nearly four years. Are all the priests there so curious?"

Nidintulugal did not answer.

"I suppose there is no harm in sating your curiosity, priest. It is Georgia, really, that holds my interest. And the twentieth century." The Hand of Nebuchadnezzar adjusted one of the flags, retrieved the lantern, and shuffled to the benches. He set the lantern on one, then plopped himself on the other and nodded to the men holding Nidintulugal. "It's all right. He's not going anywhere. Are you, Nidintulugal? You won't try to flee from me, will you?"

"No."

"See? It's all right. Take his knife, though. One thing I've learned from all my years in Babylon is that Shamash priests do not lie. They'd rather die first. So if Nidintulugal says he will stay put, he will. The boy is another matter."

Nidintulugal was grateful that the Hand was watching Sigmund now. The Hand might have noticed his darting eyes and quickened breath, might have discovered that indeed he was not being truthful—again. A third time Nidintulugal had lied, for he truly intended to flee from the Hand of Nebuchadnezzar with Sigmund. He could accept whatever punishment was due him for all his deceit. But the boy deserved no ill.

Sigmund continued to struggle, the hood of his robe thrown back, and his skin streaked. Arshaka watched the boy, a mix of amusement and ire on his fleshy face. He held out his cloth to Nidintulugal. "Take it, take it." He waved it like a pennant.

"Come on."

Nidintulugal plucked the cloth with two fingers.

"Wipe off his face. I want to see him better. Do it!"

Nidintulugal complied, but only because he saw no harm in the task. He gently rubbed the dye off Sigmund's face and neck, no easy thing to do given that the boy kept fighting against the men who held him.

"He's a bad man, Niddy. Shouldn't do anything he says."

Arshaka chuckled. "A little more. There, that's enough, priest." He rocked back and crossed his arms in front of his chest. "Better, much. Now that's the face that I remember."

"Remember?" Sigmund stopped struggling for a moment. "I've never seen you before. But Shilo and Niddy told me about you. Never seen you ever. Wish I weren't looking at you now."

This time Arshaka's laugh was deep and long, sending a chill through Nidintulugal. The priest had never heard the Hand of Nebuchadnezzar make such a sinister sound. He passed the dye-smeared cloth to one of the men who'd held him. Then Nidintulugal rubbed at his arms; there were deep scratches where his captors had dug their nails in.

"But you have seen me, Sigmund ... Sig. When I was younger and we lived in Kennesaw, not terribly far from each other, if my recollections serve me."

Sigmund leaned forward, his face pinched as he took a good look at the Hand of Nebuchadnezzar. "No." He shook his head vehemently. "I would have remembered someone as ugly and rude as you. Why, I think if I had a dog as ugly as you, I'd shave its..."

"Enough!" Arshaka roared. He was on his feet, shaking his fist at Sigmund. Spittle flew from his doughy lips, and he glared so harshly that Sigmund leaned away.

One of the men had Nidintulugal's knife, pointed at the priest to make sure he wouldn't threaten the Hand. Nidintulugal stood between Arshaka and Sigmund, but he took a few steps back so he could see both without turning his head.

"It doesn't matter," Arshaka said, "whether you remember me." He talked in English, and Nidintulugal could not understand him. "I remember you, Sig. And I remember the puzzle we found in that old man's house. I remember traveling to England and seeing the dragon-of-a-man."

"Pendragon."

"Yes, Pendragon."

Sigmund shook his head. "I don't know you."

"I went back to the old man's house and took a few pieces of the puzzle. You always thought your brother had lost the pieces. Maybe he did—some. But I kept a few, for a reason I didn't understand at the time."

"...Artie?"

Arshaka nodded. "At last you see me."

"Artie?"

"I discovered that I could use the pieces to travel. And at length, again for a reason that remains a mystery, I picked Babylon to journey to."

"Oh..." Sigmund started sucking in mouthfuls of air, shaking his head more, this time in disbelief. "This can't be real. You can't really be Artie."

"I've been here for decades, Sigmund."

"But you're... *old.*" The last word was said as if Sigmund had just bitten into a lemon.

Arshaka returned to the bench and sat down, spat on the floor and looked to Nidintulugal. This time he spoke so the priest could understand him. "Sig and I were friends, priest, back when we both lived in Georgia. He moved away with his parents, to Wisconsin. '

Nidintulugal mouthed the word *"Wisconsin,"* growing more confused.

"And I moved here." Arshaka rubbed his chin thoughtfully. "But I have aged, and Sigmund has not. That's puzzling." He brightened. "No, I understand. Sigmund traveled here as a child. I traveled here rather than go to college. I stayed, delightful place, this. Sigmund...who knows how old Sigmund *really* is, or where his adult self has settled."

Arshaka rested his elbows on his knees now. Nidintulugal guessed that the Hand might be nervous, or anxious. Always in motion, and sweating more than from the stuffiness of this room. Anxious over a boy? No, anxious over something that was to come.

The eggs and the demons. Nidintulugal shifted back and forth on the balls of his feet. He wished that Shilo were here. Maybe together they could find a way out of here. There was magic about her.

"Why do you really need the boy?" Nidintulugal drew Arshaka's attention.

"Yes. Because of Kennesaw. Because of Georgia." Again the Hand used a language the priest understood. Because I've forgotten whatever magic I commanded that let me travel through time and across continents. Because Sig here hasn't forgotten."

"You want to go home."

"Not perceptive enough, Shamash priest. I want to go home, but only briefly. There are some things there I want to bring back, things beyond this culture's ability to produce." He gave another deep, malicious laugh, and Nidintulugal shivered. "Oh, this culture is a relatively advanced one, a good bit of it thanks to me." He pointed at the ceiling. "These gard..." Arshaka stopped himself. "I better not tell you too much, priest, in the event I decide not to kill you."

"The boy..." Nidintulugal pressed.

Arshaka ignored the priest and again rose from the bench. He smoothed at his skirt. "Sigmund... Dear Sig, all you have to do is take me back to Georgia. Anytime after World War II would be just fine."

World war? Nidintulugal pictured the image the dragon had painted of demons flowing across the land.

"There's a piece or two of technology I want to pick up."

Sigmund redoubled his efforts to break free. "I'm not gonna help you do anything, Artie. Yeah, I can see who you are. The eyes're the same. But that's it. You've gotten old and fat and smelly and—"

Arshaka roared, "you foul-mouthed worm!"

Sigmund giggled, but it was a frightened laugh. Still, it succeeded in making the Hand of Nebuchadnezzar even angrier.

"I couldn't help you even if I wanted to, Artie. I didn't get here under my own steam this time. Either Shilo brought me, or a dragon, maybe both of 'em working together. Can't say for sure, as I didn't see the dragon."

"Dragon?"

"Yeah, from what I understand, you stole her eggs. Right?"

Arshaka's face was red with fury. He stormed toward the boy and lashed out with his fist, striking Sigmund in the side of the face. The men holding Sigmund nearly dropped him—so strong was the Hand's blow. The boy spat blood and tried to bring his arm to his mouth to wipe it off, but the men wouldn't allow it. He spat again and pieces of teeth came out. There was pain in the boy's eyes, but he didn't whimper.

Nidintulugal once more thought the boy and Shilo were of a similar mien. "Do not hit the boy again," the priest warned.

"And what will you do about it?" Arshaka didn't take his eyes off Sigmund. "I want that technology, do you understand? And you can cooperate, or you can die."

"Everybody dies," Sigmund answered.

Arshaka hit him again.

"Take them to one of the chambers below. I will call for them later." Arshaka picked up the lantern and headed back through the doorway, pausing just beyond it. "I do not need you, Sigmund, for my plans to be realized. But your help would make things go quicker and smoother. And there would be far less pain for everyone concerned."

The lantern flared over the diorama, and the man with the knife pulled it down from a hook. He gestured with the knife for Arshaka to go through the opposite doorway, the one with the steps disappearing into darkness.

"Where are you taking us?" Nidintulugal used a civil tone. "I have no concern for myself. But I do not want the boy harmed further."

The man with the knife opened his mouth, revealing that he had no tongue. His fellows did likewise.

"Yuck," Sigmund said. 'That's just disgusting."

Nidintulugal knew Arshaka had either done the deed or had ordered it. He doubted he could ever hate a man more. The priest started down the steps, listening to the footfalls of the two men behind him.

"Double disgusting with a big dollop of ick on top," Sigmund said. "Artie sure got nasty in his old age."

28

Men of Clay

"Arshaka, that rich man who was after me, he's from the South, from our time." Shilo talked mainly to herself, though she didn't mind that Kim listened in. "He's called the Hand of Nebuchadnezzar, and I understand that he's in charge of Babylon while the king's gone. He's terribly powerful."

"Bet he likes it when the king is gone."

She nodded. "It took me a while to admit it, but I can't figure another explanation for it. He's from the future—our present. Well, your or my present or thereabouts." She stepped carefully along the slope of the narrow passage, as it was uneven and there were muddy depressions.

"So what's he doing here?" Kim walked too close behind her, bumping into the backs of her legs. "There's no plumbing and electricity. No air-conditioning, no hot showers, no television, no macaroni and cheese. Why'd anyone ever want to come here? Nidin said Arshaka's the one who probably stole the dragon's eggs ... or since he's rich, had them stolen. You think he traveled through time, like us, but to hurt things, not to help out like we're doing?"

Shilo thought about that a moment. "I don't know why he traveled through time, but I get the idea he's been here for several years. I don't think he originally set out to get the eggs. I think he found out about them, though. And somehow he's going to use the baby dragons to unleash demons." She shuddered. "Why would anyone want to do such a thing?"

Kim made a *tsk-tsking* sound. "You're not really into history, huh?"

The question hurt. She loved history.

"I mean, I ain't read that much about it, Shilo, but I'm not stupid. Ever heard about Stalin? Hitler? Mussolini?"

"Point made." She stopped at a gauzy curtain. Odd to find such a thing hanging in a tunnel, she thought. "But have you ever heard of Arshaka in a history book?"

Shilo couldn't see Kim shake his head. "Of course not, Shilo. That's 'cause the guy hasn't done his thing yet. But if he unleashes these demons, and if we make it back home, then we'll probably find him in the history books. Probably be bigger than Hirohito and Caesar, Napoleon, and all of 'em. People from the future have no right to meddle in the past. It's not their time, and it's not their place. History could be changing right now, you know."

She thought him wise for his age, and she was pleased that her father had such a friend. "If Arshaka unleashes the demons, Kim, there might not be any home or history books." Shilo held her breath and touched the edge of the curtain with her free hand. The dripping sound was louder—annoying in its volume—and was directly ahead of them. She drew the material back slowly.

The lantern shone through the gauze, casting the room beyond in an eerie light and reminding her of one of the better haunted houses her dad had taken her to. She stepped through, careful not to catch the lantern on the curtain and start a fire. There was no one in the room, and she let out a deep breath of relief. Kim came through behind her, then walked past, stopping when he reached the center.

It wasn't really a room; it was like the chamber of a cave, though it had been excavated by man, not nature. The walls were dirt, and here and there she saw tree roots protruding like bent and broken fingers. There were two other passages leading out, both dark and making her think they looked like black eyes staring malevolently right at her. What bothered her the most, though, was its contents. Crude shelves lined two walls, stretching up to a ceiling that she guessed was at least ten feet high. One shelf was covered with clay bowls, some as small as a cereal bowl, others large enough to bob for apples in. They'd all been thrown on a pottery wheel. The wheel sat off to her right.

That's where the dripping sound came from. A contraption like a vat hung suspended near the ceiling. It was above a trough that looked like a double-sized bathtub, and it was next to the pottery wheel. There was a spigot at the bottom of the vat, and it regularly plopped gobs of liquid clay into the tub. Because the tub was metal and the gobs had several feet to fall, they plopped rather loudly.

"Hey, Shilo, that's where the squishy sound's coming from."

"I figured that out." The clay in the massive tub was too wet to work with. But she spotted two smaller tubs beyond it, half-filled with clay that looked more firm. "Drying it out some, looks like." She didn't want to stay here long, fearing someone would come to check on the clay or to throw some more of the ugly bowls.

There were more than a dozen tall, thick candles in the room, and a lantern hanging near the vat, all of them unlit. She sniffed the air, trying to tell if they'd been burning recently. All she could smell was the clay and the earth of the chamber, and her own stink from going so long without a bath.

"Need to be moving on," she told Kim. "But I want to get a closer look at what's on the shelves." She met his gaze, her eyes daggers.

"I know, don't run off. Don't touch anything." Softer: "Stop acting like my mother."

Shilo smiled. It had been some time since she'd smiled—all this worry and danger had kept her from it. She stepped closer to the shelf with the pottery. There was something about the bowls that niggled at the back of her mind. Something a little bit familiar.

"In Meemaw's attic." She'd seen some like these, though the ones above the attic store were clearly old—ancient, chipped, and the marks on them faded in places. Noticed them the night she went up in the storm and discovered the puzzle in the old sea chest. "What are they for?" The ones in Meemaw's attic had not bothered her and had not been worth more than a passing glance. But these were somehow disturbing.

The other shelf contained objects that sent a tingle down her spine. There were eggshells of various sizes, though none larger than a big duck or heron egg, all poked in the bottoms and their contents drained out. Wait… there was one the size of an ostrich egg, but only half of it was intact. And there were bones—finger and toe bones mostly, but a few larger pieces, including a lower jaw and a few chunks that looked like puzzle pieces.

"Ugh." She realized they were sections of a skull. "This is not good stuff."

"Gives me the willies for sure." Kim ogled the assortment, too. "Don't worry, I ain't gonna touch anything." He shoved his fist in his mouth to stifle a yawn. "What's it all for, Shilo? You got a clue?"

She shook her head. "No, Kim. Not a—"

"They are demon bowls, young woman. You should know that. Used throughout Babylonia. And they are not to be trifled with. Those on the shelf are of a dark magic, and so should command your respect."

The speaker was better than six feet tall, perhaps the tallest man Shilo had seen since arriving in Babylon. She couldn't tell his age, though she put him at more than thirty. His brown skin was smooth, and his long hair and beard, both decorated with dark wooden beads, were shot through with streaks of silver. Her gaze was drawn to his hands, which she could clearly see as he lit two of the thick candles. The hands were thin, like a woman's, the fingers long and circled with tattoos that were made to look like rings. Like the bowls, there was something about him that instantly set her on edge.

"I am Belzu-Mar, caretaker of the Old One, guardian of the Secrets of the Clay, and Esteemed Recorder of the Demon-Script." He stood back from the candles and stared at Shilo and Kim, critically appraising them. "And you do not belong here, either of you. May I show you the way out?"

"Yes, please!" Shilo said, feigning an expression of relief. Again, she didn't want to go, but she doubted this man would just let them keep exploring. They could leave with him, and she could wrap her robe tight around her so her streaked skin wouldn't show, and then they could come back in later.

"I should ask, perhaps, how you came to be in this chamber." Belzu-Mar nodded politely. "But that is not important. I am leaving myself, to retrieve the Old One from the western quarter. We've work to finish, and—"

"Who's the Old One?"

Shilo cringed when Kim blurted the question.

"The greatest sorcerer in Babylon." "Wow."

"He does not trifle with young ones."

"Did he make these bowls?" Shilo immediately cursed herself for asking something.

Kim's curiosity had infected her.

"Yeah, does he use the wheel and all this goopy clay?"

Belzu-Mar looked mildly surprised. "Some of the bowls, he makes— inscribes. The best of them are his." His gaze narrowed.

"Will you show us the way out now?" Shilo was worried they'd asked too many questions and wouldn't be permitted to leave.

"That would be best, I think." Belzu-Mar picked up the tallest of the lit candles and held it toward the farthest dark opening.

Shilo wondered if that was the one he'd come through. He hadn't been carrying a light. Could he see in the dark? Or had he been in this chamber and they hadn't noticed him? Had he been listening to their conversation?

"What's down that way?" Kim pointed to the other opening.

One question too many, Shilo thought.

"Perhaps my first thought is important now," Belzu-Mar said. "How did you two come to be down here?" He stared intently at Shilo, seeing something perhaps he hadn't the first time. "And what is wrong with your skin?"

"A rash," Kim spoke up for her. "It's contagious. So you don't want to touch her."

"We fell down into the mountain because we got too close to the buckets at the top. We were trying to see how the water conveyor worked." Shilo thought that fashion of the truth might stop him from worrying about her skin. *The clay!* She could use that to make her skin look darker. She should have thought of that right away, tended to it immediately, and to a splotch on Kim's hand. This tall stranger wouldn't have been so suspicious of them.

"Fortunate you were not injured." He took three measured steps toward them. "It is a long fall to the bottom. You must have landed on a ledge."

"Yes," Kim said, nodding so vigorously his hood fell off.

"Nothing broken?"

"We should follow you out of here," Shilo said. *Then turn around and come back inside.* "Would you mind?"

"I should ..." Belzu-Mar returned. There was the slightest hesitation, then Belzu-Mar turned back to the dark passage. "Come, clumsy, curious young ones. I've no more time for you. Set the lantern down. You won't be needing it once you are outside."

Kim raised his eyebrows and shrugged, pointed to the man's back and mouthed: *"What should we do?"*

Shilo didn't have an answer for that, but she did as the man said, setting the lantern down by the shelf. The light it cast upward made the bones and eggs look creepier.

"You had best not return here," Belzu-Mar warned them. The corridor he led them down narrowed after the opening, becoming no more than two feet wide. It turned to what Shilo guessed was west, and started to ascend. "If you fall down the hole again, the Hand of Nebuchadnezzar could decide that you are worth dealing with. And that would be unfortunate for you."

"What's he doin' down here? The Hand of Nebuchadnezzar?" Kim couldn't contain his curiosity. "You know, what's he doing way underground? With these bowls and stuff?"

Belzu-Mar turned, his face sad and his shoulders slumped. "I warn you not to touch the subject again. You had best forget you saw this place, young man. This is a place of bad dreams."

Shilo remembered Kim from her dream in Slade's Corners.

"There are three kinds of courage," the boy had said. "Courage in the blood. Courage in the veins. And courage in the spirit."

The more she thought about it, leaving with this man and finding a way back in now seemed like a bad idea. While Belzu-Mar was letting them go, he might find a way to prevent their return. And she didn't like the notion of him going to get the man who made demon bowls—the bad version of them.

The Old One, Belzu-Mar had called him.

The name sounded … evil.

"What about the dragon eggs?" Shilo found her "courage in the spirit." All her thoughts about them not doing enough planning, and that the dragon's pair of added helpers were too young … all of that was her fear speaking. Sigmund and Kim weren't too young. And how could one properly plan for something like this anyway? "Is the Old One going to break up the dragon eggs and put them in demon bowls? Is he going to poke the bottoms and drain the contents, killing the baby dragons inside?"

Angry lines, looking like jagged lightning bolts, sprouted on Belzu-Mar's forehead and at the edges of his mouth. "That is enough, I must—"

Shilo didn't give him a chance to curse at them, or threaten them, or say that he was now taking them to the Hand of Nebuchadnezzar. She darted forward and with both hands grabbed the candle from him and tugged it away. In the same motion she rammed her heel down on his instep.

Kim squeezed next to her. "What got into you?" he asked as he drove a rigid hand into the man's stomach and copied her move by slamming his foot down on the man's other instep.

Belzu-Mar wheezed and doubled over, reached out to his sides to grab the walls of the tunnel. He groaned and opened his mouth wider, and Shilo could tell he was going to holler for help.

She formed a fist with her free hand and punched his jaw, gasping when she heard either bones or teeth crunch. "Omigod." She stepped back as Kim punched the man in the stomach twice more.

"Don't hurt him," she said.

"Don't hurt him? You hit him first. Hit him pretty good for a girl." Kim clasped his hands together and brought them down hard on the man's shoulder, and Belzu-Mar slumped to his knees. "How do you not hurt someone if you hit him? Sheesh." Softer: "But I didn't kill him. He ain't even knocked out." Kim stood over Belzu-Mar, ready to hit him again if he tried to get up. "He's just a little woozy."

"A lot woozy. So what do we do with him?" Shilo was thinking to herself. "We can't just let him lay here. Someone will find him. Wait..." She looked back toward the clay chamber. "Help me drag him."

Kim raised an eyebrow, but bent and grabbed both hands. "I don't need help. I don't think he's that heavy. Just tall and ugly." Still, the boy huffed as he dragged Belzu-Mar back into the room, Shilo leading the way and holding the candle.

"So, just what do we do with him?' Kim held Belzu-Mar's wrists. "Don't move, buddy!"

"Over here." Shilo set the candle down, careful to leave it lit. "Help me get him up."

This time Kim didn't offer to do it himself. They got a grip under Belzu-Mar's armpits and wrestled him into one of the small tubs of clay. It made a sickening sucking sound as they pushed him in up to his shoulders. Belzu-Mar started to struggle, shaking off the wooziness.

"Hold him down." She ripped off a piece of her robe along the hem.

Kim placed his hands on either side of Belzu-Mar's neck. "You're not going to kill him, are you, Shilo?"

Belzu-Mar's eyes widened and he opened his mouth to holler. Shilo stuffed the wadded-up cloth in his mouth.

"Of course not. But we can't let him just wander off and get the guards or the Hand of Nebuchadnezzar." She shuddered when she thought of the vile, wealthy man.

"He can get out of this," Kim warned.

"Not without help." Shilo dropped to her knees next to the tub. "Keep holding him." She touched the tips of her fingers to the surface of the clay. "Please, God, let me manipulate this."

She closed her eyes and reached deep inside herself, finding a magical glow and picturing it the shade of the light the dragon gave off. She felt the clay ooze around her fingers, like the nuts she had melted. Then, as she withdrew her hands, she felt it harden.

"Serious wow," Kim pronounced. "You turned it into concrete."

"Just hardened it. When someone comes along, they can chip him out. I left just enough space around his chest so he can breathe."

"Major wow." Kim was clearly impressed with her. "Now what?"

I really want to find my father, Shilo thought. *That's what.* She worried that if her father died in Babylon, she might simply disappear ... her father never getting back to Georgia, never marrying and having children. But maybe that couldn't happen—maybe dying here wouldn't change anything. Time travel and all the ramifications were too much for her to worry over. And as much as she still wanted to find her father just because she loved him and wanted him safe, there was still the matter of saving the world from the wave of demons.

"Someone else might go get that Old One." Kim watched Belzu-Mar silently fume. "So the bad bowls might get made anyway. We've got to stop them."

Shilo picked up the lantern, scowling to see the oil running low. "We'll have to use those candles."

"Fine. I'll get 'em." Kim moved away from the tub, and Shilo stepped up to it.

She yanked the gag out of Belzu-Mar's mouth. "The Old One you talked about ... what is he planning to do with the dragon eggs?"

The man smiled thinly. "Dark magic to be certain. I am not a sorcerer, evil child, so I cannot precisely say."

Evil child? Shilo's face reddened in anger. "You have to know something."

"I have told you enough."

She waved the gag at him.

"Where are the eggs?"

He closed his mouth defiantly.

"If you don't tell me, I'll—"

"What? Torture me?"

Before he could shut his mouth again, she shoved the cloth back in.

"Kim and I will find the eggs on our own then." She saw that Kim had a candle for each of them. Bending down, she blew out the lantern and took one of the candles. "Hope you can see in the dark," she told Belzu-Mar.

Then she and Rim took the other passage, which grew equally narrow and which filled her senses with the heady scent of newly dug earth. She brushed the dirt wall with her free hand and felt that it was cool, almost damp.

"They didn't dig this very long ago," she whispered.

"Hope it doesn't fall in on us."

Kim shuffled behind her.

"Hope Sig's okay."

"I do, too, Kim." *You can't imagine just how much I hope that he's okay.* Shilo walked faster, alternating between glancing straight ahead and looking down. The floor was uneven and had ruts here and there that were from shovels. Sharp rocks protruded, and after stepping on one and feeling it go through her sandal, she took care not to step on any others.

The tunnel was short and opened into a chamber slightly smaller than the clay room. However, unlike the previous room, it was occupied.

Oil burned in a large brazier, lighting the room and making the guard's metal breastplate gleam. The guard grabbed up his spear and pointed it at the pair.

"Who are you? What are you doing here?" He looked at Shilo's smeared skin. "What—"

"Skin condition," Shilo said, suspecting that he wouldn't believe it. *Should've used some of that clay.* She set her candle on the floor and held her hands up, as if she were surrendering.

Kim set his candle down, too. "Take a good look at what's in here, Shilo."

"I see them."

"You know, there's another tub of clay back there."

"I know," she whispered. "Get him!"

The guard hadn't expected the pair to attack him. Kim hollered, and the guard turned to face him, giving Shilo a chance to dart to his side. She managed to grab the spear out of his hands, just as Kim shot forward and kicked the man hard between the legs. He wasn't as easy to subdue as Belzu-Mar, but they managed.

Neither was he as easy to drag.

Then Shilo and Kim scurried back to the chamber and stared at the four dragon eggs arranged carefully on a large bed of straw.

29

THE DEMON OR THE EGG

The chamber felt uncomfortably warm compared to the tunnel and the clay room. Shilo realized the brazier was giving off more than light... "To keep the eggs warm, to incubate them."

But she wasn't sure that was necessary. Didn't lizards just bury their eggs in the sand somewhere and scamper away? Maybe whoever stole the eggs didn't know better or wasn't taking any chances... or maybe they knew a lot more about dragons than she did.

They were huge, as far as eggs went. Three of them were a little more than two feet high, the fourth at least three feet. The bottom half of each shell was covered with letters she couldn't read and ugly drawings of creatures that were half-men, half-monster.

"I ain't carrying the big one," Kim whispered. "I don't think I could get my arms around it."

Shilo wished her father and Nidintulugal were here—they could each take an egg and get out of here. Together they would find a way out. She scanned the room, seeing the eggs, the brazier, a low stool that the guard had probably been sitting on, and an old wooden plate on the floor that had likely held his lunch. There was a narrow table—a desk perhaps. It was opposite the eggs, and several objects were arranged on it. There was also another passageway leading from here, and Shilo peered into the darkness, wondering what it led to.

"Why did they go and paint them like that?" Kim shuffled closer to the eggs. "Like dipping Easter eggs, but in a bad way."

"A very bad way." Shilo joined him and held the candle close. "The marks are like the ones on those bowls."

"The demon bowls?" Kim visibly shuddered. "This really can't be good."

"Oh, my." Shilo grasped that these eggs weren't going to be broken up and put in demon bowls... they were going to *be* the demon bowls. There was a faint indentation on each egg, running around the center just above where all the symbols started. She touched the shell, the top first, and then the bottom.

"They've strengthened the bottom, Kim, just like I made the clay hard. When the eggs crack open, I think only the top will break, leaving the bottom intact."

"Why?"

Shilo shook her head. "They want the bottoms to be bowls."

"Duh, yeah. But the bad demon bowls, right?" Kim gingerly touched the largest egg.

"What if when the baby dragons hatch, the spells on the bowls are released?"

"Calling all manner of demons," Shilo said, "to be under someone's control."

The enormity of her task settled deep in her chest.

Ulbanu's vision of the demon swarm was frightening enough, but seeing these eggs and the spells written on them intensified everything.

As much as she wanted to find her father and Nidintulugal—*needed* to find them—it was more important to deal with these eggs right now.

Kim had been talking to her, but she'd missed what he said.

"What?"

The boy grimaced. "I said ... what should we do?"

Shilo didn't answer right away. She touched the closest egg again, running her fingers along the bottom half and tracing the marks. She searched for the magic inside of her and tried to melt the letters, like she'd melted the nuts.

"Nothing's happening," Kim said.

Shilo tried harder. She felt like she was on fire, but put everything she had into it. Sweat beaded up all over her, and her chest felt like a furnace was being stoked deep inside.

"Still nothing, Shilo."

She pictured the writing melting and the figures of the men-monsters fading. She imagined that all the ink or paint or whatever had been used feathered like watercolors in the rain. Then she felt Kim grabbing her around the waist as she started to wobble. The candle in her hand slipped, and she

204

just barely managed to catch it. She steadied herself and changed the grip on the candle.

"Can't ruin the writing, can you?"

Shilo shook her head.

"But you can't give up."

She wasn't about to. Shilo had wanted out of Wisconsin, had wanted to be with her dad, didn't want him dead—but she hadn't wanted any of this. It would be easy to quit, to go back to the dragon's cave as fast as her legs or the ox could take her, and tell Ulbanu that there was nothing she could do ... now could she please go home?

But in Babylon she'd managed to find at least one kind of courage—courage of the spirit, and that wasn't letting her run. Out of the corner of her eye, she saw Kim take a whack at the base of an egg, using his hand in a chopping motion. He mouthed *"Owl"* and grabbed at his fingers.

He had the right idea to destroy the "bowls," even if that meant killing the dragons inside.

"Kim, listen down that tunnel. Let me know if you hear anything." *Please, please don't let him hear anything.*

Kim hesitated a moment before going to the passage they'd not been down. He stood sideways so he could both see her and hear what might be going on in the unknown tunnel.

"I don't hear anything."

Shilo felt the leathery smoothness of the egg, the top half slightly cooler than the bottom. Her fingertips registered the temperature, and she wondered if her magic enhanced the sensations. There had to be something about the eggs that wasn't ready. Belzu-Mar said he had to retrieve the Old One, the sorcerer who fashioned demon bowls, and who, she suspected, had written the spells on these eggs. So maybe the sorcerer wasn't quite finished.

She stepped to the side of the largest egg on the end and craned her neck so that she could see behind it. Shilo didn't know what to look for, as she really didn't know anything about demon bowls. But she couldn't see anything amiss.

"Wait a minute." She held the candle as far behind the eggs as she could. The two eggs in the middle were not wholly inscribed. The eggs on the end were painted with the images and mysterious symbols and letters all the way around, and halfway up. But the other two were not complete in the back. She came around to the front again, set her candle on the floor, and gingerly turned first one, and then the other, of the unfinished eggs. Then she picked up the candle again and held it close to an egg.

"That's why he had to go get the Old One. Maybe the Old One's so old he wasn't able to finish everything all at once. Or maybe he ran out of the funny paint."

The fingers of her free hand danced on the incomplete edges, and she felt her chest turn into a furnace again. She closed her eyes and pictured the ink feathering, and when she opened them, she saw that the ink was indeed running and the images of the half-men, half-monsters were fading, then disappearing. So while she hadn't been able to affect the marks on the completed eggs, she could ruin the spells by focusing on the unfinished sections.

She knew quite a bit of time was passing because the candle was burning shorter, the hot wax dripping across the back of her hand. It hurt, but she didn't set the candle down—she didn't want to waste a single moment. One egg erased, she started on the other incomplete spell.

"I think I hear something," Kim whispered. He'd set his candle down just inside the opening and blown it out, and he was standing off to the side now, so someone looking down the tunnel couldn't see him. "Someone talking, I think. But I can't make out what—"

Shilo put a finger to her lips, then concentrated harder. She was soaking wet from sweating so much, and she was exhausted. Magic took a toll, she realized, wishing it was as easy as David Copperfield and the other celebrity magicians made it look. But theirs was not real magic. More and more of the images faded and melted, leaving a shine on the shell where they'd been.

"I hear footsteps, Shilo."

Panicking, she motioned for him to join her, and then whispered in his ear, her words a hurried buzz. "I know I told you not to run off ever again, but I'm taking that back. That tunnel Belzu-Mar was leading us down, well, he said that it went to the outside. And I don't think he was lying." She picked up one of the eggs she'd erased and held it out to him. His arms couldn't quite encircle it.

"Kinda heavy," he said, looking around the side. "But I can manage."

She wedged her candle between his hand and the shell so he'd be able to see. The brazier gave her more than enough light in this room.

"Take this egg outside?"

"How about to just inside the way out?" She shook her head. "Does that make sense? Do you know what I mean?"

"I ain't stupid. You want me to leave it inside a doorway. Then come back for the other one, right?"

She nodded. "Hurry, but be careful, Kim. Don't drop it. Please, please, don't drop it." She glided to the passage and stood just to the side, listening intently. She heard Kim's soft footfalls, and looked to see that he had left. She heard other footfalls, someone coming down the tunnel—two or three someones, from the sound of it. Her heart hammering wildly, she returned to the eggs, crouching at the end where the largest one was.

She knew it wasn't good cover, especially since someone would notice one of the eggs missing. But she couldn't leave the eggs, and she couldn't stop trying to use her magic. She ran her hands across the surface, deciding since she couldn't affect the spell, maybe she could instead affect the egg itself.

The lower half of the egg was hard, like wood, and she worried that if the spell had made it thus, there was nothing she could do about it. But after a moment, she felt the texture change slightly, becoming bumpy like a hen's egg. She thumped it—definitely thinner. So while she couldn't affect the writing, she could indeed affect the egg itself. How much thinner should she make it?

Just a little, to be sure, to be safe, she decided. If the dragon hatched, it would break the bottom of the egg and ruin the bowl and hopefully any vile demon-summoning magic with it. She stretched a hand up and touched the top half of the egg, making it harder. She wanted to be doubly sure the bottom half would break. Shilo was about to take her hand away when a shriek cut through the air.

She poked her head around the egg and saw the wide, angry eyes of Arshaka. She jumped to her feet, mouth working, but no words coming out. She didn't know what to say.

"Insolent worm." Arshaka's words were venomous, but they were soft and controlled. Shilo sensed he was ready to erupt.

In a handful of strides he was on her, grabbing the front of her robe and lifting her, slamming her up against the dirt wall behind her. Still, his voice was low: "How dare you try to undo this? You've no cause for it. And you've no comprehension of what this is about."

Still she couldn't speak, fear freezing her tongue. She didn't blink, could scarcely breathe.

He looked over his shoulder, at two men in gray skirts who had accompanied him. "Get the others. Go get them now."

They whirled on their sandaled feet and retreated down the corridor.

"Where is the missing egg, Shilo?"

She shrugged.

"You're responsible for its disappearance. Where is it?" Still a civil tone.

In a moment there might be an army in here, Shilo thought. No doubt they'd bring chains and weapons, and might very possibly kill her.

Wrinkles formed at the corners of Arshaka's eyes and finally he spoke, much louder: "I ... said ... where ... is ... the ... egg?"

Shilo heard a hissing sound, and realized it was his breath. Like a teapot left too long on the stove, he was starting to boil over.

"The egg, worm! And what have you done with the spell on this one?" Arshaka was angry enough to order her death; she could see that in his dark, sparkling eyes. "Worm!"

He shook her and thrust her against the wall again, striking the back of her head and making her dizzy. "I don't need this, the eggs. I can have all of Babylon without this. But the spells, the dragons, the demons, will make all of it so much easier and more pleasant. What ... have ... you ... done?"

Somehow she found her voice. "I ruined your plans," she said. "At least some of them."

"Some," he admitted. He set her on her feet, but kept one hand wrapped around a fistful of her robe. He dragged her to the front of the nest. With his free hand he gestured to the two eggs with the intact spells. "But not all."

Please, please don't let him discover I've weakened the big egg. Shilo wished Nidintulugal and her father were with her, then instantly changed that thought—bad enough that she was going to die because she'd challenged Arshaka. The priest and her father didn't need to share her fate. She hoped Kim wasn't coming back, and she prayed the boy could find his way to Ulbanu with one egg and then get home.

"I've two eggs left, worm. Two spells to call the demons to start my blessed war. Demons from the egg will be stronger than ones summoned by mere bowls. They will grow and multiply upon their hatching. Glorious!" Spittle flecked at the corners of his lips. "You've not entirely undone me!" He spit at her.

Shilo had never been spit at before, and had never been handled so badly. The back of her head hurt from when he'd shoved her against the wall, and all over she was feverish from using so much magic. Could she use her magic to hurt him in return?

"I will kill you," he hissed. He shook her one more time, then pushed her away so hard she flew back against the desk. The impact sent the items on it spilling and hurtling to the floor—vials of sand and ink, wooden beads that made a clacking sound like hard candies dropped on the floor of a movie theater, smaller eggs that shattered and spilled their yolks, and objects she couldn't name fell.

"Unless…" He stared down at her, hands clenching and unclenching so tight his knuckles had turned white. "Unless you cooperate, Southern girl…Shilo…I want to go back to Georgia. Not now, the eggs are too close to hatching. But when they're done, and when the war has started. There are some things in Georgia, in America, that I want."

Machine guns. Shilo didn't know why that thought instantly popped into her head. *Grenades. Bombs. Nuclear weapons.* He wanted modern weaponry— somehow she knew that, to help foster this war he was planning.

"I can't," she said, forcing the words out. Her throat and mouth were so sore and hot.

"Can't…or won't?" He loomed over her now, foot coming down on her robe, like he was pinning a bug.

"Can't. Only the dragon can send me back. And she's certainly not going to send you back. You took her eggs!"

He laughed, a chilling, deep sound that bounced off the floor and walls. It was like something she'd expect to hear in a horror movie, but this was so much worse because it was real.

"Why do you need modern weapons?" Shilo pulled the warm air into her lungs. She was so uncomfortably hot. "If you have demons, why do you need weapons?"

His eyes narrowed and he bent closer. She could smell his breath, fetid and making her gag. "Weapons and Kevlar, chemicals. Mostly chemicals, Shilo. Bottles of chemicals. Chemical warfare is far more effective than bullets, child. Think what my demons could accomplish by spreading chemicals across countries that resist me! I'll slay the people and leave the blessed buildings intact. I'll put those loyal to me in the buildings and cities!"

'You're insane," Shilo said.

The two men in gray skirts returned, followed by four more in similar dress, who dragged Nidintulugal and Sigmund. Shilo made a move to rise, but Arshaka planted a foot on her stomach.

He spoke to her in English now. "Perhaps you'll change your mind, Shilo, about finding your way back to Georgia."

"Don't take him to Georgia! Don't tell him how!" Sigmund called. He fought only feebly now, his energy sapped from struggling so much earlier. "He's from Georgia, Shilo, and he forgot how to go back and—"

Arshaka turned. "Shut your mouth, Sig, or I'll crush your pretty friend."

Sigmund glared at Arshaka. "I should've never shown you that puzzle, Artie."

Arshaka gave him a lethal look and applied a little pressure to Shilo's stomach. She squirmed, grabbed his ankle, and tried to push him off.

"The boy!" Arshaka sneered. "Him first."

The two men wrenched Sigmund's arms up and behind him. The man with the knife pressed it against Nidintulugal's side to keep him from struggling.

"Stop," Shilo said. "Please stop. Don't hurt him."

Arshaka removed his foot. "Stay down, girl."

"Please don't hurt him." She didn't move.

"The boy will stay healthy if you cooperate."

"You can threaten him, threaten me," she said. "But I can't get back home without the dragon. That's the truth."

Arshaka looked undecided for a moment. "You realize you're worth nothing to me, either one of you, if you can't take me home. We didn't need a dragon to get home when we used the puzzle before. So you can't possibly need a dragon now."

"He's forgotten how to travel, Shilo. That's why he needs us," Sigmund cut in.

Shilo gave Arshaka the coldest stare she could muster. So he had used the puzzle before, maybe was from Sigmund's neighborhood, maybe had snuck into the old man's house.

Arshaka steepled his fingers under his chin. "You'd best remember, Shilo, Sigmund, how to travel, or you won't be getting any older." He brightened, smiling wide and warmly, and he rubbed his hands together. "These eggs are not far from hatching, and if the dragon whelps survive, they'll be hungry." He paused and stared at Shilo. "The demons most certainly will be hungry."

The Hand turned to the two men who'd originally accompanied him into the chamber. "The Old One should have arrived by now. He was to finish inscribing two eggs; now he must fully inscribe only one. Siighi, retrieve the Old One and Belzu-Mar. Perhaps they do not know the eggs are so close to hatching."

Arshaka watched the man grab up the unlit candle, light it at the brazier, and leave. Shilo sucked in a breath. He left the way Kim had with the egg; he'd discover the men trapped in the tub.

"It's so hot," Shilo whispered. Arshaka alternately watched her and Sigmund now. She propped herself up against the leg of the desk, and with one hand grabbed the front of her robe and fluttered it, as if trying to cool herself. She was worried for Kim … and for Sigmund and Nidintulugal and for everyone if the demons arrived.

"The heat is for the eggs," Arshaka said. "And because the coming demons enjoy it warm."

"Of course demons would like it warm," she whispered.

Arshaka didn't see her other hand snake forward and touch the hem of his robe, didn't know she was working her magic.

She thought about the clay in the other room that she'd hardened around the two captured men, and thought about the nuts she'd melted and the egg-shell she'd made more brittle. She felt herself growing even warmer, and she held her breath and coaxed Arshaka's clothes to become like steel and the hem of his long robe to meld with the dirt of the floor.

"All of it steel," she breathed.

"What?" The Hand felt his clothes stiffen around him, and though he tried to back away from Shilo, he wasn't fast enough.

She concentrated harder, and within the passing of a few heartbeats Arshaka was effectively trapped. His right arm was bare, and so he could move it. He tried to turn his head, but the swath of yellow material held it like his neck was in a cast. He flailed his arm furiously.

"Kill them!" he shouted. "The priest first! Make it hurt!"

Only one of the men had a weapon, and this was the knife that had been taken from Nidintulugal. The man drew his arm back, then thrust it forward. But Nidintulugal reacted quickly. The priest dropped, his weight pulling at his captors and ruining the man's aim.

The knife found flesh, but the wrong target. The blade buried itself in the side of the other man. The grip on the priest loosened, and he extricated himself by springing up and jumping back.

"Kill the boy!" Arshaka spat. "Break his neck!"

30

BAD SPELLS

"No! Don't hurt him! Don't touch him!" Shilo screamed and pulled herself up on Arshaka's immobile arm. "I'll kill your beloved Hand if you touch that boy!"

This made the two men holding Sigmund pause.

Behind them, the man who'd been stabbed clutched at his side, blood spilling out from between his fingers. The other pulled the knife out and swung it again at Nidintulugal. This time the priest grabbed the man's wrist and brought his knee up, cracking it against the man's arm. The knife clattered to the floor. Nidintulugal kicked at the man, sending him away, and grabbed the knife.

The man who'd been stabbed collapsed and stopped breathing.

"Three of you left in here," Shilo said. "If you want to keep living, and if you want the Hand to live, you'd best listen to me."

"To me!" Arshaka shouted. "You'll listen to me! She won't kill me, you fools. She's just a girl. She's—" His eyes widened.

One of the eggs, the smaller one with the complete spell, started to crack.

"Kill the boy!" Arshaka repeated. "Do it now, I say!"

Nidintulugal rammed the knife into the back of one of the men holding Sigmund. He tried to pull the blade free, but it was wedged too tightly in a rib. Releasing the handle, the man fell, gasping and twitching. The priest turned to the other man holding Sigmund and grabbed him below the shoulders. He fought hard, and Nidintulugal could barely hold him.

Shilo had made it over to the final guard. She'd hardened his skirt and pushed him to the floor. Like a turtle that had been turned onto its back, he struggled to get up, but could go nowhere.

Two dead, Nidintulugal told her as he continued to wrestle with a guard. "As a result of my actions."

"Better than all of us dead, Niddy," Sigmund said. The boy helped restrain Nidintulugal's opponent. "Hurry, Shilo, give him a concrete skirt, too."

Concrete? That's just what she did.

All the while Arshaka continued to holler.

"Don't you have a way to shut him up?" Sigmund was looking to her to solve the problem.

"No, I—" She ripped another piece of cloth free from the hem of her robe and stuffed it in his mouth. "I guess I do have a way to shut him up."

Arshaka's face was so red it looked like he was going to explode.

"The egg—" Sigmund prompted.

Nidintulugal was not looking at the eggs. He stared at the two downed men and the growing pools of blood. There was blood on his hands and on his robe, and a smudge on his face where he must have wiped at the sweat.

Shilo wanted to talk him through this and console him, but the eggs were the more pressing concern. A large spiderweb crack had appeared in the top of the smaller egg, and the black writing on the bottom half had started to glow.

"Oh, my," she hushed. "I don't know what to do. I don't know… Fath… Sigmund. I don't—"

"Well think of something!" the boy said. "You're the one with magic."

Think. Shilo grabbed the egg at the bottom and squealed. "Hot!" She pulled back, but only for a heartbeat. Then she grabbed the egg again, her mind racing with prayers and thoughts of making it as thin as tissue paper. She closed her eyes, not wanting to see what was happening and not wanting to watch her hands burn.

She felt them burning—she'd accidentally burned herself more than once trying to cook. Those incidents had been nothing. She imagined that her skin was frying away. Still, she wouldn't release her grip. Was this a second kind of courage—courage of the blood? In the dream Kim had told her she would have to find her courage.

Shilo threw her head back and opened her mouth to scream, but with the last bit of her will she kept quiet. And then she felt her thumb break through the shell.

"Niddy, she's breaking the bad spell! Look!"

Shilo thrust all of her fingers against the shell, feeling each one break through. It was like plunging her fingers into boiling water, and she pictured her hands melting away.

Can't keep this up, she thought. *This will kill me.* But if she succeeded, Sigmund might live, Nidintulugal, too. Was that another kind of courage—being willing to sacrifice yourself. In the back of her mind she remembered something else Kim had told her in the dream.

"And yet if you value your life and want to hold on to your father's memories—if you don't want to risk everything you know, you must never heed her call."

But Shilo had heeded the dragon's call, and now she was risking everything. She started breaking away bits of the shell, as if she were peeling a hard-boiled Easter egg. Only this egg sizzled and popped and gave off the worst odor she'd ever smelled in her relatively short life. It was the scent of sulfur and charred flesh and things dead and rotting.

She tried to gag, but nothing came up. Then she tried to breathe, but her chest had grown too tight. Finally, she tried to open her eyes. But all she saw was blackness. Hot and total, it swirled around her and sucked her down.

"Demons!"

Safe in the stifling, scalding darkness, Shilo heard the word repeated. It was Sigmund shouting, and she fought her way back to reach him.

"Niddy, those've got to be demons!"

Shilo floated in the darkness; it was syrupy, and it resisted her attempts to pull out of it. Her arms felt like lead, trying to tug free. *Water,* she thought. *Let the blackness be like water.* She pictured the water that ran in the troughs down the sides of the Hanging Gardens, and the Euphrates River. Somehow she manipulated the blackness. It wasn't so thick anymore, and it didn't suck her down.

Buoyed, she felt her head breaking above it, opened her eyes, and witnessed a horror that held Nidintulugal and Sigmund dumbstruck. Emerging from the shattered egg were red-skinned demons.

The chittering, writhing mass oozed out of the nest and onto the floor. Each creature was roughly the size of a Softball, and each was a little different—one had a broad face and a wide nose with four nostrils, Mr. Spock ears, and no lips, but plenty of teeth. Another had a heart-shaped face with wide blue eyes and nostrils, but no nose. And one had two heads, one of them malformed with only one eye and ear. Some of them had wings, others webbed

215

fingers and toes and gill slits on their necks. They had some things in common—scaly skin the shade of fresh blood, curved talons on their hands and feet, gleaming white teeth that looked needle-sharp.

The man on the floor, trapped by his concrete skirt, could not scream as they flowed over him; he had no tongue.

But Sigmund screamed. The boy threw his hands over his mouth and stumbled backward. The demons swarmed over the corpses of Arshaka's other men, and Nidintulugal reached into the mass and retrieved his knife. One started climbing the priest's leg, and he stabbed at it. The demon howled shrilly, the noise hurtful, then it withered and disappeared in an oily puff of smoke. Nidintulugal started stabbing at more.

Sigmund tried to shake off his fear, jumping and coming down on a demon. "They can die!" he called to Shilo. "But there's so many of them."

She risked a glance at Arshaka, who was futilely trying to spit the gag out of his mouth. *He could control these demons*, she thought. *He knows the spell and knows how to order them around. He can stop this slaughter.* She stepped toward him and raised her arm to pull the cloth out, saw the relief in his eyes and instantly stopped herself. Arshaka would order the demons to continue the slaughter.

Shilo looked back to the broken egg. The form of a small dragon, its stomach missing, sickened her. She started stomping on the demons too, crying out when one tore at her robe and bit deeply into her leg.

"Hurry! We've got to kill them before they get out of this room!" Shilo wrinkled her nose when she crushed one of the skulls of the two-headed demon. "If they get out into the city, who knows what'll happen." A glance back at the shattered egg. More demons were emerging from where the dragon's stomach had been.

She fought her way toward the eggshell, even as she fought against the bile rising in her throat. She'd never been in a more disgusting, horrid situation. The stench pounded at her senses, so strong she swore she could taste it. She managed to reach the baby dragon corpse, where more demons continued to emerge. These monsters were only the size of golf balls. But as she watched, they started to grow.

Shilo placed her hands on the dragon's body ... it was just an object now, no life to it, just a gate the demons were coming through.

"Sigmund, the other egg—the big one with the writing on it. Break it!" She hated the order, knew doing so could well kill the baby dragon inside. But she couldn't risk that the egg would break on its own and that demons would spill out. The monsters clearly could exist without a bowl being intact. "Break it now!"

She bit hard on her lower lip to keep from crying out and returned her attention to the baby dragon corpse. The tiny demons emerging from the carcass swarmed up her arms, chewing and clawing at her. She wanted to brush them off, but didn't budge. Instead, she did her best to ignore the pain and focused on the dragon corpse. *It was a thing now,* she told herself again. An inanimate object. Like the nuts and the clay and the garments, it was something that could be manipulated.

"Melt," she said. "Run like water." As the tiny demons continued to bite at her, the corpse did just that—it melted. A silver-gold smear, it trickled into the nest. "No more demons coming out." She stepped back and started plucking the tiny demons off her arms, hurling them to the floor and stomping on them.

Shilo was engrossed in the grisly task, but she took a quick peek to her right, seeing Sigmund repeatedly strike the large egg like it was a punching bag. The egg cracked, but she couldn't hear it; the demons were making too much noise. Finally scraping the last one off her, she spun to see Nidintulugal struggling with one that had grown to the size of a basketball.

How big could they grow?

"Did any get out of this room?" she shouted.

The priest shook his head. "I do not think so."

"One at least!" This came from Kim, who stood by the brazier, holding the broken body of a demon who'd grown to half the boy's size. "Caught him in the clay room, chewing on the face of that Belzu guy. Had to deal with a guy without a tongue, too." He dropped the dead demon and started stomping on the red wave surging his way.

"Don't let any more get out!" Shilo called.

"Eww... gross!"

Shilo turned her attention back to Sigmund. He'd broken the egg and peeled the shell off the baby dragon. It struggled to live, mouth opening and closing, neck flopping around and feet twitching. Its belly roiled, and Shilo likened it to a pan of Jiffy Pop.

"Kill it, Sigmund!" She cursed herself for saying it, but she knew the demons were going to erupt. Perhaps their only chance of stopping the demons was to kill the dragon host, which was going to die anyway. "Be quick!"

Nidintulugal, covered with blood, pushed Sigmund aside. "I will do it." The knife in his hand flashed once across the baby dragon's throat. The priest and Shilo watched as the writhing in the dragon's stomach slowed, then finally stopped.

Behind them, Sigmund and Kim kept stomping. They were making a game of it and trying to keep score.

"Do you think it's over?" Shilo looked at Nidintulugal. She hoped all the blood on him belonged to the demons and the man he killed, and wasn't his own. She felt blood on herself, too, and saw that Kim and Sigmund were splattered.

"I do not know if it is over, Shilo. Must we break open this one, too, and kill the dragon inside?" He pointed to the last intact egg.

"I don't want to. I hope not. The spell is off it. So let's just get it out of here, put it on the cart, and get it out of Babylon."

'The other egg's by the back door," Kim said. "I left it there, just like you told me. Oh…was that a person?" The boy stared at the Hand of Nebuchadnezzar's stiff clothes.

"Oh." Shilo felt weak and rocked back against the blood-drenched nest.

Only the hardened robe and scarf remained of Arshaka. All trace of the man was gone.

"The demons must have swarmed him."

"And feasted well, Shilo," Nidintulugal said.

"Ewwww," Kim said.

"Let's get the hell out of here." This came from Sigmund.

The floor was covered with a red pulpy mass that had been the demons. Shilo slogged through it to make sure none were still alive. She bent and searched through the goop around the base of Arshaka's robe, coming up with eight gold, bejeweled rings and a thick gold bracelet. She put them all in her pocket.

Then she touched the stiff robe and willed it soft again, ripped it in half and passed one section to Nidintulugal.

'To wrap that egg in," she told him. "Don't need the common folk seeing it." She gave the other piece to Kim. "For the egg by the door."

Then she sloshed toward Sigmund and put her arms around him and hugged him tight. He returned the embrace, neither talking for a few moments.

"Yeah, let's get the heck out of here," she said.

218

31

THE DRAGON MAGE

They had little trouble getting out of the city. Shilo used Arshaka's smallest ring to trade for a change of clothes for each of them and for a bag full of nuts, which she used to color Sigmund, Kim, and herself. She used her magic to strengthen the cart, and to smooth the wheels so they might travel faster, and she gave up Arshaka's bracelet for a small crate of food and a big jug of goat's milk—all of them were terribly hungry and thirsty.

They ate along the road, Kim and Nidintulugal walking on either side of the ox, leading it. Only once did they go off the road—this when they heard voices ahead. They hid in the tall grass until a dozen men passed, led by Ekurzakir. From the conversations, Shilo could tell they'd been looking for her and the priest, and that the Hand of the Hand was terribly angry.

For most of the rest of the way, Shilo and Sigmund walked behind the cart, chatting endlessly about Georgia and baseball, Neil Diamond songs, and history. It was like they were old friends.

"So where do you live in Georgia?" Sigmund finally asked.

"I used to live in Marietta." There was a touch of sadness in her voice. "I loved it there. I really loved my father. Now I live in Wisconsin with my grandparents. They're good people."

Sigmund dug the ball of his foot into the ground. "Wisconsin. Ugh. From time to time my folks talk about moving there. Cows and snow." He let a silence settle between them, before he added: "Wisconsin, huh? Maybe I'll see you there sometime."

They swung wide around the village of Ibinghal, fearing that a guard or two had been left behind to look for them. Then they hid the ox and cart in the foothills and carefully carried the eggs up to Ulbanu's cave.

Shilo marveled that the egg she toted felt just about as heavy as that bolt of cloth.

The dragon was pleased to see them. And Sigmund and Kim were awed in Ulbanu's presence to the point their knees shook.

"My dragon ... Fafnir ... was not near so big as this," Sigmund said. His voice cracked, and he leaned back against Shilo for support. "Wow. Double wow."

"Triple wow," Kim added. "Everything in the world was worth seeing this. All the hurting and the demon-killing. It was all worth it."

Ulbanu wrapped her tail around the eggs and pulled them close to her.

"Are they—" Shilo didn't quite know how to phrase the question.

"The dragons inside the eggs live. No demons beat in their hearts. They are but a few days from hatching. And they owe their lives to you." Ulbanu purred. "I shall name them Sigmund and Shilo."

"Neato-keeno," Sigmund gushed. "I'd like to stick around and see them hatch, but I better be getting back. My mom'll be worrying."

"Mine, too," Kim added. "Four times wow."

"But maybe we'll come back sometime," Sigmund said. "If you don't mind."

Ulbanu let out a breath, warm and dry, sounding like sand being blown by a strong wind. It fluttered their robes and threw their hoods back. "I would relish your company, Kim, Sigurd Clawhand."

"Neato-keeno," he repeated, raising his hand and waving. "Be seeing you then."

"Wait a minute." Shilo grabbed him. "The dragon has to do something to send you back, to send all of us back!"

"Nah," Sigmund said. "Artie ... Arshaka ... the Hand of Nebuchadnezzar, he forgot how to use the magic. I figure he stayed here too long, didn't travel enough, was too far from the puzzle. See, there's this puzzle that's a magical focus. Anyway, Artie just forgot how. But me and Kim, we just learned it. So it's still fresh." He gave her a wide smile. "So I'll be seeing you, Shilo. Hey, if I ever have any kids, I'll name one of 'em after you ... just like Ulbanu's doing."

He started to fade. Kim, too.

"I love you, Sigmund ... Sigurd Clawhand." She prayed he heard her before he completely disappeared. Shilo stared at the empty space for several minutes, listening to herself breathe and the dragon purr.

"So they could travel on their own." She raised her gaze to stare into one of the dragon's massive eyes. "Did they come here on their own?"

"I did not bring them. I merely asked if they would help."

"And me?"

"You do not need me to send you home, Shilo."

Shilo's face reddened.

She intended to berate Ulbanu for implying that the dragon would send her back, that she couldn't get back on her own. And that for the dragon to do the sending, Shilo would have to retrieve the eggs. There were a dozen mean things that flitted through her mind. But she dismissed one after the next, dominoes in a line she knocked down.

The dragon wanted her eggs saved, and wanted dragonkind helped—so any deception could be forgiven. In the process, Shilo stopped a wave of demons and found three kinds of courage.

"So I can get home on my own, Ulbanu?"

"You always could. It is inside of you, the magic. You only need to look for it." The rumbling of the dragon's voice sent pleasant vibrations against the bottoms of Shilo's feet.

"I guess you're right," Shilo said. "I can feel it, the magic." She reached into her pocket and pulled out seven of the heavy rings she'd retrieved from Arshaka. She pressed them into Nidintulugal's hand. "Nidin, these ought to be worth a lot around here."

He looked at them and felt their weight. "Worth a great deal, Shilo."

"What are you going to do?" She looked up into Nidintulugal's eyes. "Not going back to the Temple of Shamash, are you?"

He shook his head. "I do not know—"

"I would wish him to stay here," Ulbanu said.

Nidintulugal and Shilo turned to again face the dragon.

"There is magic in you, Nidintulugal of Shamash. More even than in Shilo and the one called Sigurd Clawhand. You have felt it before. It drew you to follow her the first time to my cave. And it compelled you to help her and to fight the demons."

Nidintulugal didn't say anything; he just kept staring. Shilo noticed a sheen of sweat forming on his face.

"I can teach you, Nidintulugal of Shamash. And in exchange you can help me raise my young. Together, we will watch for demons."

"A mage," he finally said. "Myself, a mage?"

"A dragon mage," Shilo said. She stood on her toes and kissed his cheek. "A real hero."

Nidintulugal blushed and opened his mouth to say something. Shilo put her finger to his lips. "More powerful than me and my father. You'll do Babylon proud, Nidin." She paused. "And I might come back to check up on you … if I get the hang of this time-and-space traveling."

"We both would welcome you, Child of Sigurd."

Shilo smiled wide.

She liked the sound of that title.

She woke on the floor of her bedroom, head on the puzzle she'd assembled. The image she'd slept on was of a singular dragon, one cobbled together from the pieces of the gold and silver dragons depicted on the lid of the puzzle box. She touched the dragon with her fingertips and concentrated. All the pieces fused together and the surface smoothed and sparkled.

"I think I will come back for a visit, Ulbanu," she said. "Provided this all was real."

"Shy …" It was her grandmother standing outside her door, gently tapping. "I'm going to open early this morning. Hurry with your shower and come down for breakfast."

Shilo looked to her window. Sunlight streamed in.

Was it possible?

Had she really journeyed to Babylon and spent days there while only hours passed here?

She had fused the puzzle.

The back of her hand was tanned, as was her arm, though it was streaked a little. The dye from the nuts! The bottoms of her feet were scarred and calloused. And she reeked!

"I *was* in Babylon." She stood and padded to the window, looked out just as Big Mick was putting up a sign advertising Wisconsin cheese soup.

"I'm not in Hades anymore," she said. A look back at the fused puzzle, still sparkling.

Maybe she ought to have it framed.

During her lunch break she intended to visit the attic, to look at some of her dad's things and to check out the clay bowls she'd spotted. She wanted to make sure they were the good version of demon bowls—she was pretty sure that they were. Maybe her father had made a few more trips back to Babylon, and they were souvenirs he'd brought home. And then there was the matter of those rabbit ears. She'd test her magic and see if she could manipulate them to give her grandparents better reception.

But she'd have to be careful with her magic.

"Shy..."

"Coming, Meemaw." Softer: "Such a tale I will tell you today. And when I'm done, you'll think that if I had Pinocchio's nose, it would stretch all the way across the street and to the front door of Big Mick's Pub."

One of the best-loved and most famous science fiction and fantasy authors of all time, Andre Norton was named Grand Master by the Science Fiction Writers of America and was awarded a Life Achievement Award by the World Fantasy Convention. She wrote over a hundred novels which have sold millions of copies worldwide, including her Witch World, Beast Master, Solar Queen, and Time Traders series, among others. She passed away in 2005. More can be learned at www.andre-norton-books.com.

Jean Rabe is the author of over thirty books of fantasy, mystery, thriller, and suspense. In addition to her original series she is known for her *Dragonlance* and *Forgotten Realms* novels and her collaborations with Andre Norton.

Made in the USA
Middletown, DE
10 August 2020

14999867R00136